Breaking
the speed **Limit**

NEW YORK TIMES AND *USA TODAY* BESTSELLING AUTHOR
MELANIE MORELAND

Breaking the Speed Limit by Melanie Moreland
Copyright © 2022 Moreland Books Inc.
Copyright ©1170982
ISBN Ebook 978-1-988610-84-9
Paperback 978-1-988610-90-0

MORELAND
BOOKS INC.

Edited by Lisa Hollett—Silently Correcting Your Grammar
Cover design by Karen Hulseman Feed Your Dreams
Photographer Eric D Battershell
Model Johnny Kane
Cover content is for illustrative purposes only and any person depicted on the
cover is a model.

Dear Reader,

Thank you for selecting Breaking The Speed Limit to read. Be sure to sign up for my newsletter for up to date information on new releases, exclusive content and sales. You can find the form here: https://bit.ly/MMorelandNewsletter

Before you sign up, add melanie@melaniemoreland.com to your contacts to make sure the email comes right to your inbox! **Always fun - never spam!**

My books are available in paperback and audiobook! You can see all my books available and upcoming preorders at my website.

The Perfect Recipe For **LOVE**
xoxo,
Melanie

ALSO BY MELANIE MORELAND

The Contract Series

The Contract (Contract #1)

The Baby Clause (Contract #2)

The Amendment (Contract #3)

The Addendum Coming to Radish 2022 - Wide Release 2023

Vested Interest Series

BAM - The Beginning (Prequel)

Bentley (Vested Interest #1)

Aiden (Vested Interest #2)

Maddox (Vested Interest #3)

Reid (Vested Interest #4)

Van (Vested Interest #5)

Halton (Vested Interest #6)

Sandy (Vested Interest #7)

Vested Interest/ABC Crossover

A Merry Vested Wedding

ABC Corp Series

My Saving Grace (Vested Interest: ABC Corp #1)

Finding Ronan's Heart (Vested Interest: ABC Corp #2)

Loved By Liam (Vested Interest: ABC Corp #3)

Age of Ava (Vested Interest: ABC Corp #4)

Men of Hidden Justice

The Boss

Second-In-Command

The Commander

Reynolds Restorations

Revved to the Maxx

Breaking The Speed Limit

Shifting Gears

Insta-Spark Collection written by M Moreland

It Started with a Kiss

Christmas Sugar

An Instant Connection

An Unexpected Gift

Harvest of Love

An Unexpected Chance

Following Maggie (Coming Home series)

Mission Cove

The Summer of Us

Standalones

Into the Storm

Beneath the Scars

Over the Fence

The Image of You (former title My Image of You)

Changing Roles

Happily Ever After Collection

Heart Strings

DEDICATION

For my friend who insists

Gabby is simply another way

to say Stephanie.

You really need a hobby, Gabby, Stephanie-whatever.

He's yours.

Have fun.

ITALIAN TRANSLATIONS

Siamo fatti l'uno per l'altro - We're made for each other
Sei tutto per me - You're everything to me
Cuore mio - my heart
Sei più bella di un angelo - you are more beautiful than
an angel
Tesoro –treasure/darling
Amore – Love
Sempre – Always
Bastardo – Bastard
Stronzo - asshole
Oh Dio – Oh God
Bambino – child
Ti amo – I love you
Ti adoro - I adore you

CHAPTER ONE

Stefano

I sat back, studying the design I was sketching out. I rubbed my tired eyes and, scowling, gave in and reached for the glasses I'd recently acquired. I hated using them, but I had to admit, once I slipped them on my nose, the lines on the paper in front of me were much clearer.

I liked to hand-draw my ideas before using the software we'd recently had installed. I felt the flow of the design under my fingers, using that to guide me. My boss, Maxx, felt the same way, and his wife, Charly, laughed, informing us to "get with the times." She'd shaken her head in frustration when I agreed with Maxx as we discussed it over dinner one night.

"Holy moly, I thought you'd rub off on the curmudgeon here, Stefano, not the other way around."

I had chuckled. She was droll and funny. She kept us all in line and ran the shop like a well-oiled piece of machinery. Maxx had hired her to help him sort out his house and garage, and in addition, she sorted out his heart. He was crazy in love with her, and anyone close to them could see it.

The sounds of shuffling met my ears, making me smile. Without even looking, I called over my shoulder, "You're not supposed to be in here. Fumes."

Charly appeared in the doorway, a grin on her face. Her red hair tumbled over her shoulders, and she was sporting a pair of loose denim overalls emblazoned with the garage's logo, over a pink T-shirt. She rested her hand on her rounded stomach, and her eyes were bright.

"I'm pregnant, Stefano, I don't have a cold. I sniffed—I knew you didn't have any paint open." She came closer. "What are you working on?"

I showed her the layered design for a restored bike Maxx was working on. The customer was into everything classic on the bike —skull and crossbones, black, white, and silver, and I was trying to come up with a twist to make it unique. The client was British, so I was weaving in the Union Jack under the design in a couple of places, the colors muted but visible. I was pleased so far and hoped he would like it.

"Oh, cool." She handed the paper back to me and gripped the edge of the table as she attempted to hoist herself up onto the stool beside me. Chuckling, I helped her settle, making sure she was fully seated before perching on the edge of my own stool and regarding her.

"Maxx know you're out here?"

"He's reading a book to Thomas. Mary's doing the dishes. She told me to go relax. I saw the light on in here, and I thought I'd come check on you."

"Ah," I replied, waiting. She didn't disappoint.

"Are you okay, Stefano? You seemed quiet at dinner."

I smiled at the woman who was like another sister to me. Maybe even more. She was a caretaker and constantly fussed over everyone—especially Maxx. She ran him as well as the garage, and he wouldn't have it any other way. She was the light to his dark, and she kept him smiling and happy—most of the time. She compared him to a growly grizzly bear, although at times, I was certain, most of that was for her benefit. She loved to rile him up, and he never disappointed her. It made for some interesting moments in the garage. We had all learned to deal with it and grown used to seeing him flip her over his shoulder and carry her into the house. We chose to ignore what happened once the door shut behind them.

"I'm fine," I assured her. "Working through this design. You know how I get."

"You only ate one helping. Was my lasagna not up to Rosa's standards?"

I had to laugh. My mama had taken Charly under her wing, making her an adopted member of the Borelli family. She taught her many of my family's recipes, and Charly, in turn, had taught my mother and sisters the art of baking pies. It was a win-win situation for everyone, except my waist. Luckily, Maxx had a great workout area in his barn, and both Brett and I took full advantage of it.

"Your lasagna rivaled my mama's. And I will deny saying that until the day I die. The piece you gave me was massive. Plus, I ate salad and a huge piece of pie. Stop worrying." I leaned forward and pressed a kiss to her forehead. "You do far too much of that."

She shrugged. "It's what I do." She patted my arm. "One helping won't keep these muscles going. You're going to give Maxx a run for his money soon."

Since coming here, my physique had changed. I had always been in shape, but working out with Maxx, following his regimen, I had filled out. My shoulders were broad, my biceps muscled, and my waist trim. I wore a beard now, trimmed close to my face, and I kept my hair short. I had more tattoos than I used to. My mama insisted I looked like a gangster, especially when I drove my motorcycle. She hated it even more than she hated my car. I loved them both. We agreed to disagree on that subject.

"I think I'll survive one smaller meal."

She frowned, displeased by my answer. I stayed silent, not wanting to give her any more ammunition. Luckily, she was Charly, and she understood. She dropped the subject—at least for now.

Her eyes widened, and she rubbed her stomach. "Oh, someone is busy."

"May I?"

She laughed and pulled my hand to where the small hand or foot was moving. I chased it over her stomach, chuckling at the rapid movements. "Soccer. I think she's playing soccer."

"She's been playing a lot." Charly shook her head. "Thomas was active in the daytime and quiet every night. She is the exact opposite. She starts around this time and keeps me up most of the night." She sighed, rubbing her bump. "Don't you, baby girl?"

I felt a strange flutter in my chest. Dull and achy. I rubbed at my sternum, unsure what caused the sensation.

4

I heard the door opening at the other end of the building and heavy footsteps headed our way. I looked at Charly, who was smiling, her eyes once again dancing with mischief.

"You had to poke the bear, didn't you?"

"No idea what you're talking about."

"Red!" Maxx bellowed in his gruff voice. "What are you doing in here?"

I hung my head, trying to hide my amusement. Maxx appeared, grabbing the doorframe. He was massive, filling the space. "Paint fumes, Charly. What have I told you about paint fumes?"

"There are none. Jeesh, I checked before coming in, big man. Stop chapping my ass."

"I'm going to chap your ass. With my hand."

Charly was almost vibrating on the stool in giddiness. "Promises, promises," she teased.

"Jesus, can you two take the foreplay somewhere else? I'm trying to work."

Maxx crossed the room and grasped the denim straps on Charly's overalls. He lifted her up, kissing her hard. "You were supposed to be relaxing. Sitting on the porch. Not wandering around. Why are you never where I leave you?"

His words were spoken without anger. I could hear the underlying adoration in his voice.

Once again, the odd sensation in my chest welled, and I frowned. Maybe I needed a Tums. I was getting old if lasagna was causing heartburn.

Charly gazed up at Maxx, her love shining in her eyes. "Maybe I like it when you come find me."

I cleared my throat. "Still here, people. Right here."

Maxx chuckled and shot me a grin. He had zero embarrassment when it came to his wife. He bent and scooped her into his arms. She gasped but laughed and rested her head against his broad shoulder.

"We'll leave you to work," he said with a wink.

"Have a good night," I replied.

"I put leftovers in your car!" Charly called. We all drove trucks belonging to the garage since it was great advertising, but on the weekends, I preferred my own car.

"Thanks," I called back, seeing how close their heads were and knowing neither of them was listening.

I watched them walk away, already lost in each other. I rubbed my chest, the odd sensation not dissipating.

I stared at the design, deciding to head home. I wasn't accomplishing much, sitting here and stewing.

Tomorrow was Sunday. A nonnegotiable afternoon spent at Mama's. I'd be surrounded by my siblings, their spouses, and children. There'd be lots of laughter, teasing, and food. I'd spend a few hours being climbed on by the kids, scolded by my mother for not having any of my own. At least one of my sisters would casually mention a friend she wanted to introduce me to. That would set off yet another scolding from my mother for not being married and bemoaning the fact that eight grandkids wasn't enough. My brothers had only daughters, so no one was carrying on the great last name of her beloved Antonio Borelli, *God rest his soul.* I needed to produce a son to make sure the line continued. I stopped trying to point out if I ever had kids, they could be girls as well. Mama simply didn't listen. It was the same every week, and although I was used to it, lately I was tired of hearing it.

Maybe I'd take Brett with me. At least then the clucking was divided between us.

In the meantime, I headed to the small house I shared with Brett. I'd have a couple beers with him, maybe watch a movie. Convince him to join me tomorrow.

Another exciting Saturday night in the life of a carefree bachelor.

Wasn't it grand?

CHAPTER TWO

Stefano

I headed home, the sun just beginning to lose its brilliance in the late evening. I loved summer—the heat and long days. I liked hiking in the vast emptiness around Littleburn and Lomand, discovering small, private places I could escape to. I had grown up in a suburb of Toronto and lived over the garage I worked at in a busy section of the large city. I had always been restless and edgy. Since living out here, even though it was only a short drive to get to Toronto, I was more relaxed. I liked the open spaces and the quiet. The different pace of life. Knowing my neighbors' and customers' names. Being greeted by name when I walked into my favorite bar or store.

I drove leisurely, in no hurry. Under me, the engine of my rebuilt Mustang growled low and powerful. I had to admit, another reason I loved this area was being able to take the car and let it go on one of the long, deserted roads. But today, I was just headed home and enjoying the drive with music playing and the windows open.

I noticed a small, older SUV pulled to the side of the road, and I slowed down. It was sitting at an odd angle, the back hatch open and the driver bent over inside, searching for something.

I pulled over, coasting close, and cut the engine, unable to take my eyes off the vision in front of me. The driver was a woman, wearing a skirt. A short one, from the looks of it. She was bent over, her creamy thighs exposed, the short skirt pulled so high, I caught a glimpse of lace stretched over an ass I could only describe as spectacular. It was rounded and full, and I had no doubt it would be a handful to grip. And for some reason, I wanted to do just that.

I slid from the car and called out. "Hey—can I help?"

The spectacular ass slid out of the hatch, and the driver stood. She turned to me, her eyes wide, clutching part of a jack. I froze mid-stride as she turned, my muscles locking into place at the sight of her.

She was average height, but at 6'2", I towered over her. She wasn't thin or plump, but somewhere in between, with heavy breasts, a sweet indentation at her waist, and rounded hips. Deep brunette-colored hair was pulled away from her face, masses of tiny curls escaping everywhere. She had a heart-shaped face, with curved cheeks and full lips that were currently frowning. Her skin was like cream, and I had the urge to reach out and touch it to see if it felt as soft as it looked. Her eyes were huge and dark—darker than mine and wide-spaced. She looked upset and a little frightened. I knew my size intimidated strangers, especially, I supposed, if you were a woman stranded on the side of the road at night. I held up my hands in supplication and offered her a friendly smile.

For a moment, our eyes locked, and the rest of the world faded away. We stared at each other, her dark eyes wide and alert. Her gaze lit something within me. Something hot and fierce. She licked her lips, causing my eyes to focus on them. I found myself wondering what they would taste like—how they would feel underneath mine. Her eyes focused on my mouth briefly, then she shook her head. "You scared me."

"Sorry, I didn't mean to startle you. I thought you'd heard me coming." I indicated my car. "Kinda hard not to hear that engine."

A look of derision crossed her face. "Toys," she muttered. "Men and their toys."

I frowned. My car wasn't a toy. It was a fine-tuned piece of machinery, and I was proud of it. But I ignored her. "Can I help?" I repeated.

She shook her head. "Nope. I got this."

I ignored her and walked closer. I dropped down to my knees and inspected the flat tire. I whistled in alarm at the rim.

"How long have you been driving on the flat?"

She crouched beside me, and her scent wafted across my nose. It was alluring and sexy. She wobbled a little, and I put out my hand to steady her. Her skin was soft and her eyes widened, our gazes locking again briefly, her eyes flaring with something. She stood and grimaced. "I was trying to get home and thought I would have it fixed in the morning. But it seemed to get worse."

I stood, shaking my head. "It's worse, all right. You've damaged the rim. You'll probably need an entire new one."

She frowned, pulling in her bottom lip in vexation. "Damn," she whispered.

"You should have pulled over right away. Called CAA. You never drive on a flat. You're risking yourself and other drivers," I scolded her.

"Thanks for the public service announcement. I've learned my lesson. You can go now." She turned her back, beginning to move things around in the back again.

I blinked at her dismissal.

"I'll change your tire."

"I said I was fine, whoever you are. I've got this." With a grunt, she lifted out the other part of the jack, inspecting it. I watched as she studied the two pieces, trying to figure out how they went together. She huffed and reached back into the hatch, pulling out the owner's manual, flipping the pages, squinting at the small print. She was obviously independent. It made her even more appealing to me somehow.

"I can have that done before you even find the right page number," I offered, amused by her stubbornness.

"Oh, you're still here? I thought there was a gnat flying around my head," she muttered, otherwise ignoring me.

I tried not to laugh, but a small chuckle escaped my lips, nevertheless. Reaching around her, I picked up the jack and stepped away. I was shocked when she turned and grabbed it.

"I said no."

I tried not to notice how close we were. Our chests were almost touching. I felt her breath on my face before she stepped back, but I noticed how her breathing had picked up, matching mine.

I studied her, then glanced at the waning light. "It will be dark in twenty minutes or so. You won't have even figured this out. I'll have the tire changed and you back on the road in ten."

She pursed her lips. "Some sort of expert, are you?"

I smirked. "You could say that."

"I can do this myself."

"Really? Do you know how to get the spare out?"

She glanced at the trunk. "Um, lift it?"

I shook my head. "Nope. You have to unscrew it. It drops down underneath, and you have to pull it out. Which means you need to get on your knees in the dirt and gravel to do so." I let my gaze wander down to her rounded knees. Her pale, unblemished knees that would be cut and bleeding by the time she was done.

I couldn't allow that to happen. I also had to ignore the image of her on her knees for another reason.

Where the hell had that thought come from?

"Damn," she breathed again.

"Ten minutes," I repeated, tugging on the jack.

She sighed. "Fine, Mr. Expert."

I winked. "Watch me and learn."

It took me a little longer. The spare was stuck, but I had WD-40 in my trunk, and after a few squirts, it was free. Her jack was cheap and useless, so I grabbed mine to use. I had to use the lubricant again on the lug nuts, then things went quickly. I installed the donut, placed the badly damaged tire in the back with the useless jack, and shut it. She watched me the whole time, her eyes wide, mumbling under her breath, the words too low for me to hear. When I was done, I stood, wiping my hands off on my jeans. I turned, catching her wide-eyed stare. Knowing she had been watching me and liking what she saw made me grin. I liked that being caught caused color to soak into her cheeks. It only made her sexier.

I threw her a wink, went to my car to grab a business card, then handed it to her.

"This is a great service station. They won't rip you off."

She squinted at it in the growing darkness. "Reynolds & Co. Restorations and Repairs."

I pointed in the direction I had traveled in. "About ten minutes down this road."

"I usually go to Mr. Lube or Pennzoil. Whoever has a deal on oil changes."

I tried not to shudder. "I promise you, this place is the best. Reasonable and, as I said, they won't rip you off. Easy terms if you need it," I explained.

Her shoulders straightened and her eyes flashed. "I never said I needed help."

"Of course not. Simply letting you know."

She held up the card. "Friend of yours?"

"You could say that."

She sighed and ran a hand through her hair, grimacing when her fingers hit the knot at the top, as if she'd forgotten it was up. "What do I owe you?"

I wanted to ask her for her number, but I had a feeling the answer would be a resounding no.

"Nothing."

"I have to give you something."

"Nope. Glad I was coming along and could help."

She frowned. "I don't like being beholden to anyone."

I tilted my head and met her eyes. Once again, the fire in them lit me up. Hidden in the dark gaze was desire—desire she was directing at me. Desire I returned fully.

I had no idea what came over me. One minute, I was standing beside her. The next, she was in my arms and I was kissing her.

Shock rendered her stiff, then suddenly she was kissing me back.

It was spectacular.

Her lips were full and soft. Her curves fit against me as if she was sculpted just for me. I slid my tongue along her bottom lip, and she opened for me. She tasted of chocolate and something sweet. Addictive. Her tongue was velvet against mine. I slid my hand up her neck, feeling the rich silkiness of her hair under my fingers. They itched to pull out the clips holding her hair back and play with her curls. She wrapped one hand around my bicep, her fingers digging into my skin. The other, she ran through my hair, making me tremble. She whimpered low in her throat, and I grunted in approval.

Then she stiffened again and pushed away. I moved back, my breathing ragged. She stared at me, her eyes huge. Then suddenly, she lunged, and we were locked together again. My pulse raced the way my Mustang did on an open stretch of highway. My body hugged her curves the way the car hugged the road, the speed and hum of the engine pure adrenaline.

She was the same.

Until she pulled back again, this time stepping away. My arms felt strangely empty without her in them. "Consider the debt paid," I rasped, reaching out to touch her again.

She slapped away my hand, her eyes shooting daggers my way.

"You are so…"

"Sexy?" I asked. "Incredible?" I opened my arms, waggling my fingers. "Come back, and I'll show you how incredible."

Her hands curled into fists, and she punched me. Right in the stomach. I glanced down, trying not to laugh. I barely felt it even though I knew she'd put a lot of force behind the punch.

"You need some boxing lessons as well as some basic car maintenance lessons," I stated dryly. "Is that the best you've got?"

She let out a muffled shriek and pushed past me, slamming her door shut. I heard the locks engage then the engine gun to life. I frowned—it really needed a tune-up, the timing was off, among other things. I tapped on her window, but she refused to roll it down.

"You need some service on the engine!" I shouted. "Call the garage."

She flipped me the bird and drove away, scattering gravel as she went.

I stared after her, tempted to hop in my car and follow her. But I resisted—I had a feeling I had already done enough damage.

I tugged a hand through my hair in vexation.

What the hell was I doing kissing a stranger? I didn't do things like that. My mama had brought me up to respect women, treat them well. Not haul off and kiss them because they were feisty, sexy, and talked back. Mama would be appalled at my behavior. I was appalled at myself.

I had to be overtired. That was it.

Yet, even as I got in my car and drove home, all I could think about was how her lips felt on mine. How she fit in my arms, her luscious curves pressed against me.

How she tasted.

And how much I wanted to do it again.

Bad behavior or not.

CHAPTER THREE

Gabby

I watched the stranger in the rearview mirror become smaller as the distance between us grew, until he disappeared as I went around a bend in the road.

What the hell had just happened?

What had I *allowed* to happen?

I'd known the tire was bad when I got out of the SUV, and any hope I'd had of making it home without changing it was gone.

I had been struggling so hard to get the jack out of the back I hadn't even heard the black muscle car pull in behind me. The stupid jack was steadfastly stuck, and I was wasting precious daylight trying to get it unstuck, growing more anxious by the second.

The sound of that deep, melodic voice made me spin around, and the sight that met my eyes was unexpected.

I wasn't sure I had ever seen a man that imposing before. Or as sexy. His T-shirt stretched over his pecs and abs, showing off the definition of his physique even in the fading light. A tattoo peeked out from under the sleeve of his shirt. Dark hair and eyes, a wide smile, and his deep voice made something inside me tremble. I had to blink to clear my head. Desire, long dormant, woke up, jarring me with its power. I clutched the jack, planning on using it as a weapon if needed, but he had simply offered to help me. I was grateful until he examined my tire and began lecturing me. It reminded me too much of what I had run from, and unlike my younger self, I wasn't going to take it. I snapped back at him, which seemed only to amuse him, and we spent the next few moments in barbed banter. Somehow I sensed only teasing and genuine concern in his words. There was no anger or nastiness in his tone.

Finally, I gave in, watching in amazement as he took control, changing the tire with ease. He grunted as he used some cross-looking thing he got from his trunk to loosen the bolts, then made the rest of the work look like child's play. His form was spectacular as he worked. His ass was tight and high. His arm muscles flexed and bulged. His thighs bunched. He was sexy and strong.

He'd handed me back my jack, calling it a piece of shit, and I'd clutched it against me like a talisman to ward him off. He tossed everything in the back hatch, handing me a business card he'd gotten from his car and giving me yet another lecture on what I should or shouldn't do when it came to car maintenance.

That got my hackles up yet again. All I wanted to do was get home. I didn't have the time or patience to explain to him I was doing the best I could. I had a cheap cell phone. No CAA. It was an expense I couldn't afford. I could barely keep the SUV on the road, but I needed it for work, so I had to give up other things in order to do so.

I offered to pay him for his time, hating to be in debt for anything. Once again, we sparred, then suddenly I was in his arms with his mouth on mine.

I should have exploded with outrage. Stepped back and slapped him. Screamed in his face.

Instead, I kissed him back. Not only did I kiss him, but for one glorious moment, the entire shitstorm my life had been lately disappeared. He held me close, as if I were precious. His mouth was wicked, capable of rendering me a mass of quivering limbs and stirring up emotions I hadn't felt for a very long time—if ever. Want, desire, and need filled me. I whimpered, and he pulled me closer, his hand cupping the back of my neck firmly, yet with great tenderness.

I was shocked to realize how right it felt to be in the stranger's arms. How much I wanted to stay there. I was so out of my mind, I kissed him again.

Until reality hit and I pushed back.

His eyes were rich chocolate—deep, dark, and filled with desire. He looked so sexy, his lips wet from mine, his hair disheveled from my fingers. There were red marks on his arm from my nails.

And, my God, I wanted him.

Until he opened his mouth.

"Consider the debt paid," he murmured, the sound deep and rumbly. He lifted his hand to touch me as my common sense kicked in, and I slapped it away.

"You are so…" I spat.

"Sexy?" he asked, one eyebrow lifting. "Incredible?" He opened his arms, beckoning with his long fingers. "Come back, and I'll show you how incredible."

He was both, but I wasn't giving him the satisfaction of knowing that. Then before he could move, I punched him in the stomach. Hard. Hard enough I felt the ache in my knuckles that would no doubt worsen over the next few hours. He simply glanced down with a smirk.

"You need some boxing lessons as well as some basic car maintenance lessons," he said. "Is that the best you've got?"

Angry, I pushed past him and climbed into the car, slamming the door and locking it. He appeared by the window, tapping on it, but I refused to meet his eyes.

"You need some service on the engine!" he shouted. "Call the garage."

I flipped him the bird and drove away, scattering gravel behind me. I hoped one of the rocks would leave a mark.

I drove home as if the devil himself were chasing me.

I parked and hurried inside. My landlady was sitting in the rocking chair, busy knitting, the monitor beside her. She looked up with a frown.

"You're early. Is everything all right?"

I smiled ruefully. "Ziggy is having trouble again. Something with the electrics in the kitchen. We had to close early." I sighed. "On the busiest night of the week, of course."

"Of course." She patted my hand. "These things happen."

I nodded. "They do. How was he?"

Mrs. Scott smiled. "Good as gold, as usual. He played with his cars and ate his supper like an angel. Even had his bath."

I handed her some cash, but she shook her head. "No, dear. I was happy to have him today." She patted my hand again. "You need it more than I do."

"But…" I began to protest.

She shook her head. "No. I told you the deal. I prefer barter."

"Laundry?" I guessed. I lived on the top floor of an older house, and Mrs. Scott lived on the main floor. The machines were in the basement, and Mrs. Scott had trouble with stairs. So, I traded off some babysitting for odd jobs like laundry, shopping, cutting the grass. I was even able to do some minor repairs like leaky faucets and stuck windows. She, in turn, looked after Theo when I had the opportunity to pick up extra shifts, which helped me a great deal. Other nights, Mrs. Wilson next door looked after him, then brought him home and tucked him into bed. Her teenagers took turns sleeping on the sofa in case he woke up and needed something, returning to their own place when I got home. Most of the time, they were still awake when I arrived, using my TV to play video games. It was the only time it was ever turned on. I couldn't afford cable, and if the previous tenants hadn't left it in the corner, it would never be used. I helped tutor her kids, and she charged me a low price for caring for him. He loved going there, so the arrangement worked out well for now.

Everything in my life was centered around "for now." I hoped one day I wouldn't have to be breaking the figurative speed limit to get through every day. I had no idea what it was like to have a day when I didn't have to pray that I'd have no disasters, that I would have enough money to feed my child and myself, and that I could keep him safe and not be looking over my shoulder constantly. I liked it in Lomand. People were friendly but not intrusive. I had been lucky when I'd calculated how far I could go with bus fare and stepped into the little town. It, and the people, had been good to me, Mrs. Scott especially. Theo was never upset when I left him with her, and he thought of her little spare room as his second bedroom.

Mrs. Scott's voice interrupted my musings. "Laundry, yes. And I was wondering if we could make some of that vegetable soup of yours. I'd like some for dinner this week."

I made great vegetable soup, and Mrs. Scott loved it. So did Theo. I also made an awesome beef and barley, as well as a few others. The best part was how far I could stretch it on my budget.

"Sure. I'll check the market and see what they have in this week."

She shook her head. "I was there today. There's an entire harvest in my kitchen. You come get it and make it." She met my eyes. "That's the deal."

I gave in easily, because there was no point in arguing with her. "Okay. We'll make a big batch tomorrow."

Sunday was my one day off, and occasionally, I got another night, depending how busy Ziggy's bar was. I worked from six to closing at Ziggy's in Lakeside, except on Saturdays when I started at four. If I was lucky, I picked up shifts at Zeke's here in Lomand, but those were harder to come by, and unless they were at night, my childcare cost me a bundle. I managed to make do every month and, thanks to Mrs. Scott's trades and my tips, put a little aside for emergencies.

Mrs. Scott smiled at me. "You get your boy, and I'll see you tomorrow."

I went to the spare room and looked down at my son. His hair was similar to the color of mine, maybe a little darker, and he looked like me, except for his eyes. They were hazel in color—a mixture of his father's and mine. That and his lean build were the only traits he had inherited, thank God. He was sunny and sweet and his patience seemingly endless.

Very un-Wayne-like. His temper was constantly ready to blow, and he thought patience was some sort of flower. How I had never seen his true nature until I was trapped was a mystery. But I had gotten out, and I never planned on going back.

I lifted Theo, burying my nose in his hair. He smelled like bubble bath and little boy. *My* little boy. I loved him so much my heart threatened to burst with it. Carefully I carried him to the hallway, pausing in the doorway before I shut Mrs. Scott's door.

"Thank you."

She smiled. "Goodnight, dear. I'll see you tomorrow."

I nodded and carried Theo up the steps, his body a dead weight in my arms. I wasn't sure how much longer I would be able to do this, but I hated the thought of waking him to move him to his own bed. At five, he was growing like a weed, and I knew the day would come soon I wouldn't be able to lift him, but I could still manage. I tucked him in and gazed down at his sweet face, brushing the hair off his forehead. I bent low and kissed him then headed to my room.

I got ready and slid into bed, my body tired but my mind still wide awake. I had to fix the tire on the SUV. I needed it to get back and forth to work. Using the old iPad I had, I checked out the website for the garage the stranger had recommended. There was a picture of the owner, another huge man with a great smile. He was leaning against a red wall, the company logo over his head. His name, I surmised from the little I skimmed, was Maxx Reynolds. And he had two partners, a Brett Conner and a Stefano Borelli. I read a little more, flipping a few pages. The customer reviews were glowing. They offered classes for women, designed to answer questions and help them understand how their cars worked. The classes were free, but there was a waiting list for them. I filled out my information, using Mrs. Scott's phone number. She allowed me to do that and save a monthly rental fee on a home phone I didn't want. I never gave out my cell number unless I had no choice. The fewer people who had that number, the better. I rarely got calls on her line, but if one came through, she passed on a message. Luckily, she had Wi-Fi and let me use it as well, so I had email I could get on the old tablet I had. That was about all it was good for. I filled in that information as well and decided I would take my car to the garage and get it fixed. I looked at the card, the memory of those dark eyes and teasing mouth coming to mind. Given his physique, he must work out with the owner of the shop at the same gym, which would explain how he knew them. There were other pages about motorcycle restoration, but I had no interest in that, so I signed off. I would call in the morning and ask for a quote on replacing the tire.

I slid under the sheets, drawing them up to my chin. Unbidden, the image of the stranger came to mind. His powerful build. His rich voice. How gently he had held me in his big hands. The way his mouth worked mine. How lost I had felt in his arms.

And yet, strangely at home.

I rolled over and punched the pillow. I had to stop thinking about him again. Chances were, I would never see him again. And if I did, I needed to turn and walk the other way.

Once bitten, twice shy.

I ignored the little voice that whispered the stranger could be different.

I couldn't take that chance. I had too much to lose.

I shut my eyes, determined to sleep.

That was easier said than done.

CHAPTER FOUR

Stefano

M onday, I kept making excuses to drop in to the front office. I told myself it was because I needed coffee, but even Charly called me on my BS.

She looked up at me, her green eyes wise. "The coffee isn't located on the appointment page, Stefano. What are you looking for?"

I shifted uncomfortably on my feet. "Ah, anyone call today about needing a tire? A new customer?"

She narrowed her gaze. "Maybe."

"I, um, helped someone Saturday night. Gave them the number here. Just idle curiosity."

"Was it a woman?"

I stepped closer. "She called? Did you fit her in soon? The tire was really bad."

She grinned. "I knew it. Coffee, my ass. *Holy moly*, you liked her."

I frowned. "I did not. Like I said, the tire was really bad. It came to mind, and I was just following up on it."

Charly's eyes danced with glee. "Maxx calls me a bad liar. If your ears got any redder, they'd be on fire. You want to know if she's coming in."

"She shouldn't be driving on it. It's dangerous."

She leaned back. "And you're worried." She waggled her eyebrows. "What will you give me to tell you if she is coming in?"

"Stop chapping my ass," I growled. "Did she make an appointment?"

Charly tilted her head, regarding me. "Well, she called—if it's the same woman. She said she had a flat and thought she needed a new tire. I'm calling her back with a quote."

"What's her name?"

She shook her head. "Nuh-uh. Not telling. That's private."

I glared at her and ran a hand through my hair. "Look, Charly. The tire was toast. She'd driven on it and damaged the rim badly. There is no doubt she needs a new one." I paused and huffed, recalling her statement about going to whatever place was the cheapest for oil changes. "I got the feeling she didn't have a lot of money to fix it."

She frowned. "What do you want me to do?"

"We have a bunch of tires out back. There's one that would fit. I checked it. Give her a deal and charge me the rest."

Her eyes widened.

"She reminded me of my sister Gianna," I lied. "I would like to think if she was in trouble, someone would help her. And I think she needs help."

Not that she would accept it, I added silently.

"Your *sister*," she repeated.

"Yes. My sister."

"Okay then, Stefano. I'll tell her it's her lucky day and we have a used one in stock. I'll give her a decent price and make sure she's looked after."

"Thanks."

Charly turned to her computer, then glanced over her shoulder. "Anything else?"

"No." I turned to leave, then paused. "Charly?"

"Yeah?" she replied, her voice amused.

"Could you, ah, just give me the heads-up when she's here?"

"Because you want to make sure we look after your sister-type-friend?"

"Yes," I ground out.

"I can do that."

"Thanks," I snapped.

Her laughter followed me all the way back to the restoration area.

I flung myself into my chair and rubbed my eyes. I shouldn't have even asked—but I couldn't stop thinking about the woman I'd kissed.

I felt an odd need to somehow help her. The instinctive knowledge she would refuse any offer I made—much the same way she didn't want me to change her tire—persisted, but I had to try.

When I had gotten home on Saturday, I found the house empty, Brett out with friends. I stewed most of the night, worried if the woman had made it home. Wondering if she would call the garage. Pondering the idea of dropping by the local Mr. Lube to ask if she had shown up there.

Except that would make me a stalker.

And the fact was that I didn't chase after women. I wasn't in the market for a relationship, and from the way she brushed me off, neither was she.

But that kiss…

It was etched in my memory. The feel and taste of her. The softness of her body against mine. The way her lips molded, pliant and soft, moving with my mouth.

Dammit, I wanted to kiss her again.

And more.

Sunday, I had been distracted—and grateful for Brett's presence. My family liked him a lot and hadn't seen him for a few weeks, so they bombarded him with hundreds of questions. Even luckier was the fact that my sister Izzy was determined to set him up with a friend, rather than focusing on me. I was beginning to hope they had determined I was a lost cause and would direct their attention on to Brett for a while. He was actually a year older than I was. Surely a thirty-five-year-old needed the help more?

He took it all in stride, eating enough to please Mama, smiling and accepting their clucking and fussing easily. He even agreed to take Lola's number, although I wasn't sure he would ever call her. I knew he had been seeing a girl, but knowing his track record, that might have changed. I would have to check. I was certain I'd gotten away scot-free until Mama caught me alone in the kitchen, getting a drink.

"What's up with you?" she asked, her accent thick. "You off today. Too quiet."

"I'm fine," I replied, kissing her cheek. "Thinking about work."

"Ah!" She gestured with one hand, flipping it in the air. "You should be thinking about the future. A wife. Children." She spoke faster, pointing at the driveway. "Not driving bike like young man and doing nothing. You waste time, Stefano. You need family of your own!"

She hated the motorcycle. She lectured all of us about driving one. She hated my car too, so no matter what I used to drive in to see her met with her displeasure.

"Babies, Stefano. You need to think of babies."

"Mama," I teased. "You want me going around just planting babies in women?" I grinned at the shocked look on her face. "I can if you insist, but that's not what you taught me growing up."

She slapped my arm. "Stop!"

I laughed and hugged her tight. "One day, Mama. Just not today."

She huffed. "I hate you alone."

Her words struck something inside me.

"I'm not alone. I have our family. And lots of friends."

She shook her head, gazing up at me sadly. "No the same, Stefano. No the same. Find your own family. Your future."

With a sigh, I kissed her again. "I'll try, Mama. I promise."

For some reason, the woman I'd kissed seemed to come to mind every time I thought about Mama's words.

Why, I had no idea.

Tuesday morning, Maxx came to my area, a frown on his face. "We're two men down and have a full docket. You have some free time to help cover?"

"Sure. I'm still waiting on some approvals, and I can push back a few things."

"Great. Brett's taking bay one. I'll take bay two, and you can have three."

"Like old times."

"Yep."

"Lou and Ward okay?"

He grimaced. "They were out last night with their bowling team. Apparently shared a bad platter of wings. The whole team is suffering."

I tried not to laugh, but I had to. "Sounds shitty."

Maxx chortled. "Don't get Charly going. She's having far too much fun with it already."

I clapped him on the shoulder. "Of course she would. Let's hit it."

Once in the garage, I glanced at the board and whistled. It was full. I frowned, not seeing anything about a tire change, then shook my head. I needed to put it and her out of my mind. She was so stubborn, she was probably ignoring my advice and going to Mr. Lube—or even worse, driving on the donut. I didn't know her, and she wasn't my responsibility.

No matter how much I enjoyed kissing her.

The morning went quickly, music playing, customers coming and going. Charly was in her element, bossing everyone around, laughing, and running the office with her usual deftness. My next customer came in, and after talking to them, I sent them to the waiting room and began working on their car. I grabbed one of the creepers, sliding underneath, my tools ready as I started the required repair. As usual when working, I zoned out, my thoughts focused on the job at hand. I was so focused, in fact, that I didn't notice I had company until it was too late.

"Whatcha doing?" a little voice spoke to my right.

Startled, I snapped up my head, and it glanced off the metal undercarriage of the car. I hit it so hard, I swore I saw stars.

"Shit," I snarled, meeting the shocked gaze of a little kid as I rubbed the tender spot.

"That's a bad word," he whispered, cupping his mouth as if telling me a secret.

"Um, yeah, sorry. You startled me."

"I wanted to see."

"Who are you?"

"Theo."

"Nice to meet you, Theo, but you shouldn't be under the car, little man."

"Why not?"

"It's not safe."

"You are."

"I'm an adult."

"I'm smaller. I fit better."

The kid had a point—stubborn little bugger.

"You aren't authorized."

He frowned. "I'm only five." He picked up a socket wrench. "I don't know what that is. But I can help!"

He was pretty damn clever for a five-year-old. I rubbed my aching head. "You need a uniform to work here."

He looked disappointed. "Can you get me one? My mommy says I'm a good helper." He held up another tool. "This is a screwything!"

"A screwything?"

He nodded. "My mommy has some. She gets mad and swears when she can't find one. I help her. I can help you." He looked around. "Don't tell her I said she swears. Mommy says that's bad."

"I won't tell her."

He wiped his hand on his cheek, and I noticed the smear of oil.

"Okay, kid, out from under the car."

I slid out, and the kid crawled out beside me. I sat up and he stared, his eyes wide. "You have a boo-boo," he said, pointing to my head.

I crossed my arms. "I'm not surprised."

"I'm sorry I scared you. I just wanted to see." His bottom lip began to tremble.

Dammit, I hated to see a kid cry. I ruffled his hair. "It's okay, little man. I'm a big guy. I can take it."

"You have lots of muscles," he agreed, rubbing his nose, then peering under the car. "How'd you fit under there?"

Before I could respond, he added, "Is your uniform magic?"

I laughed, touching the coveralls. "Maybe."

"Can I have one?"

"I don't have any in your size."

"Oh." Again, the lip quivered. "I wanted to help you. I like cars."

I was about to respond when Charly appeared, peeking around the car. "Aha. Found him, Gabby!" she called out.

I heard hurried footsteps, and a woman rounded the end of the car, looking upset. I froze when I saw her, my heartbeat increasing. It was *her*. The woman from the other day.

And her name was Gabby.

Lovely.

"Theo!" she scolded. "You scared Mommy!"

"I was looking at the car," he protested, tapping the fender. "It's pretty."

The kid had that right. The car *was* pretty—he obviously had good taste.

"You weren't supposed to leave the waiting room." Her gaze drifted to me, and suddenly color saturated her cheeks as our gazes met. Two sets of dark eyes appraised and locked, both shocked, one pleased, while the other looked uncertain.

Gabby was even more beautiful than I remembered. Her hair was down, tiny corkscrew curls wild and thick hanging just above her shoulders. The lights in the garage caught strands of gold and red scattered in the dark brown, making it unique and pretty. Her face was pale aside from the slashes of crimson on her cheeks, and her lips were as full and tempting as they had been the other day. She was dressed in jeans with a loose T-shirt hanging low over her hips. She was appealing and sexy. And glaring at me.

"What are *you* doing here?"

I grinned and rose to my full height, towering over her. "I work here."

"I-I didn't know that."

"Why do you think I gave you that card?"

"I thought it was your friend's place."

"Maxx is a friend, but it's part mine as well."

"Hmmph."

I crossed my arms. "So, if you'd known that, you wouldn't have come?"

"I never—I never said that. Don't presume to know what I'm thinking." She lifted her chin in defiance, which somehow only turned me on. I liked her spunk.

I lifted one eyebrow sardonically. "I wouldn't dare."

"Good," she sniffed, attempting to sound haughty. All it did was make me want to kiss her. Taste her mouth again. I tried not to stare at her lips. I also tried not to smile when I noticed she was staring at mine.

Charly's gaze bounced between us. "Stefano is one of our best. He's very talented."

"I'm sure he is," Gabby drawled, her sarcasm evident. I wanted to remind her how talented I was, but I was a gentleman and refrained. I didn't want to shock Charly.

A hand tugged on my pants, and I glanced down, suddenly remembering the kid. Theo.

It hit me. She had a kid. If she had a kid, she was…

Holy shit. Was she married? *I had kissed a married woman?*

"You did what?" Charly asked, looking around, confused. "What married woman?"

I groaned, realizing I had said that out loud. I ran a hand through my hair, grimacing as I hit the lump forming on my forehead.

Charly noticed. "Yowsers, Stefano, what did you do to your head?"

"I scared him," Theo offered, pointing to the car. "I wanted to see what he was doing under there."

His mother's face became paler. "Are you all right?" she asked me. Once again, our eyes locked, a strange connection flowing between them. It felt like a physical thing; I could feel it everywhere. As if she was touching me—all over.

"Charly," I said, not taking my eyes off the woman in front of me. "Take Theo and get him a garage shirt. I promised him one. Maybe a hat."

"Can I work on the car with you, then?" he asked.

"I'll show you a couple of things," I replied.

Charly huffed, hating the fact that I was sending her on an errand. Little Miss Know-It-All wanted to stay and find out what was going on. The bottom line was, I'd tell her later anyway and she knew it, which was why she offered Theo her hand.

"Okay if I give him a shirt, Gabby?"

"Um, sure?"

Theo looked ready to burst from excitement. As soon as they disappeared around the car, I leaned close to Gabby, catching her appealing scent.

"You're married?" I hissed. "You're married, and you kissed me?"

"What? No!" Her dark eyes flashed. "Let's get something straight, buddy. *You* kissed *me*."

"You didn't object."

"Whatever," she huffed.

"So, you are married?"

She ran a hand over her eyes. "No. I. Am. Not. Married."

"Good."

"But *you* kissed me," she repeated.

"You kissed me back." I took a step, needing to be closer. "Then you kissed me again. I liked it."

She shook her head. "No."

"No?"

"Not again." She pushed on my chest. "Do not get closer."

"Can't resist me?"

"I can resist you just fine."

I dropped my eyes to where her hand lingered on my chest. She had long, elegant fingers, the nails short and blunt—bare, no polish. No jewelry of any kind. Not even a faint line where a wedding ring would have been. Whoever Theo's dad was, he was long out of the picture. If, in fact, he had ever been in it. Gabby was obviously independent. Maybe she'd had a child on her own.

I covered her hand with mine, liking how her skin felt against mine. "Is that so?"

She yanked away her hand. "Yes. And stop being nice to my kid. It won't get you anywhere."

"I was nice before I knew he was yours," I retaliated. "Even when he startled me and gave me this goose egg."

She looked up, her annoyance turning into a grimace. Her eyes softened and she appeared worried. "I'm sorry. Does it hurt?"

"A little."

"Maybe some ice would help."

I inched closer. "Or you could kiss it better—" I paused "—*Gabby.*"

Her eyes flashed. Desire overrode annoyance on her part. Her lips parted and her breathing picked up.

Then it happened again. My brain shut down, and I reacted to her close proximity. The next thing I knew, her mouth was underneath mine, her lips soft and full. She gasped, and I took advantage and slipped in my tongue, stroking along hers. I slid my hand over her back, settling it on her hip, keeping her close. She whimpered, winding her hand into the short hair at the back of my neck, tugging. I grunted in approval, slanting my head and kissing her harder. I had to bend at the knees a little, and she leaned into me, her breasts pressing against my chest. We both made a sound of pleasure, and I tightened my grip on her waist.

Until the sound of running steps and an excited "Mommy, look!" pulled us apart. Theo sped around the corner, wearing a slightly too big red T-shirt, emblazoned with the logo. And a matching baseball hat. "I got a uniform! I can help Stefo!"

I chuckled at the shortening of my name. Stefano was a big name for a kid.

Gabby blinked, shell-shocked, her mouth swollen from mine. She shook her head and cleared her throat. "No, not today, sweetie. We have to go. Mommy has to work."

"But, Mommy—"

She cut him off. "Not today," she stated firmly.

Charly smirked as she followed Theo, the look on her face saying everything. She wasn't going to be satisfied until she knew the whole story.

"Your tire is changed, Gabby. Maxx wants to see the vehicle in a couple of days if you can drop by."

"Why?"

Charly blinked, not expecting that question, and I stepped in. "We always check on the alignment and fit when we replace a used tire after the car is driven for a couple of days. It's part of the service," I improvised. We never had to since the vehicle would be double-checked before it left. But she bought it.

"Oh."

"So, I can come back?" Theo asked anxiously. "Help Stefo, Mommy? I like cars," he pleaded.

I grinned down at the smiling face of the little interloper. He was my ace in the hole right now. "Yep. You can help me next time. Wear your uniform." I met Gabby's eyes. Her furious, piercing eyes. "As long as it's okay with your mom."

I knew I put her on the spot, but I wanted to see her again. I wanted to get my hands on her SUV.

And her.

She huffed out a sigh. "Fine. I'll drop by."

Charly grinned. "Okay. I'll write you up." She held out her hand. "Come on, Theo. I'll show you how the machine works."

He grabbed her hand, following her.

Gabby trailed after him, pausing when I laid my hand on her arm. "See you soon."

"I know what you're up to," she hissed. "It won't work. I won't like you because you're sweet to my kid."

I leaned close. "No, you already like me. You're just not willing to admit it yet."

"Don't put words in my mouth."

I couldn't help it. It was as if I lost my mind whenever she was close, and the words were out before I could stop them. I leaned down, my lips close to her ear. "Is there something else you'd like me to put in your mouth?"

Her eyes went wide, and she made a muffled shrieking noise before brushing past me.

I chuckled as I watched her walk away. Her jeans hugged her ass nicely. It was full and round, and next time I kissed her, I planned on touching it.

I planned on touching a lot of her.

She just didn't know it yet.

CHAPTER FIVE

Gabby

I tried desperately to hold on to my anger the rest of the day.

How dare he? How dare he be there? The nerve of him, all tall and sexy, charming Theo, helping me get great service on my SUV.

Letting his eyes roam over me as if he owned me. Those dark, sexy eyes that smoldered and beckoned.

Kissing me.

That big, egotistical Italian jerk.

I grumbled under my breath as I filled my tray with drinks for my table. I refused to admit I enjoyed the way I felt as he looked me over, his eyes lighting up as if he liked what he saw. A lot.

I wouldn't allow myself to acknowledge that I sighed when he kissed me. That it felt as if everything had settled again and I was at peace. As if I was supposed to be in his arms.

I refused to admit that. In fact, I needed to stop thinking about him. Period.

Jerk.

I forced a smile to my face and served the tray of beers to the large table, teasing and joking with them. I depended on my tips, so I made sure to treat my customers right. It was busy for a Tuesday night, and I was pleased. Busy meant more tips for me, which gave me a little breathing room in the budget. I was grateful to have gotten the extra shift tonight. It was rare they came up.

I saw a new set of customers in the corner, and I grabbed some paper coasters and an appetizer menu and approached the table, my smile firmly in place. As I set down the coasters, I launched into my usual spiel.

"Hey, guys. Welcome to Ziggy's. Drafts on special this evening. Appy's half price if you're hungry. I'm Gabby, and I'll be looking after you tonight."

A blond man smiled at me. He looked familiar, but I wasn't sure why. A younger man was with him, and he grabbed the menu.

"I'm starving. We need a bunch of stuff."

"Sure, Chase. Order whatever you want. We'll eat." The blond looked up. "Three drafts and whatever my friend here wants. We'll need lots of napkins." He winked. "The kid's messy."

"Three?" I repeated, just as I felt someone behind me. Someone big. Someone who felt far too close and smelled far too familiar. Like the woods on a fall day. Crisp. Clean. Inviting.

"Well, well, if it isn't my lucky day," a man murmured close to my ear.

I spun, meeting the dark eyes of Stefano. Instantly, I realized why the other two table occupants looked familiar. I had seen them at the garage earlier today.

I narrowed my eyes. "What are *you* doing here?"

He stepped back, holding up his hands, his eyes dancing with mischief. "Having a beer and some snacks with my boys."

"I've never seen you in here before. Are you following me?"

"Following you from where, exactly? We had to deliver a car and pick up some parts from a junkyard, and we saw the sign on the way back and decided to stop in. We're hungry." A smile played on his full lips. "But seeing you is an added bonus."

"Sit down, Stefano, and quit harassing the pretty waitress."

Stefano grinned. "I like harassing her. She likes it too."

I sniffed. "Don't count on it."

"Can I order?" The young one spoke up. "I'm really starving."

Stefano brushed past me—brushed being too strong a word. He laid his hand on my arm, sliding behind me, his chest pushing into my back. I felt his heat and his strength. His muscles as they rippled. My breath caught, and I had to take a moment before I responded. He sat down, his gaze never leaving mine. He indicated the blond man. "That's Brett." He pointed to the one desperate to order. "The hungry one is Chase. We work in the garage." He smirked. "This is Gabby, a new customer of ours, boys. Say hello."

They both nodded and did exactly that, and despite my annoyance, I had to smile at them. I directed my attention to Chase.

"What would you like?"

He ordered half a dozen items, rattling the list off fast. "Double order of hot wings, nachos with extra jalapeños, onion rings, chicken fingers, poutine, and deep-fried pickles. Extra dipping sauce."

"How about something healthy?" I asked before I could stop myself.

Stefano grinned. "Throw in some carrot sticks."

"Wow."

Brett laughed. "We'll work it off tomorrow."

It was impossible not to notice how incredibly built they all were. Stefano was cut and powerful. Brett was slimmer but muscular, his pecs and arms well-defined under his tight T-shirt. Chase was lean but toned, his forearms flexing as he held the menu.

"Unless, of course, you want to work it off with me tonight," Stefano drawled, still staring at me.

I resisted the urge to stick out my tongue at him. "Good luck with that. I'll get your order in."

I pivoted and hurried to the bar, ignoring his low laughter.

"Just another customer," I muttered. "Just another customer." I had to be polite and serve them. That was my job. And it wasn't the other men's fault that Stefano got under my skin. I would ignore him and direct my inquiries to them. What was the expression Charly used yesterday that had made me smile?

Right. *Easy peasy.*

I would ignore Stefano.

I put a rush on their food, hoping they would eat and leave quickly.

But I should have known better.

They devoured the food, getting a second plate of nachos. Chase had another beer, but Stefano now sipped tonic water while Brett had a Coke. And they lingered.

I felt Stefano's eyes on me the entire time. After eating, they moved to the back of the bar and shot some pool. I could hear their laughter, somehow pinpointing Stefano's low guffaw easily and knowing exactly where he was at any moment, no matter how busy I was serving drinks or clearing tables. Eventually, they returned to their table, and I got them more drinks. I helped out Gus in the kitchen for a short time, and when I returned, the table was empty, the check sitting on the scarred wood with a signed credit card slip and a pile of cash.

I was shocked at the flash of disappointment I felt that Stefano had left and not said goodbye. I lifted the money, my eyes widening at the generous tip. The bill was signed by Brett, and I wondered if it was he or Stefano who left the extravagant addition. I was distracted from my thoughts by the sound of Stefano's laughter, and I snapped up my head, seeing him by the pool table, casually leaning on a cue stick, looking far too sexy for my peace of mind. Lara, the other waitress, was standing in front of him, chatting. She was close to him. Too close. I heard her high-pitched laughter and watched as she twirled a lock of hair around her finger while she flirted with Stefano.

I was across the bar in an instant, my feet carrying me before I even realized what was happening. "My customer, Lara. If he needs anything, I can get it."

She glanced at me. "I cashed them out for you."

"Thanks. I got it from here."

She frowned. "I started a new ticket."

"I'll make sure you're looked after," Stefano interrupted smoothly. "Gabby and I are old friends."

Lara pouted. "I can be your friend too."

He smiled, and jealousy tore through me. "Always happy to make a new friend, but I think Gabby's got me covered." He glanced at me. "Right?"

"Yes."

Lara flounced away, and Stefano tilted his head. "Well, that was interesting."

Sanity returned, and I was shocked at my behavior. Why did I care if Lara served him? Why on earth had I stomped over and acted like some jealous, jilted lover? I liked Lara, and we got along well. What was I thinking?

What the hell was this man doing to me?

I met his amused eyes and straightened my shoulders.

I held out the stack of money. "You left too much."

He eyed the cash and shrugged. "It was Chase's turn to tip. I had nothing to do with it."

"Give him some back."

He held up his hands, shaking his head. "Nope. You treated us well, and he likes to show his appreciation. We all do. We understand how hard it is to work in the service industry. You don't want to insult him, do you?"

I couldn't shake the feeling he had more to do with it than he was admitting. But I wasn't going to argue. I shoved the money into my apron pocket. "Tell him I said thank you."

Suddenly, Stefano was right in front of me, too close for me to ignore. The scary part was that I wasn't sure I wanted to ignore him. "Now can we get back to your little jealousy fit?"

I felt the heat in my cheeks, but I refused to admit anything to him. "You were my ticket."

He laughed low and deep in his chest, reaching out to tuck a stray curl behind my ear. "Sure, Gabby. Your ticket."

He leaned closer. "I'll be your ticket to anything you want. You just have to ask."

I wanted to push him away. To snap at him. But he smelled so good and he was such a warm pillar of strength in front of me, I couldn't seem to find it in me to do either.

"Tell me something. Is Gabby your name or your nickname?"

"Gabriella," I replied. "Gabby is easier."

"Hmm. *Gabriella*. It suits you." His scent washed over me as he inched closer. "I like it."

My name being called brought reality crashing down. I was standing in the bar, far too close to a man who drove me crazy. A customer. I wasn't supposed to get close to customers. I wasn't supposed to get close to anyone.

I stepped back, gazing in shock at Stefano, shocked by how I could have forgotten where I was. Why I was there.

"I'll check on you later," I said and turned, hurrying from him.

"I look forward to it," he called.

I sped up, trying to get away.

Stefano was suddenly far more dangerous than I had expected.

I felt his stare the rest of the night. He sipped tonic, played pool with a couple of regulars, and chatted with Ziggy.

Lara kept fluttering around him, driving me insane. She was the moth to his flame, and she wanted to get burned. Badly. He was unfailingly polite, always listening to what she had to say but refusing to let her get too close. He was a master at dodging her wandering hands, easing away when she stepped too far into his personal space. Often as she stood in front of him talking, I found his eyes directed toward me. He threw me a wink at one point as I was polishing glasses, covertly lifting his eyebrows in amusement.

I tried not to laugh at his drollness, but I failed.

I came from the kitchen carrying the last tray of glasses, surprised to find him gone. I glanced at my watch, realizing last call had happened and we'd be closing in twenty minutes. I quickly finished the glasses, cashed out, and gathered my coat.

"See you tomorrow, Ziggy."

"You get to leave first next shift you work with Lara."

I frowned. "Why?"

He snorted. "You don't think I didn't see you doing all the work while Lara was busy trying to get noticed? She can close tomorrow and do all the things you did tonight she shoulda been helping you with."

"Thanks." I glanced around the bar. "I assume she left?"

"Yeah, the big guy finally succumbed." He sounded bitter.

My stomach clenched and my throat tightened. Stefano had left with Lara? The room seemed to shift, and I reached out, clutching the edge of the bar, holding it so tight my knuckles were white.

"Oh," I breathed out.

"He seemed like a decent guy. I hope he knows what he's doing. She's a lot to take on," Ziggy huffed, then snapped off the overhead light on the bar. "I should know."

He walked away, mumbling. He and Lara had an on-again, off-again relationship. Both of them were stubborn, and Lara liked to flirt, which caused them a lot of problems. At times, it was amusing to watch. But this wasn't one of those times.

I stepped outside, the door closing behind me. My legs felt heavy and my chest ached.

I shouldn't care who Lara went home with. Who Stefano chose to sleep with. It didn't matter—it was none of my business. Obviously, he was as big a flirt as Lara, which shouldn't surprise me, given his actions during our brief encounters. The two of them deserved each other, and I was better off out of it, I assured myself.

The bar lights shut off behind me, leaving just the one overhead light in the parking lot. The other one was burned out, occasionally flickering as if to remind Ziggy to fix it, but it did little good.

Five vehicles were left in the lot. Ziggy's van, the two cars belonging to the kitchen staff were parked on one side, and my SUV and a truck were farther down, parked on the other side under the burned-out light. I sighed and trudged toward my car, my steps lumbering and slow.

I was being ridiculous. I had no idea why the thought of Stefano leaving with Lara was upsetting me so much, yet it was. I grabbed the clip from my hair, letting the curls loose, and tossed the clip into my bag in anger. I refused to let the actions of a man upset me anymore. I had done that long enough. I tossed my head in defiance.

The sight of a tall, large body coming around the side of the truck parked beside mine startled me, and my steps faltered, my breathing suddenly fast with panic. Until I heard the voice breaking the silence of the night.

"You walk out to your vehicle alone every night?" Stefano crossed his arms. "I would think Ziggy would at least walk you out. Make sure you were safe."

I stopped in my tracks at his words—why would he care?

Why was he here?

"Not your concern," I snapped.

He glanced around. "He needs to fix these lights. You shouldn't be parked in the dark."

I walked past him. "I'll be sure to tell him that."

"I'll speak to him about it. It's not safe."

"Don't bother." I opened the passenger door and flung in my bag.

"It's not a bother," he replied from right behind me.

I tamped down the feeling of warmth that he cared enough to be worried. Very few people worried about me anymore. Instead, I found my anger and spun around, facing him.

"Finished already? That must be the shortest hookup on record," I tsked. "Maybe you need to cut back on the steroids if they're affecting your performance, big guy."

He frowned. "Hookup?"

"With Lara," I spat. "Or did you already forget her name? Look out for her, Hulk. She's a lot of work."

For a moment, he looked confused, then a smile broke out on his face. He reached out and tucked a curl behind my ear. I slapped his hand away, but he only chuckled.

"You're cute when you're jealous."

I gaped at him, aghast. "I-I'm not *jealous*."

He moved closer, crowding me. I stepped back, the cold metal of the SUV hitting my back. Stefano braced his arms on the hood, caging me in.

"I came out to wait for you, hoping your little friend would take the hint. She didn't. Instead, she followed, so I told her exactly the way things were, and she left." He traced his finger along my cheek. "I never touched her, and I never will. I don't play around, *Gabriella*." He whispered my name, the sound a caress falling off his tongue. "You understand what I'm saying?"

I swallowed, my throat suddenly dry. "W-what?"

"I told her I was here for you. *Only you*. I made sure she got in her car safely and left. That's all, *Tesoro*."

I swallowed at the way the endearment rolled off his tongue. Once again, all I could do was stutter. "M-me?"

He cupped my cheek, his thumb drawing circles on my skin. His touch was tender. His eyes, however, were intense. Dark, piercing, and focused entirely on me. He bent and brushed his mouth to mine. Soft, sweet, light as a feather. It made me want more.

"You," he repeated.

"You–you didn't…" I let the words trail off.

"No."

Relief flooded through me. His words sank in. *Only you. Tesoro.* He was right. I was jealous. It had been eating me up inside, thinking he was touching her. That she would know the wonder of his mouth, the way his body felt pressed to hers. I had hated the idea.

I stopped thinking and, for the first time in a very long while, only felt.

Reacted.

I flung my arms around his neck, lifted up on my toes, and I kissed him. His shock was evident, and then he recovered. He wrapped his strong arms around me, lifting me easily, and he took control, slanting his mouth over mine and kissing me back. Deep, possessive, and intense. His tongue invaded my mouth, stroking along mine. His breath filled me, warming me from the inside. He groaned low in his chest as I slid my hands into his short hair, tugging him closer. As close as I could get him without crawling under his skin. He gripped my ass with his hands, kneading firmly. I held him tighter, lost to the moment. To him.

He was hard and solid against me, his muscles like bands on his torso. His arms were huge—too big for me to wrap my hands around, but he held me with a gentleness that was comforting yet sexy. His scent, that crisp, woodsy scent, surrounded me. His taste filled my head, his touch settling my mind. He was solid. Warm. Safe.

And wanted me as much as I wanted him.

I whimpered as he ground against me, his bulge evident, hitting me exactly where I needed it. I had been wrong—he had no problems with steroids. The odd thought caused a giggle to erupt from my throat, and Stefano pulled back, frowning.

"Why the hell are you laughing right now, woman?"

"I guess there're no, ah, issues here." I flexed, rubbing against him.

"Only that we're not some place private," he growled. "What I want to do to you…" He trailed off, covering my mouth again.

I groaned at his touch. His kiss. Pinning me against the SUV, he slid one hand into my hair, fisting my curls as he worked my mouth. His other hand ran over my thigh, cupped my ass, and slid between my legs, touching, teasing, lingering. The ache, low in my belly and spreading, became acute. Intense. My body became a mass of trembling limbs and aching need. For him.

He shifted me higher, opening me up more, and I felt his fingers delve under the short black skirt of my "uniform." Up and down, he slid them along my thigh, going higher, deeper, each time until he slipped his long fingers under the satin of my panties, touching me where I ached the most.

I gasped into his mouth, and my head fell back. Stefano licked, kissed, and bit at my neck, sucking my lobe into his mouth, whispering low, dirty words into my ear.

"Feel you, *Tesoro*. How wet you are. Soft. You're so soft." He glided his fingers over me, finding my clit and stroking it. "So beautiful in your need. You feel so good on my fingers. Hot. Silky. So wet, baby. You have no idea how turned on I am right now. How fucking beautiful you are."

I was lost in a sea of sensation. His mouth. His body. His magical fingers on me. The air around us was cool, but in his arms, I was on fire. He slipped one finger inside me, making me whimper. He added another, pressing his thumb to my clit and rubbing tight, intense circles on it, his touch sure and perfect. I began to shake, my entire body reacting to him. To his touch. He sped up his movements, covering my mouth with his, his tongue once again twisting with mine.

Colors exploded behind my eyes as my orgasm hit me. Hard, potent, and powerful. My body locked down as it raced through me, obliterating everything in its path. I bucked against his hand, my muscles spasming around his fingers. I screamed my release into his mouth, his lips swallowing my cries. I gripped his shoulders, tightened my legs around him as I rode out the sensation. The pleasure was so great, I almost passed out.

Until it ebbed. Trailed off into low tremors that shook me. His mouth gentled, his kisses becoming tender touches, sweet presses of his lips. He slid his hand from me, wrapping me in his embrace. "You are so beautiful when you come for me," he murmured into my ear. "So fucking beautiful. I can't wait to get you naked and in my bed and feel you come all over my cock."

It hit me. What happened. What I had *allowed* to happen. Our gazes clashed, his filled with understanding.

"Don't. Don't freak out." He kissed me. "That was perfect. *You* were perfect."

"I can't–I don't…" I groaned, letting my head fall to his neck. Why did he reduce me to this stuttering woman, incapable of thinking or talking straight?

"I know, *Tesoro*. I know. You do the same to me."

Jesus. Now I was saying my disjointed thoughts out loud.

"I mean, I have never—" I waved my hand "—done *that* in a parking lot." Embarrassment flooded my system. "Oh my God, let me go."

His arms tightened. "No."

"Please."

He set me on my feet but didn't release me.

"Look at me," he commanded.

I lifted my eyes to his, startled to see how close his face was to mine.

"Thank you," he murmured. "For trusting me." Then in a gesture I didn't expect, he pressed his lips to my forehead, his mouth lingering.

I tried to find my anger. My indignation. I couldn't. All I felt was contentment. Satisfaction. My body felt as if every muscle had turned to liquid. Once again, the feeling of being safe and protected welled within me. I wanted to stay in his arms forever.

Sadly, I knew that wasn't possible.

I pushed at his chest, and he eased back. My gaze dropped to his crotch, and I wanted to groan. Tentatively, I slid my hand along his waistband, but he caught it in his large palm, shaking his head and kissing it.

"Not tonight."

"But that seems unfair. It looks, ah, uncomfortable. I could help you with that."

He rested his head on my shoulder, turning his face so his breath blew over my skin. "Jesus, you have no idea how tempting that is." He kissed the juncture of my neck. "I want you alone, not on your knees in a parking lot. You mean too much for that."

"But—"

His mouth silenced me, his lips sliding over mine sensuously. "Soon," he promised. "You must be tired, and you need to get home."

Reality struck like a bolt of lightning. "Theo," I gasped. I had to get home. Panicked, I pushed at him, digging in my pocket for my keys. "I have to go."

He didn't argue, instead, walked me around to the driver's side, waiting until I slid in. I turned the key, hitting the steering wheel in frustration when it didn't turn over. It did this sometimes, and it took several attempts to get it going. I tried again, cursing low as it clicked and nothing else.

"Your battery is dead."

"But I just got it," I insisted, turning the key.

His hand covered mine. "That won't work. Trust me."

"What am I going to do?" I mumbled. Normally, Ziggy would drive me home, except I knew he would be drowning his sorrows over Lara already.

Stefano held out his hand. "Come with me."

Strangely enough, I did.

We pulled up in front of the house. Stefano bent low, studying the Victorian-style residence. "Nice."

"Mrs. Scott has lived here for forty years. She has the main floor. I live upstairs."

He nodded. "I live not far from here."

"Oh, not in Littleburn?"

"No, we're only ten minutes away from there, and I like Lomand."

"Yes, it's a nice town."

"And you mentioned your neighbor looks after Theo?"

"Yes, her son Alfie has his turn tonight." I indicated the flickering light behind the upstairs blind. "He's still playing video games. He'll go home once I'm inside." I pointed to the larger house next door. "He lives there."

He nodded. "Okay. We'll get our tow truck to get your car in the morning. Do you have errands tomorrow?"

"I always have errands. And I have a shift."

"Do you ever get a night off?"

"Sundays. Sometimes a Tuesday or Wednesday. Depends how busy it is."

"You work too hard."

I narrowed my eyes. "I do what I have to do."

He held up his hands. "Just stating a fact. I'll pick you up at nine and take you to the garage. You can have a loaner for the day while we figure out what's going on."

I hesitated. "I, ah, have a budget. It's not very big."

He nodded. "Most people do. I'll keep that in mind. Hopefully it's just a loose cable or something." He paused. "Give me your cell number, and I'll make sure to call before we do anything over a hundred bucks."

I squirmed a little, unable to meet his eyes. "I can give you Mrs. Scott's number, and she'll take a message."

"That's fine." He slid his fingers under my chin, making me look at him. "Go inside, get some sleep. I've got you, okay? We'll get the car fixed and figure this all out."

"This?" I asked with a frown.

"You and me."

"Ah," was all I was able to offer. I had a thousand protests, denials, and reasons why there wasn't an us. Why there couldn't be an us. But somehow, they were all jumbled in my head, and I couldn't get the words out.

It had to be the orgasm from earlier—it messed with my mind. I felt off-kilter and unsteady, as if my brain was detached from my body.

He leaned close and kissed me. "Go inside, *Tesoro*. I'll be here in the morning. Everything is going to be okay. I promise."

I walked to the door, turning when I got there. He was watching, waiting for me to go inside. Right there, just as he promised.

I climbed the steps, thanked Alfie, and followed him down to lock the door behind him. Stefano was still there, the truck rumbling. He waited until Alfie was home, then he drove off.

His protective ways made me feel warm. I presented a tough front to people. I had to. I had to look after Theo and watch out for us. I made do with what I had, and I didn't complain, mostly because I had no one to listen. Stefano's assurances that everything would be okay were nice words, but I knew better than to believe him. The endearment he called me—I thought it meant sweetheart or something. I would have to look it up. It sounded nice rolling off his tongue. But he shouldn't be calling me nice things.

Stefano seemed to know how to make me feel as if he saw what I was hiding. It was as if he wanted to take some of the burden off my shoulders. It was a strange sensation, and one I couldn't trust.

I had the oddest thought as I climbed back to the second floor.

I would miss Stefano more than anyone else in my life once he was out of it.

Because there was the strong possibility I would have to leave at some point. Or he would walk away when he found out why I kept running.

It felt inevitable.

CHAPTER SIX

Stefano

I dragged Chase with me to get Gabby's car at six. By seven, I was under the hood, shocked the car was even running. It needed a lot of little things fixed—expensive little things. Belts, hoses, clamps, spark plugs, rusted parts. I rattled off the list as Chase wrote it down, whistling when I stopped. Then I added a complete tune-up, another tire on the back, a new battery, and a set of windshield wipers.

"The repairs are more than the SUV is worth," Chase observed.

I wiped my forehead, knowing he was right. Except I knew she couldn't afford a new vehicle. It was obvious she knew nothing about cars and had no clue how bad it was. She'd been making Band-Aid fixes to keep it going, but it wasn't going to last much longer.

Chase glanced at his watch. "I have to go and start my pickups."

"Thanks for coming in early and helping."

"No worries." He laughed. "Not like I have a long way to go."

I laughed with him. Chase lived in the small apartment over the garage. When Maxx had made a bunch of renovations, he'd added the apartment upstairs to replace the small room at the back of the garage. That area became part of the new, larger parts storage space. The new upstairs spot was a self-contained unit, and Chase was a happy tenant.

He left, and I went to get a cup of coffee, sipping the strong brew.

Maxx appeared, plucking the list from my hand. He whistled as he looked it over. "SUV's not worth it."

I sighed and rubbed my face. "That's not the worst of it. I looked under it. The rust is bad. Really bad."

He crossed his arms over his massive chest and looked thoughtful. "If we gave it a good tune-up and replaced the belts and battery, it would run smoother. Give her a little more time."

"I hate the thought of her driving it. I'm not even sure she should."

"What if we found her a better one?"

I met his eyes. "I have the feeling she's living check to check, Maxx. Any sort of new vehicle isn't in the budget. I was going to fix this up and only charge her for a few cables and cover it myself."

"You care for this girl."

I thought of last night. Her indignation when she saw me. The way we constantly sparred. Her unexpected reaction to Lara's flirting.

How she fell apart in my arms. The feel of her on my fingers. The scent of her in my nose. The taste of her in my mouth. How badly I'd wanted to take her home and keep her with me all night.

"There's something about her," I muttered.

Charly waddled in, seemingly larger than she was the day before. She looked tired, but she was grinning. "About whom? Who are we gossiping about? Holy moly, is it Gabby?"

Maxx chuckled, shaking his head. He bent, kissing Charly's forehead, and settled her into the chair. "Relax, Red. If you get too excited, you'll go into labor. Stefano and I are talking about a car."

"Gabby's SUV. I saw it. Chase told me you were at the bar last night and she's a waitress. He said you stayed behind to talk to her and you towed her car here this morning." She leaned forward, eager. "What's going on?"

I had to groan. Chase told Charly everything. Every. Damn. Thing. There were no secrets here. He adored her, and they were close—she was like a mother to him. Of course he would rat me out.

Maxx picked up his coffee cup. "I'll just leave you to it. I'll reread the list and do a ballpark figure."

"Bastard," I muttered as he strode from the office. His laughter floated back, but he never stopped.

Charly waited, expectant.

I ran a hand through my hair and decided to keep it short and simple. "Yes, we went to the bar she worked at—a total coincidence. Her car wouldn't start. I drove her home and brought the SUV here. It's in bad shape. Really bad."

"But she can't afford many repairs," Charly finished for me.

"And she's proud. Stubborn. She won't accept charity. Especially from me," I added.

"And you like her. Really like her."

"Are we in grade eight?"

She grinned, not put off by my words. "Just getting the facts." Charly seemed lost in thought for a moment. "What if it's not charity?"

"I'm listening."

"I need to talk to Maxx, but I have an idea."

"Okay."

She held out her hands. "I need help up."

I gently pulled her from the chair, then bent and kissed her cheek. "Thanks, Charly."

She smiled, her eyes dancing. "So much more fun than ordering spark plugs."

She headed toward Maxx, and I returned to the SUV, thinking. I had a feeling Gabby was going to be upset when I gave her the news. Very upset. I contemplated lying—simply fixing everything, telling her it was done and not explaining how bad it was. Paying for it myself. Except I hated lying. And she would, somehow, find out, and I had a feeling part of her mistrust with people was that she'd been lied to before. And the bottom line was, the vehicle shouldn't be driven anymore.

Charly appeared by my elbow, smiling. "Maxx agrees with you. The vehicle is in bad shape. When you get Gabby, bring her to see me."

"What do you have in mind?"

She shook her head. "I'll talk to Gabby first."

I trusted Charly completely. "Okay. I'm going to get her soon."

"Great."

She padded away, almost dancing in her excitement. Maxx leaned on the workbench, watching her, his adoration evident in his stare, a small smile playing on his mouth. I half expected him to follow her and shut the office door before he kissed her senseless the way she liked. When she disappeared from view, his smile dropped, and I had to hold in my laughter as he did exactly what I expected. He could barely stand to have her out of his sight. I heard her giggle before the door shut, and I knew Charly was having a good morning.

I realized the time and grabbed the set of car keys for the garage van. I didn't want to be late picking up Gabriella—she was dealing with enough stress, and I didn't want to add to it.

Even if when she was annoyed, she was adorable, and somehow, we ended up with our mouths connected.

I knocked on the door, smiling down at the little old lady that opened it.

"You must be Mrs. Scott."

"And you have to be Stefano—or, as Gabby refers to you, the PITA," she announced, crossing her arms and gazing up at me, not at all worried over the vast difference in our sizes.

She barely came up to my chest, her snow-white hair gleaming in the sunlight. Despite her frosty tone, her blue eyes danced with humor and her face was kind. A multitude of laugh lines crossed her face, like a delicate spider web of etched merriment embedded in her skin.

"Guilty as charged," I admitted. I bent my knees, lowering myself to her level. "But she gives as good as she gets, you know."

She sniffed. "I wouldn't expect otherwise. You gonna do right by her?"

"I'll try," I replied honestly. "If she lets me."

She tapped her foot. "How are you at changing lightbulbs?"

I blinked at the abrupt shift in conversation. "An expert."

"Come in."

For the next ten minutes, I followed the tiny woman around and swapped out some burned-out bulbs. Then she mentioned a clogged drain in the kitchen and a loose cupboard door. I promised to return soon with some tools to take care of both.

Appearing satisfied, she nodded. "Gabby's upstairs. The steps are to the right, behind the door you came in."

I tried not to laugh. The old fox knew exactly what she was doing, waylaying me. I bent and kissed her downy cheek. "I'll be back tomorrow."

"See that you are."

I climbed the steps, pausing outside the door at the top. I knocked, grinning when Theo opened it, beaming up at me. He wore his red shirt and hat. "Stefo!"

"Hey, little man."

Gabby appeared, looking upset. "Theo, you never open the door without Mommy," she scolded.

"But I heard him. I knew it was Stefo!"

"You should listen to your mom. She knows best," I advised.

"Why?"

I crouched down. "Moms are special. They. Know. *Everything*," I whispered, unfurling my fingers in a ta-da fashion.

His eyes went wide. "Like when I say I brushed my teeth but didn't?"

I looked up at Gabby and winked. "Yep. Exactly like that."

"Whoa," he breathed.

"Get your backpack," Gabby instructed, tenderly running her hand over his head. "We have to get going."

He disappeared down the hall, and I stepped into her place. She watched me warily as I moved closer, capturing her waist and pulling her close. I kissed her full mouth.

"Hello, *Tesoro*."

"Um, hi," she replied, looking nervous and quite adorable. Her wild curls were loose, and she wore a frilly, girly blouse and skirt. She was pretty, feminine, and very sexy.

"You look lovely."

"Oh." She swallowed, seemingly at a loss for what to say. "I have lots of errands."

I chuckled and kissed the end of her nose. "Get your stuff and we'll go."

"How's my SUV?"

"Charly has all the numbers. She'll talk to you when we get there." I recited exactly what Charly told me to say.

"Oh God, it's that bad."

I had to be honest. "It was more than I thought it would be."

She went pale, and I stepped forward to give her a hug. She came into my arms easily, which I liked, and she accepted my embrace. In fact, she wrapped her arms around my waist and held on tight. She sighed, her voice so quiet I could barely hear her.

"I'm not sure how much more I can take."

I held her tighter and kissed the top of her head. "It's gonna be fine. I promise." I stepped back and cupped her check, dropping a kiss to her mouth. "Get your stuff."

Theo came down the hall. "Wanna see my room, Stefo?"

"Sure, bud." He grabbed my hand and dragged me to his doorway. His twin bed was against the wall, and the large room was painted a light blue. He had toys and puzzles, games, trucks, and cars scattered everywhere. He held up one of his small treasures.

"This is my favorite," he confided. "I love cars."

I hunched down and took it from him. "Good choice." I lowered my voice. "I have a real one just like this. Maybe one day I can take you for a ride."

His eyes grew big. "Really?" he whispered.

"We'll have to ask your mom. But not today."

"Okay."

I stood and followed him back down the hall. There was a small eat-in kitchen, a compact TV room, and another bedroom.

Gabby had obviously given Theo the largest room so he could spread out his toys. Her room held a double bed, a night table, and a dresser. That was it. The TV room contained a love seat and a chair, plus the TV and a couple of small tables. It was neat, tidy, but very sparse. The only room that showed any extras belonged to Theo. I had no doubt that Gabby made sure he came first in everything.

I would have to see what I could do to change that.

Gabby was waiting, and we headed downstairs. Mrs. Scott waited, reminding me I'd promised to come back. I assured her it hadn't slipped my mind and I would see her very soon.

"I forgot. My tap is dripping."

"I'll be sure to bring a wrench."

She reached up and patted my cheek. "That's a good boy."

I had to bend so she could reach me. I chuckled at her words, thinking no one had called me a boy for a very long time.

In the van, Theo laughed as I made a big deal of pulling out the kid seat assembly that was built in. I strapped him in, pretending to have trouble picking him up.

"You're big," I huffed.

He laughed in delight. "Mom says I'm growing like a weed."

"A huge one." I ruffled his hair, then opened the door for Gabby. She stepped in and I grinned. "Should I buckle you in too?"

She shook her head primly. "I can manage."

"Just checking."

En route to the garage, she turned in her seat. Theo was busy enjoying the DVD that was playing, so he was ignoring us.

"I'll talk to Mrs. Scott. You don't have to do her repairs. She's testing you."

I waved her off. "It's all good. I'm pretty handy. Gotta make a good impression."

"I think you already did."

"With her or you?"

She turned and crossed her arms. "Mrs. Scott is easily impressed."

I reached over, laying my hand on her thigh. "And you?"

She lifted one shoulder, gazing out the window. "I'm tougher."

I squeezed her leg lightly. "I'll have to try harder."

She didn't say anything, but as I went to pull my hand away, she covered it with hers. She kept looking out the window, her fingers idly stroking the back of my hand. It felt nice, so it stayed there the rest of the drive.

At the garage, Theo sat with Maxx, who was working on an engine. He had run around, greeting everyone like old friends, clearly excited to be there. He was fascinated, asking a hundred and one questions that Maxx was answering in his low, patient voice. I went with Gabby to the office to talk with Charly, knowing Theo was in good hands.

"Okay, so I'm going to be honest," Charly stated.

Gabby swallowed as she sat down. "Good. I prefer honest."

"Your SUV is basically toast. It's not worth the cost of the repairs it would require to make it safe."

I gaped at Charly. I thought she'd at least break it to Gabby gently or fib a little. Say something positive.

"But it was running yesterday. Can't you just fix what is broken?"

Charly shook her head. "It's way more than a bad wire. The vehicle isn't safe, Gabby."

Gabby's shoulders tensed, and I felt her anxiety. Before I could say anything, Charly leaned forward.

"That's the bad news. But holy moly, have I got some good news."

"Do tell," I muttered.

"We want to buy your SUV. And Maxx is willing to make you a great deal."

The news surprised me, yet it didn't. I knew why she was making the offer, but since Gabby didn't, she wouldn't accept it so easily.

"I don't need charity," Gabby said, lifting her chin in that stubborn way I was beginning to recognize. "Just fix what you can for my budget, and I'll figure the rest out later."

Charly leaned forward—at least as far forward as she could these days. It was more of a tilt.

"As a friend and a fellow mother, I can't let you do that. The SUV isn't safe for you to drive Theo in."

Gabby jerked at her words but stayed silent. Charly regarded her steadily. "Listen to my offer, Gabby."

Gabby crossed her legs, swinging her foot, her voice tight. "Fine."

"Maxx wants to buy your SUV for our classes. We've been wanting to start some basic hands-on learning, and your SUV would be perfect. It still runs but needs a lot of work. It would suit the situation really well." She sat back. "And in return, Maxx has a great little SUV he would trade you for it."

"That hardly seems like a good business proposition for Maxx."

Charly held up her hand. "I'm not finished."

Gabby nodded, her shoulders tight.

"I want to wrap the vehicle with the garage info. So, basically, you'll be a driving ad for us. Considering you work at a bar and drive around Lomand and the surrounding area, the visibility for us is great." Charly rubbed her stomach. "You told me you used to be in charge of merchandise control where you worked."

"Yes."

"I'm going to need some help with things when this little bundle shows up. Ordering parts, inventory. You would have access to the system and could do most of the work from home with a laptop we provide. Once every two weeks, you come in here and do a physical inventory. You can bring Theo with you." She waited a moment. "We'll agree on a number, figure out the trade, the value of the ad on the vehicle, and how many hours we're talking to make both sides happy."

Gabby was silent.

Charly's voice changed. It became quieter, assuring. "No charity, no handouts. We need a car to practice on, you need a better vehicle. I need help, and you could do the job. Seems easy peasy to me."

"Could I talk to Stefano for a moment?"

"Of course." Charly held out her hands, and I helped her from the chair. "I need to pee again," she announced. "Then I'm going to get a snack. You talk and let me know."

She left, shutting the door behind her. I sat across from Gabby and waited for her to talk.

"Did you put them up to this?"

"No. I had no idea. Charly isn't lying, though. Maxx has been looking for a practice vehicle to expand the classes. Hands-on, so women know how to change an air filter or a spark plug. A worn hose." I paused. "I'll be honest, Gabriella—your SUV has a plethora for us to use."

"So why not just fix it in a couple of classes and I can drive it? I'll pay for the parts."

I shook my head. "First off, the underbody is badly rusted and could give way any time, so it's too dangerous for you to keep driving. It won't be on the road, but the engine will be used from now on. Secondly, we'll reuse the SUV—constantly. Replace the good with the bad for the next class. Readjust so the engine sounds bad but runs the way it is now. Show them how it sounds after. We find if they see it, hear it, maybe work on it a little, it helps them understand more."

"Makes sense, I suppose."

"It was Charly's idea. The whole concept of the classes was hers from the start. She's brilliant that way."

"You're very fond of her."

I met her eyes. "I adore her the way I adore my sisters. I consider her a friend—my family. Nothing more." I drew in a deep breath. "Not the way I feel about you."

Our gazes held, then she dropped her eyes. "I didn't expect all this," she confessed with a wave of her hand.

Instinctually, I knew she wasn't only referring to the cars. "To quote someone much smarter than me—my mama—life has a way of bringing us what we need when we need it," I stated dryly.

"You think I need you?" she asked, her eyes flashing, a proud jut to her chin.

I tilted my head, hearing the panic in her voice. "Maybe I need *you*, Gabriella. Ever consider that?"

"No."

I stood, beginning to feel angry. She was more than proud. Obstinate came to mind. So did pigheaded. "Maybe you should. Talk to Maxx and Charly. Listen to the numbers with an open mind. Stop being so stubborn when someone wants to help you."

She tossed her head, still inflexible. "Usually help comes with a cost."

"I don't know what happened to you in your past that makes you so wary, but I'll tell you this right now. Nothing being offered to you has a hidden price tag for you to pay. No one will ask anything of you except what you agree on." I clenched my hands. "And even if you tell me to leave you alone and you don't want to be a part of my life, the offer is still there for the SUV."

"So, if I say no to you, you're telling me your friends would still help me?"

"Yes, I am."

"I find that hard to believe."

"Who did this to you?" I asked. "Who made you so wary of people, you can't think of anything but the bad?"

She looked away, not answering. But I saw the flash of pain in her eyes and the way she curled in on herself. I hated it. I liked the vibrant, sparring part of her personality. Her feisty side. Her wittiness. Not this worried, hesitant side. My annoyance deflated, and I moved in front of her.

"Go talk to them. Whatever you decide, I'll support you. But keep an open mind." I cupped her cheek, bent, and kissed her forehead. Her hand flew up, grabbing my wrist, and our eyes locked. I had so much to say to her, but this wasn't the time or the place. I wanted to hear her story, but I wasn't sure she trusted me enough to tell it. We seemed to be at an impasse, and until she was ready, I had to be patient.

I kissed her again and strode from the room before I did something stupid.

I had a feeling I'd already done enough.

CHAPTER SEVEN

Gabby

Maxx stared at me, his head tilted to the side as if studying a puzzle. "Trust me, Gabby. I'm not doing this out of the goodness of my heart."

I looked around the interior of the vehicle, tamping down the unusual feeling of excitement. It was ten years newer than the one I drove. The instruments all functioned, and there were no cracks on the dashboard. The seats weren't torn—in fact, they were leather and had seat heaters. The radio worked. And when I turned the key, it purred.

"This seems so much better than mine," I admitted.

Beside Maxx, Charly smiled. "That's the point."

"Your SUV had low mileage, but it hadn't been maintained long before you bought it. It was the rust eating away at it that made it dangerous," Maxx explained. "Add in all the little things that needed doing, it was a disaster waiting to happen." He patted the hood. "This little beauty has higher kilometers but has been maintained properly. It'll run for another few years—especially if we take care of it. And since you'll be representing the garage while you drive it, it will be."

"It was all I could afford."

"Understood. But now, you can drive something better. I can use your car. You can help my wife and me get more advertising out there. Everybody wins because we're taking care of one another," Maxx offered, his voice low and patient. "That's how we work here."

I tightened my hands on the steering wheel, swallowing down the sudden lump in my throat. Stefano's words played through my mind.

"Life has a way of bringing us what we need when we need it."

And I needed this car. I needed to keep Theo safe. The thought of not worrying that the SUV would break down on my way home or wondering if it would start after a long day of work would ease so much stress. Charly had shown me figures, a neat, well-structured document of the expenses needed to fix the car, the value of this one, and how it would be offset. I had studied it hard, not finding anything that would worry me. It was, as Stefano said, clear. No hidden price tags. I glanced at the couple standing beside the car. Maxx was a huge man, bigger than Stefano, and Charly looked tiny beside him. His arm was around her, resting on her bump, his love evident and his expression open and kind. Charly was warm and friendly, and I liked her a lot. I liked them both.

Maybe Stefano was right and I needed to stop being so stubborn.

I slid from the car and offered my hand to Maxx. "I accept."

My errands were made easier since I didn't have to worry if my vehicle would start or not. Theo was happy and chatty, exclaiming over the soft leather and talking about his new friends. When I told him I was returning to the garage the next day, he could barely contain himself. I had to promise his uniform would be ready.

"They need me, Mom."

"Okay, baby." I hid my smile, but his excitement made me happy. I was still smiling at work, even though it wasn't as busy as I hoped.

I returned to the garage the next day. I sat with Charly, and she showed me how their system worked. It was slick and well organized. The mechanic entered the parts required, and that fed into a master sheet. Anything immediate was handled differently, but the list was printed, the parts ordered, and Chase picked them up the next day. Anything removed from the stock room was flagged in a particular way, and Charly kept the stock room full. I could easily print the lists and place the orders from home before I left for my shifts at the bar. I could use my days off to work on the stock room, which Charly said only took her a few hours since the system was so well utilized. It was obvious she was the brains behind the success. She was meticulous, clever, and ran the garage with ease. I could see why Stefano was so fond of her.

Stefano seemed to avoid me. He worked in his own space, his specialty the airbrushing and design of restored autos and motorcycles. He only worked in the garage on occasion, Charly told me.

"When we're really busy or down a mechanic. He enjoys it, but his love is the design work. He's brilliant."

The pride in her voice was clear. Her relaxed, easy way with him made their closeness evident. When she took me through his area on my tour, he had been busy, hunched over a fender of a motor-cycle, his arm sweeping in small arcs, his face a study in concentration. I watched him for a moment, then we moved on. He was either deep in the zone or ignoring our presence.

Theo was in his glory. All the mechanics welcomed him and made a fuss over him. I knew Stefano had spent a little time with him, letting him use a couple of tools and "help" him with a simple task. I had never seen Theo's face so happy. It occurred to me how much he must have been wanting this. Missing it. He had very little male influence in his life. Alfie was really another kid, not someone Theo would look up to the way I saw him looking at Stefano or Maxx. He was sitting with Brett, who was showing him how to use a socket wrench. Theo ate it up and added another favorite guy to his roster. He talked nonstop all the way home, excited about his day.

"Stefo's smart, Mom."

"He is," I agreed.

"Brett said I was a great helper."

I smiled at him in the rearview mirror. "You are."

"Maxx said I could come back anytime."

"As long as you behave."

"Charly gave me a cookie. It was good. I like her."

"I like her too."

"I'm going to be a mechanic when I grow up. Just like them."

It was the first time he'd ever said anything like that. He'd never said he wanted to be a fireman or police officer—nothing. They had obviously made a great impression on him.

"You can be whatever you want to be," I assured him.

"Can I get a tattoo like Stefo?"

"No."

"Hmmph."

"Kids can't get tattoos. Only adults."

"Oh." He was quiet then spoke again. "I like this car. It's nice."

I patted the dashboard. "It is nice."

"Is Stefo your boyfriend?"

That one gave me pause. "Why would you ask that?"

"Because he came to the house, and no one ever comes to the house," he stated simply. "I like him. He can be your boyfriend, Mom."

"I'll keep that in mind."

"Okay." He leaned his head back, staring out the window. "You need to wash my uniform so I can be ready for the next time. The guys need my help."

I had to hide my smile. "Okay, Teddy Bear."

"Theo, Mom. I'm five. I'm too old for Teddy Bear now."

"You'll always be my Teddy Bear."

He closed his eyes and shook his head. "Not in front of the guys, okay?"

My shoulders shook with silent laughter. No doubt he'd heard that expression at the garage and picked it up right away. "All right. Theo, it is."

I had lost track of time, and I barely had time to make Theo his supper, do some laundry, and put on a pot of soup for Mrs. Scott. I sat with him as he ate, enjoying our usual routine. I always fed him before I left. My shift was from six to one, and I liked having supper with him. It made the odd, grueling schedule seem a little more normal. I walked him next door to Mrs. Wilson, who greeted him with affection and happily accepted the container of soup I brought.

"Alfie will take him home later and stay with him."

"Thanks."

The bar was busy tonight, and the time passed quickly. Lara seemed fine, not bothered, it would appear, by Stefano's rejection the other night. It didn't take me long to figure out she and Ziggy were back on. His long looks and her giggles every time she was close to the bar made me roll my eyes. I couldn't keep up with them. It quieted down by eleven, and Ziggy sent me home early. I had made a lot in tips already, and now that the bar was quiet, I knew leaving wasn't a big deal. I had the feeling it was more to be alone with Lara than anything, but I was fine with it since it meant some extra time at home for me, and Ziggy told me he would pay out my full shift. Both things were rare occurrences.

The SUV purred to life and was a pleasure to drive. I hummed to the music, feeling calmer than I had been in a long time. Theo was happy and healthy. I didn't have to worry about the vehicle I drove. I had steady employment and a place to live. I had met some nice people.

And then there was Stefano.

He crept into my thoughts all the time. He hadn't spoken to me other than a simple greeting since yesterday, and I knew he was confused. I wasn't sure how to make him understand. I had no idea what he would do if he found out what being involved with me entailed. Why I was so reluctant to get involved with anyone. Why I might disappear in the blink of an eye.

The other night had been one of the most sensual, exciting moments of my life. Surrounded by him. His incredible body pressed into mine. His innate strength tempered with a gentleness to his touch I had never experienced. The way his mouth worked me. How his fingers felt inside me. My explosive orgasm.

I sighed as I parked the SUV in the driveway, my head filled with thoughts of him.

I let myself in, the downstairs in darkness except for the small light Mrs. Scott always kept burning for me. The double doors to her place were drawn shut, so I knew she was in bed. Some nights, they were open and she was awake, and we would talk for a while. Other times, I simply shut off the light and headed upstairs once whoever was watching Theo left. If she woke later, I knew she always looked to see if the light was out. That was her way of checking up on me.

I climbed the steps and headed to the small TV room in order to let Alfie head home, surprised not to hear the low noise of his video game playing. In the doorway, I stopped short in shock at the sight that met my eyes.

Draped across the small love seat, his legs hanging over the end, was Stefano. Lying across his chest, his little hand resting on one massive arm, was Theo. Stefano's other arm was over Theo, anchoring him close. Theo's tousled head was resting on Stefano's shoulder, and they were both asleep. Stefano's deep, even breathing was interspersed with Theo's grumbly noises.

For a moment, all I could do was stare. They were adorable. One so large and protective, the other so small and safe, wrapped in a warm, gentle embrace. Their coloring was so similar, they looked as if they belonged together.

I had to blink away the sudden onslaught of tears.

Where was Alfie, and what was Stefano doing here?

I moved closer and laid my hand on Stefano's arm. He stirred, and I whispered his name. His eyes opened, blinked, then he smiled. It was wide, open, and warm. So warm, I felt it all over my body.

"*Tesoro*," he murmured. "You're home."

Something in my chest tightened at his words.

"What are you doing here?" I asked.

He glanced down, running his hand over Theo's curls.

"Make me a coffee and I'll tell you."

"Okay."

STEFANO

I carried Theo to his room, tucking him into bed. He'd barely moved as I'd lifted myself off the small sofa, still holding him. He burrowed under his blanket, and I watched him for a moment, lifting my shoulders and stretching out my back and neck. I was way too big to be sleeping on such a tiny piece of furniture.

I had arrived just after seven and spent over an hour doing little repairs for Mrs. Scott. She trailed behind me, nattering on about the house, the upkeep, and getting too old.

"I stay now for Gabby and Theo. She helps me so much."

"I'm happy to help too, Mrs. Scott."

"Peony. I told you to call me Peony."

"My mama taught me my elders were Mr. and Mrs. or sir and ma'am. Hard to break that habit."

"You were brought up right."

"I think so."

"Gabby's trying to do the same with that little boy up there. She's crazy about him." Mrs. Scott sighed. "She works so hard. Too hard."

"Does she work every night?"

"Except Sunday and Tuesday or Wednesday unless she picks up extra shifts," she confirmed. *"She told me the only job she could find in the daytime didn't pay her enough to cover Theo's care. Shame. She struggles so hard. I worry for her."*

I grunted as I tightened the washer on the faucet. I worried too.

Mrs. Scott tilted her head, studying me as I wiped my hands on a rag. *"Maybe I don't have to worry as much now?"*

I chuckled. *"That's up to her. As you pointed out, she's stubborn."*

She moved closer, laying her hand on my forearm. Her skin was as white as snow, blue veins running under the transparent skin like a road map. Her fingers were cool, the rings loose. Her hand looked tiny against me. Her voice was solemn.

"She's more than stubborn, Stefano. She's frightened. Something's got her spooked. I recognized that the first time I met her, but she's never told me what it is."

I frowned at her words. Gabby was scared of something from her past? I hadn't considered that. I thought she was cautious, stubborn. Fear hadn't entered my mind, but now that Mrs. Scott had pointed it out, it made sense. Gabby always seemed on edge, as if expecting the worst. Leery of strangers. Afraid to accept help or to depend on someone.

"Be patient with her," she said softly. "I have a feeling you could make a big difference in her life."

I nodded slowly.

The sound of a young voice made me look up. A teenager was in the double doorway, pale and sweating.

"Mrs. Scott, I'm not feeling so well. I think I need to go home."

"Where's Theo?" I asked, moving forward.

"In his room." The kid clutched his stomach. "I really gotta go."

I patted his shoulder. "We got this."

He turned and ran, and I looked back at Mrs. Scott. "Guess I'm staying awhile."

"Theo can come down here. He sleeps in the guest room a lot."

I shook my head. "No, I think a boys' night is in order."

Her smile was bright. "I think that's a good plan."

I walked into the kitchen, meeting Gabby's gaze. She indicated the box on the counter.

"You ordered pizza?"

"Little man said he was hungry. I hadn't had dinner. It was easy."

She slammed her hand on her hip. "I do feed him, you know. He had supper. In fact, he ate two bowls of spaghetti."

I shook my head, chuckling. "I have eight nieces and nephews, Gabby. I am well aware of when I'm being played. The fact was, I was hungry, and it was fun to share a pizza with the little guy." I tilted my head, making my voice soft. "I am also well aware that you are an amazing mother. Theo is a lucky kid to have you."

Her shoulders dropped. "I'm sorry. I didn't mean to snap. It's just..." She trailed off and I hoped she would explain, but instead, she shrugged. "I guess with being a single mother and the schedule we have to keep, I'm sensitive."

"I understand." I really did, but I needed her to know I wasn't judging her. I never would. "You got off early tonight?"

She nodded. "You'll be sad to know Lara has moved past you. She and Ziggy are back together—at least for today."

"Damn. My heart." I laid my hand on my chest. "That hurt."

Her lips quirked, and she turned to the counter. "Coffee is ready."

Forgetting my earlier frustration from that morning, and unable to stop myself, I sidled up behind her, dropping my head and brushing my lips along her exposed neck. "Smells good."

"The—the coffee?"

"That too," I agreed, dragging my mouth to her ear. "You smell better."

Her hands clenched into tight fists on the counter, and I felt the tremor race through her.

"You were angry with me," she whispered.

"Not angry," I disagreed, leaning my chin on her shoulder. "Frustrated. Confused."

"I'm sorry."

"You accepted the SUV?"

"Yes." She let out a long huff of air. "I really like it."

I spun her in my arms, hauling her up my chest with one arm. Our eyes locked. Her pupils dilated, and her breathing picked up. I stroked her neck, cupping her head in my hand. "I really like you."

Then my mouth was on hers.

She flung her arms around my neck, holding me tight. She opened for me, our tongues meeting, touching, and caressing. I lifted her to the counter, moving between her legs as I slanted my mouth over hers, kissing her harder. Deeper. Wanting more of her. More of her taste, more of how she felt in my embrace. More of her low, pleading whimpers that spurred me on and made my cock hard and heavy in my pants. I pulled her flush to me so she knew exactly the way she affected me. She pulled back, gasping.

"Holy shit, you're huge."

I cupped the back of her head. "I'm going to fit inside you perfectly. Your pretty little pussy was made for me. I know it."

"I'm not... I mean, it's too—"

I cut her off. "When you're ready. When we can be alone and I can have you every way I've been fantasizing about you since the first moment I saw you. I'll make sure you're ready. So ready, you'll be aching the same way I am. You'll be so drenched for me, I'll slide home like it's the bottom of the ninth in the final game of the World Series, the score is tied, and the bases are loaded. A grand slam."

She blinked. "Did you just compare us having sex to baseball?"

I grinned. "They both have balls."

"I'm beginning to think yours are bigger. You should have them checked."

I threw back my head in laughter, the passion of the moment gone. And that was good. I needed to know her, and she needed to trust me.

I kissed her forehead. "I'll do that."

"Stefano?" she whispered.

"Yeah, *Tesoro?*"

"I like pizza too."

"Are you hungry?"

"Starved," she replied, licking her lips, her eyes on my mouth.

"Do that again and I'm taking you right here, right now," I threatened, half hoping she would. "To hell with waiting."

Her cheeks flushed and I chuckled. I held out my hand. "Come on, Gabriella. Let me feed you."

I was gratified to see the flash of disappointment on her face. It matched the same way I felt.

And it gave me hope.

GABBY

I swallowed the last bite of pizza. Stefano had heated it up, and I enjoyed watching him move around my small kitchen. He told me about Alfie being ill and deciding to stay.

"Little man was happy to see me."

"What did you do, other than eat pizza?"

He grinned, draining his coffee. "Played with his cars and trucks. And dinosaurs. We decided dinosaurs were too big to fit in cars, but the trucks worked. We pillaged some cities and destroyed a few towns. Talked guy talk." He scratched his chin. "He didn't want to go to bed, so I lay on the love seat, and he sat on my chest talking and finally fell asleep." He shrugged sheepishly. "I guess I did too."

I shook my head in amazement. He sounded so nonchalant about hanging with Theo. "Your nieces and nephews must love you."

"I adore all of them. Plus, I let them get away with shit their parents don't. I like to spoil them a little."

"I can guarantee you made Theo's night. Probably his week."

"He's a good kid. Smart as a whip. He talks like an adult."

I sighed. "He's always been smart. And since I can't afford day care, most of his time is spent with me or other adults, so he is really advanced."

"Hey," he called.

I looked up.

"He's a great kid," he repeated. "You're doing an amazing job. Don't beat yourself up."

"I just want him to be okay."

"He already is. He's happy and content. He knows he's loved." He sat back. "Just because you can't give him stuff doesn't mean he isn't okay." He sighed. "My dad died when I was young. My parents had immigrated from Italy just before my oldest brother was born. Neither of them could speak English, but they learned. My dad's English was better than my mom's since he was exposed to it every day, while she stayed home and raised us." He smiled fondly. "Even today, she has her own way of speaking."

"You're very close with her."

He nodded. "There are six of us. After my dad passed, my mom had to go to work, and it was my siblings who had to step in. We had no family here, although my parents had great friends who helped when they could. There wasn't a lot of money left for 'things.' Hand-me-downs reigned. Used toys. Leftovers. Stretching a dollar as far as it would go. But there was a lot of love, and we made it work. We all turned out okay."

"I'm sorry about your dad."

He nodded. "He was larger-than-life. There wasn't anything he couldn't do. He was the greatest guy. I remember his friends coming over and showing my older brothers how to fix things in the house, taking us for the day, I'm sure to give my mom a break. Their wives cooking and bringing things over to help my mom. We all learned to cook. To do repairs." He met my gaze. "To accept help when offered, knowing it wasn't charity—it was friendship."

I traced the top of the table with my finger. "I see."

"What about your parents?" he asked quietly.

I fought down the pain his words stirred in my chest.

"They died in a fire when I was twenty-two."

"*Tesoro*, I'm sorry."

I swallowed down the lump in my throat. "We were at a friend's cottage. Someone forgot to put the cover on the fireplace before we went to bed, and a piece of wood rolled..." I trailed off and cleared my throat. "It was a log cabin and went up fast. My parents didn't get out. The owner's wife died as well. I, ah, have some scars on my back and hip where I got caught."

He reached across the table and grabbed my hand. "I'm sorry," he repeated.

I nodded, unable to speak.

"So they never met Theo."

"No."

"His, ah, father?"

I stood. "Not in the picture," I snapped.

I carried my plate to the counter, and immediately Stefano was behind me, encircling me in his arms.

"I didn't mean to upset you."

"I don't want to talk about it."

"Okay," he soothed. He slid his hand down to mine and tugged. I followed him to the small TV room, and we sat on the love seat. He sat in the middle, pulling me down to his lap so I was straddling him. He pressed my head to his shoulder, rubbing my stiff neck muscles, easing the tension. Simply thinking about Theo's father made me feel ill.

With a long sigh, I let Stefano's magic fingers do the trick. I relaxed into his warmth. He murmured soft hushing noises and quiet words of Italian. I had no idea what he said, but his tone was low and affectionate.

"You're twenty…?" He trailed off.

"Eight," I replied. "I'm twenty-eight."

"I'm thirty-four."

I hummed at his information. Six years wasn't a big age gap by any means.

"Gabriella," he murmured after a few moments. "So, Italian?"

I tilted up my head. "Sorry, my mom just liked the name. She was Canadian, my dad was English. I got her dark hair and his dark eyes."

"Ah." A mischievous grin lit his face. "So no Italian in you." He waggled his eyebrows. "Yet."

A giggle burst from my mouth, and he chuckled. I ran my fingers along his jaw, the scruff soft under my fingers. "Yet," I repeated.

His eyes narrowed, and he lowered his head, capturing my mouth. I slid my fingers into his hair, pulling him closer. The kiss became heated quickly. He worked my mouth, taking control, slipping his hands under my shirt, gliding them over my skin. I shivered at his touch. I'd never had a reaction to a man the way I did with him. One look, one touch, and I longed for more.

I whimpered as I felt him growing hard and erect under me, his desire evident. He groaned low and needy in his throat as I reached between us, palming his erection. He gripped my ass, moving me against him, the thick bulge of him hitting me exactly where I needed it through my thin skort. I shuddered with longing, unable to stop myself from undulating over him.

He brought me back to his mouth, kissing me long, hard, and deep, his tongue pressing on mine in controlling passes. I rocked against him, the pleasure building. I gripped his shoulders, kissing him back, lost to a sea of sensation. His touch, his mouth, his heat. The strength of his body, the feel of his grip—powerful, yet so gentle—all of him surrounding me. Holding me close as if he couldn't bear to let me go. His quiet grunts and growls became more pronounced, and suddenly, it wasn't enough. I had to feel him. I lifted myself up, tugging down his zipper and reaching inside the denim. I groaned out loud.

"Commando?"

"Always."

I knew I was never going to be able to look at him without remembering that fact.

He thrust upward, his length overflowing my grip. He was hot and heavy in my hand. Soft as velvet and hard as steel. I began to stroke him, staring down in fascination as his cock wept for me, and I sped up my movements. I gasped as he slid his fingers inside my shorts, finding my clit and circling it in hard, urgent circles.

"Fuck, *Tesoro*, what the hell are you doing to me," he gritted out, tightening his hand on my neck.

I lifted my head, our eyes locking. Passion, need, and want blazed from his dark gaze. He pulled my face close to his, his breath washing over me. "I want to see you come again," he demanded, the words rough and commanding. "And I'm going to come all over you."

I pumped him and he stiffened, his fingers moving faster, and my body locked down.

He swelled in my hand, jets of hot liquid spilling over, landing on my thighs, my shirt, dripping over my fist. I gasped as my orgasm hit me, and I threw back my head, fighting against the urge to scream his name. He dragged me close, burying his face in my neck, and I felt the sharp edge of his teeth, then the wet stroke of his tongue along my skin. I rode out my pleasure until I was spent. Until I dropped my head onto his shoulder, panting and sweaty.

And messy. So very messy.

"Guess it's a good thing tomorrow is laundry day," I quipped.

He began to laugh. Muted, rolling guffaws that lifted and shook me on his lap. He eased his hand from me and sat back, then slowly slid his fingers between his lips, his eyes on me the whole time as he tasted me.

Just to tease him, I did the same thing with my finger, running it over my lips and licking his essence from them. "Hmm," I murmured.

He narrowed his eyes. "Now I want you all over again. Except this time naked."

I jumped from his lap, looking down at myself. "Sorry, that was a strike. You're out."

He rose to his feet, tucking himself in. "Is that a fact?"

I backed away. "Um, yes?"

He lifted an eyebrow, a grin pulling at his mouth. "Run. I dare you." His words, growled out in a playful voice, combined with the soft smile on his lips and the heat of his gaze, made me giggle.

Something in me lightened, and the worry I felt all the time faded into the background. I caught on to his teasing mood and dodged to the left as he reached out.

I stifled my squeal, trying to hurry past him. It didn't work, and this time, he caught me. He slung me over his shoulder, gripping my ass. "I think, *Tesoro*, the bases are loaded. It's time for the tiebreaker."

"Put me down."

"Not yet." He strode down the hall, his footsteps sure and silent. For such a big man, he moved gracefully. In my room, he tossed me on the bed, staring down at me. I knew I was a mess. Covered in him. Yet he looked at me as if I was the most beautiful woman he'd ever seen.

He also waited for me to make up my mind. If I said no, he would accept it. Of that, I had no doubt.

"We have to be quiet."

"I can do that." He lifted his eyebrow. "I can make sure you're quiet too, baby. Don't worry about that."

I held open my arms.

Stefano tugged his shirt over his head, and I caught my breath. He had a well-muscled torso, defined pecs and abs. His jeans hung low on his hips, and his golden skin had a dusting of hair that led down to the sharp vee carved into his hips.

He was more magnificent than I dreamed.

"I like your tattoos."

"I designed them all."

"They have special meaning to you?"

"I'll tell you all about them, but not now." He quirked his eyebrow.

"Your shirt, Gabby. I want it off."

I hesitated, then sat up and tugged it over my head. I wished I were wearing lingerie, sexy and lacy, instead of a serviceable plain white bra I could afford. I slid my finger under the strap, self-conscious. "It's not very pretty," I whispered.

"The woman wearing it is. What it's concealing is." His eyes gleamed in the dim light, and he dropped his voice. "Take it off, Gabby. Show me what I want to see."

My fingers trembled and fumbled with the clasp, and I inhaled deeply before I let it fall from my shoulders to my lap. Stefano approached the end of the bed, placing one knee on the mattress, the edge sinking under his weight.

"Magnificent," he growled, then lunged. In seconds, I was under him, his mouth hot and wet on my breasts. He alternated licking, stroking, and biting my aching nipples, using his hand on one while his mouth was busy on the other. He pressed me deep in the mattress, his skin hot on mine. I ran my fingers through his short, silky hair, whimpering at the way he was worshiping my breasts. I longed to feel all of him on me, wanting to taste his mouth, lick his skin, feel his cock in my hand and inside me. I had never wanted someone the way I wanted him.

Then it happened. A little voice breaking in to my fogged brain.

"Mom," Theo called out from his room, his sleep-filled voice plaintive.

Stefano pulled himself up, and our eyes locked.

"Busted," he whispered, a grin playing on his lips.

"He does this a lot," I explained. "Calls for me in his sleep. But I have to check him."

He stroked my cheek. "Of course, *Tesoro*. He comes first. Go to him." He pushed away, landing on his back. His jeans tented obscenely, and I had to shake my head to clear it before grabbing my old robe and pulling it on.

"I'll be waiting," he promised, his voice a quiet hum that followed me down the hall and made me shiver.

I hurried to Theo's room, but as I suspected, he was still asleep, clutching his favorite dinosaur, his blankets kicked off. Bending, I tucked him in, brushing back his wild curls. He needed a haircut. We both did. But his was more important. I would bribe him this week. I had done really well with tips tonight, so a Happy Meal would do the trick. He loved those, and it was rare I could afford it. I brushed a kiss to his head and slipped to the bathroom.

I glanced in the mirror, hardly recognizing myself. My lips were swollen, my hair wilder than normal. I was flushed, and I had some red marks from Stefano's beard on my neck and chin. It was my eyes that struck me. Wide, dark, and glowing. Filled with desire. Not worried, not anxious, not overthinking. I thought of Stefano's reaction to Theo's interruption. He hadn't been annoyed, upset, or even mildly impatient. He'd instead been sweet, funny, and understanding.

And he was waiting.

I studied my reflection. Was I ready for this? Making love to Stefano was going to change everything. I had no doubt of that. He was an "all in" sort of guy. He wasn't going to fuck me and run. And he wouldn't accept that from me either. He would want to be part of our lives, which meant he would have to know the truth. I would have to tell him about my past. Theo's father. What getting involved with me meant.

Then how would he feel?

I shook my head. As usual, I was getting ahead of myself. Thinking, worrying, planning a future that might not exist.

Right now, I wanted to live in the moment. There was a sexy, sweet giant of a man waiting in my bed, capable of giving me more pleasure than I ever dreamed of.

That was where I wanted to be, and for the first time in many years, I wanted to be selfish and take what I wanted.

And what I wanted was Stefano.

I quickly brushed my teeth and washed my face. Taking a deep breath, I returned to my room, stopping at the foot of the bed and trying desperately not to laugh.

Stretched out, one arm flung across the bed and the other resting on his chest, Stefano was asleep. He took up most of the bed, his feet hanging over the edge of the mattress. In repose, his face looked younger, peaceful. His full lips pursed and relaxed in time with his deep, even breathing. He emitted a small grumble every few seconds, low in his throat, that I found quite adorable.

His erection, that massive bulge, had softened, although I knew if I woke him, it would return and I would be under him in seconds. Then I recalled the fact that he had been asleep on the sofa with Theo. He had worked all day, starting earlier because of my SUV, then he helped Mrs. Scott, looked after Theo, and had given me one hell of an orgasm. He had to be exhausted.

Making a decision, I slipped downstairs, shut off the light, then returned. I set the alarm earlier than normal, then carefully, I crawled in the bed, trying not to wake him. He roused, muttering my name, pulling me against him. I hushed him as I settled into the cradle of his body.

"Sleep, Stefano. Just sleep."

With a low grumble, he tucked me closer and was gone again. I inhaled his comforting scent and sighed. I felt warm, safe, and content. With him beside me, it was as if all the fears that haunted me at night vanished. Nothing would hurt me with him here.

I closed my eyes and fell asleep.

CHAPTER EIGHT

Gabby

I woke up slowly, the usual feeling of instant panic not hitting me. Instead, I felt rested and peaceful. I looked over at the clock and sat up, startled. My alarm hadn't gone off. Stefano was gone from the bed, but I heard voices coming from down the hall. I threw on my robe and hurried toward the sounds.

Sitting at my kitchen table were Stefano and Theo. They were eating cereal, talking about cars. Theo looked up as I entered, his grin wide.

"Hey, Mom!"

"Hi, baby." I eyed Stefano warily. "Good morning, Stefano."

"Hey, *Tesoro*," he replied, calm and relaxed. "Sleep well?"

"I did," I replied. "Um, you?"

"Other than your sofa is tiny, great." He winked. "Thanks for letting me crash."

"You're welcome."

"I made coffee."

I headed to the corner, grabbing a cup and pouring some of the hot, fragrant liquid. It was a treat to have it ready and waiting for me.

Theo slid from his chair. "I gotta get dressed. Will you be here when I get back, Stefo?"

"Sorry, no, little man. I gotta head home, shower, and get to work."

Theo's face fell, and he inched closer to Stefano, his voice pleading. "I'll see you soon?"

Stefano reached out and ruffled Theo's hair. They fist-bumped and Stefano grinned. "For sure. I'll come hang with you again."

Theo's face was wreathed in smiles as he hurried down the hall. I chuckled. "He sounds like a herd of buffalo when he walks." I tilted my head. "You were far quieter last night."

He grinned, pushing back his bowl. "I had precious cargo."

"You turned off my alarm."

He held out his hand and tugged me to the chair Theo had vacated. "I woke up beside you in the night and realized I'd fallen asleep before you came back." He grinned sheepishly. "I'm sorry about that."

"You were tired."

"So were you. When I woke up this morning, I heard Theo thumping down the hall to the bathroom. I figured his next stop would be your room, so I slipped back to the sofa. When he saw me, I told him I had fallen asleep and you let me stay over. Then I got us breakfast and, yes, turned off your alarm so you could sleep." He tucked a curl behind my ear. "I wanted you to have a little extra rest."

"Thank you."

He leaned forward and pressed a kiss to my forehead. "It took everything in me not to wake you in the night and finish what we started. But I enjoyed having you tucked up against me."

"I slept well," I confessed. "I felt…safe."

He studied me for a moment, frowning. "You don't usually feel safe?"

I stared into my coffee cup. "Sometimes, no."

Silence lingered until he wrapped his hand around mine, his skin warming me more than the hot feel of the mug. "We're going to talk about that. But right now, I need to get home, shower, and head to work. What are you going to do today?"

"Spend some time with Theo. Make more soup."

"You could always drop by the garage. See Charly. I can let Theo have some mechanic helper time if you have things you need to do on your own. My day is pretty light."

"I can't ask you to do that."

He met my eyes. "You're not. I'm offering. I enjoy spending time with him. The guys would all watch over him."

"I'll, ah, keep that in mind."

"Saturday—you have plans before you head to the bar later?"

"No."

"I was thinking we'd go on a picnic to the park. We could spend the afternoon, and then you can go to work. I'll bring Theo home and spend the evening with him."

I opened my mouth to say no. But he held up his hand, stopping my words.

"Think about it."

"Why?" The word was out before I could stop it. "Why do you want to do that?"

He frowned, pulling my hand to his chest. "I want to know you, Gabby. To be part of your life. I know your life contains Theo, so therefore, he will be part of mine. He needs to get to know me the same way you do. And I need to get to know you. So sometimes it will be just us and sometimes all three of us. I want him to know he's important too."

"I don't know if I'm really what you should be going after, Stefano. My life isn't—" I waved my hand, unsure how to describe it "—my life isn't my own to give."

"I'm not sure what you mean by that."

"It's complicated," I told him. "Maybe too complicated for anyone."

"Why don't you let me decide that?"

"I can't risk Theo being hurt. If he gets too fond of you—"

He cut me off. "He already is, *Tesoro*. And I'm fond of both of you. Too damned fond, frankly, given how skittish you are. So, let's just call it what it is."

"Which is?"

"A relationship. And going forward, we're in it together."

A relationship. With Stefano.

I hadn't planned on a relationship with another man—ever. My heart rate picked up just thinking about the implications.

"I don't know if it's possible."

"What has you locked in the past, Gabriella? What are you running from?" he asked quietly, my name rolling off his tongue, sounding like a caress.

I shook my head fast. "Not now."

"Soon. I can't fight what I don't know is coming. I can't protect you and Theo from the unknown." He stood and pressed another kiss to my forehead. "Give me the information I need. Trust me enough to tell me."

I wasn't sure how to reply. Stefano held out his phone. "At least give me your cell number."

I keyed in the digits and he smiled as he took back his phone. "One hurdle down."

I heard him call out a goodbye to Theo, then his steps faded as he headed downstairs.

I sighed as I hung my head in my hands.

Fight. Protect. Those were the words he used. Did he know how accurate they might be?

The question was, would he want to stay once he knew the truth?

And was I willing to risk it?

STEFANO

"What is that?"

I glanced up from the design I was working on. Or, at least, attempting to work on. I had been at it for a while, not making much headway.

I glanced at the screen with a frown. "I'm not sure."

Charly narrowed her eyes, peering at the image. "Me either. I think you drew a one-legged dog—or is that a parrot?" She glanced at me, winking. "Is the client a pirate?"

I chuckled, erasing the image with a swipe of the mouse. "Doodling, I suppose."

She grunted as she lifted herself up on the stool beside me, using my arm for leverage. "What's going on, Stefano?" She held up her hand. "Don't tell me nothing. Brett says you never came home last night, and you've been quiet all day."

I sighed. There were no secrets here. Charly somehow found out everything, even shit we weren't trying to hide. And when you held something back, she was like a heat-seeking missile, finding information.

"Gabby?" she guessed.

"Yeah."

"You stayed the night?"

I decided a small white fib was in order. I explained about Mrs. Scott and looking after Theo. "I fell asleep on the sofa. I was tired, so I stayed. I had cereal with my little man this morning, went home and showered, and came to work."

"Okay, first off—'your little man,' how adorable. Second, bull pucky if you think I believe nothing happened since you're sporting a little mark on your neck, and third, holy moly, you're moving fast."

I hung my head, laughing low in my throat. *Bull pucky.* Another one of Charly's odd phrases. She didn't like to swear, so she made up her own expressions. I lifted my head and met her eyes. "Okay, I didn't sleep on the sofa the whole night, but we didn't, ah… That is to say, we…" I ran my hand through my hair, feeling oddly embarrassed. "I was tired, and I fell asleep while Gabby checked on Theo. So nothing happened other than some, ah, heat on the sofa."

She lifted one expressive eyebrow. "And the third?"

"It is fast. No argument there. But there is something about her…" I trailed off, thinking.

Waking up beside her had felt so natural. Feeling her tucked close, smelling the light fragrance of her shampoo, the scent of her skin. I had enjoyed my breakfast with Theo; in fact, I had enjoyed all the time I spent with him. He was funny, smart, and well-behaved. He asked a ton of questions, and his imagination was vast. He was a great kid.

And Gabby.

Kissing her was becoming an addiction. Her smart, sassy mouth that teased and argued. Kissed me back like I was her salvation. Her beautiful dark eyes that held so many secrets. I loved how she looked at her son. How she looked after we kissed. The fire I saw in her eyes when she looked at me. The quiet peace that settled over her after I made her come.

She was an enigma. One I wanted to solve.

"Stefano?" Charly prompted, interrupting my thoughts.

"Her landlady, Mrs. Scott, said something. She thinks Gabby is afraid of something in her past."

She nodded. "I thought so as well. There's an edge to her. As if she can never fully relax. Even when she smiles, it's as if she isn't fully there. As if she's expecting the smile to have to stop."

Our gazes met. "As if she is ready to bolt."

"At the drop of a hat." Charly summed it up.

"It has something to do with Theo's father." I recalled the way she'd shut down when I mentioned his dad. "I think he's bad news."

"Are you prepared for that, Stefano?" she asked. "Getting involved with a single mom is hard enough. One with baggage—maybe a potential troublesome ex? That's an entirely different ball game. Her first instinct will be to push you away—protect herself and Theo."

Charly was right, and Gabby had already tried to push me away. But I couldn't deny my attraction to her. To the draw I felt to her and to Theo. The thought of her being scared, or Theo being hurt, made me rage inside. I wanted to protect them both.

"I am," I said simply.

"Then be patient. Let her know you're here for her." Charly smiled. "We all are. I like her—I like her a lot. So does Maxx." She grinned, rubbing her belly. "She'll be surrounded by people who care, and maybe that will help her."

I smiled at the woman who was such an important part of my life. She was caring and giving. Warm. She loved hard and took care of those she made part of her life. I was lucky to be included. I leaned forward and kissed her cheek.

"Thanks, Charly. What would I do without you?"

She beamed as she slipped off the stool. "You'd be lost." She paused. "She's coming in, by the way."

"Oh?"

"I called and asked her to. Maxx wants to talk to her a bit too. She should be here soon."

"Okay. I'll watch over Theo."

"His mother too, I'm sure," she teased.

I grinned as I watched her waddle away. I turned back to the computer, then shut it off. I wasn't in the mood for modern technology. I needed to feel the pencil in my hand, watch the design come to life on paper.

Except, as I picked up the notepad, I noticed my earlier scribblings. I had written down Gabby's name in several different ways. Changed the font, used her full name, different variations of it. Entwined it with mine.

I shook my head, huffing out in relief that Charly hadn't seen this. She would have compared me to a schoolgirl crushing on a boy in her class and doodling his name in a love-sick, obsessed manner.

And dammit, she would have been right.

A while later, Charly texted me that Gabby was done for the day and would be leaving. I liked seeing her at the shop, although I knew she was there to learn and help Charly, so I stayed in my own space, only going out front to get Theo and say hello. She'd seemed a little shy and hesitant, and I put it down to all the people around us. I hoped she'd come to me but wasn't surprised that she hadn't. Disappointed, but not surprised.

Theo had sat with me, and I showed him how to adjust a carburetor. He had been so serious as I tweaked the one I was working on, explaining what I was doing, holding his hand within mine as I used the different tools and made the adjustments it needed. He asked a barrage of questions—smart ones, which somehow didn't surprise me. He listened intently as I responded, and when we were done, I took him back to my area and showed him some drawings. He was enraptured again, asking more questions, which I was happy to answer.

I think we were both disappointed when Charly let me know it was time to leave.

I walked Theo back to the garage, stopping in the entrance at what I saw. Gabby was sitting on one of the chairs in the waiting room. Chase was sitting next to her, talking. On the other side of her was another mechanic, Ward, who seemed to be part of the conversation. All three were laughing over something. Brett leaned on the doorframe, his head tilted to the side, a grin on his lips.

What. The. Hell.

She didn't come seek me out, was quiet with me, but she was having a great time with them. Laughing, chatting, looking far too sexy and beautiful to even be in their company. Did she not see the looks she was getting from Ward? The way he was eyeballing her? And what the fuck was Chase doing leaning in so close, as if sharing a secret?

The only person who should be sitting that close to her was me.

Dammit.

I stalked over, Theo behind me. Brett glanced over his shoulder, spying me, a wide grin breaking out on his face as he stepped back from the door.

"You boys on a break?" I snarled. "Looks like the docket is pretty damn full, and you're sitting here, shooting the shit with Gabby?"

Gabby's eyes widened in shock. Theo grabbed my jeans, staring up at me, his mouth a round, open O.

"Stefo," he whispered. "You said a bad word. Two of them."

"Sorry, little man," I muttered.

Chase looked at me as if I were crazy. "I'm waiting on a confirmation to pick up a part. I was getting coffee and started talking to Gabby. I was telling her how much I liked the food at Ziggy's the other night."

"I don't see a cup of coffee in your hand," I replied, crossing my arms, knowing it made me look bigger. Scarier.

"It's brewing," Brett said, his voice low. "Take a step back, Stefano. Boys are just being friendly."

"Too friendly." I glared at Ward. "Ever hear of personal space? My lady doesn't like to be crowded."

He stood. "*Your* lady? Sorry, man. I was just telling her about the bad wings we had at the other bar. She was telling me which places to stay away from. That's all." He edged past me. "She talks really quietly. I had to lean close to hear her."

"Listen better next time," I snapped.

Theo headed for his mom, who wrapped her arm around him and lifted him to her knee, shaking her head.

Chase looked at me, then Gabby, and laughed. He said something to Gabby then stood and high-fived Theo. "I'll go get my coffee now and get back to work. Nice talking to you, Gabby. I look forward to working with you." He walked past me, clapping me on the shoulder, still laughing.

"This is great," he said. "Two down."

I glared at his retreating back, then looked at Brett, who was trying not to laugh.

"What is so funny?"

"You are," he replied. "Cool, unflappable Stefano, all worked up because *your lady* is having a conversation about wings with a couple of your *friends*." He leaned close. "By the way, the whole time she's been here, she's been looking around for you, so you can pack away the jealous act. You have nothing to worry about." Then he waved to Gabby and winked at Theo.

"Looking forward to working with you again soon, big guy."

Theo gave him a thumbs-up, and I slumped against the door. I was behaving like Maxx did when Charly riled him up. Like a caveman. Worse.

I had just acted like an idiot. A total idiot. Gabby was no doubt furious with me now.

I straightened and met her gaze. She looked more amused than anything, which confused me.

"You ready to go, Gabby?" I asked.

She stood, taking Theo's hand. "I suppose I should before I get anyone else in trouble." She walked past me, and I followed her outside. She strapped Theo into his seat and came around to the driver's side. I put my hand on the door, stopping her from opening it.

"I'm sorry," I offered, bracing myself for her anger. "I don't know what came over me."

She turned, peering up at me, her dark eyes dancing. "Is that how I sounded the other night at the bar? With Lara?"

"Pretty sure I was worse," I admitted.

"You're kinda hot, all jealous and possessive."

"I didn't like them that close."

She laughed, running a finger along my jaw. "It's a small room, Stefano. They weren't trying to get close. It just happens."

She was right, but I still didn't like it. I captured her hand and kissed it. "I wanted to be sitting there with you. Why didn't you come see me?"

"I didn't want to bother you." She looked over my shoulder, suddenly shy again. "After last night…" She trailed off.

"You will never bother me. I wanted to see you." I touched her cheek. "Especially after last night."

"Next time."

I grinned, lowering my head and brushing her mouth with mine. "Next time," I agreed.

Inside the SUV, Theo groaned. "Mom, can you kiss Stefo later, like a rain check? I'm starving and I need to eat. I think my legs are gonna fall off, I'm so hungry."

I started to laugh and opened the door. "Go feed your son, *Tesoro*, before he loses his legs. There's cold pizza at home that should stop that from happening."

She slid in and I shut the door, but not before I snagged another kiss.

"I'll call you later," I assured her.

"You do that."

"Mom, does that mean Stefo is your boyfriend now?" Theo asked. "You kissed him."

She met my eyes with a smile. "I guess so," she responded, winking at me and making me grin.

Boyfriend. I could handle that.

She drove away, and with a sigh, I went inside. I had a feeling I'd be ordering pizza for lunch to express my apologies to Chase and Ward.

And I knew I wasn't going to live this down.

Ever.

Saturday, I left the garage and swung by Mary's place. She was waiting on the porch, a large picnic hamper ready for me. I hadn't wanted to ask Charly, since she was always tired, to help me with a lunch, but Mary had been excited and volunteered to help. When I'd lived with her while looking for a place when I first arrived, we'd become close. I'd asked her advice about what food to pack, and she'd waved me off, insisting on doing it herself.

"Pasta and cutlets aren't going to cut it, boy."

I had chuckled. "I can handle sandwiches."

She snorted, shaking her head. "I recall the sandwich you made me once. It fed me for a week. I'll take care of this."

I gave in easily since I wanted the picnic to be nice for Gabby and Theo.

I hefted the basket, lifting my eyebrow at the weight.

"Well, *you'll* be eating," she explained with a grin.

I bent and kissed her cheek. "Thanks, Mary."

"Bring her for dinner. I want to meet this girl. Charly says she's lovely." She paused. "And troubled."

I rubbed my chin. "I think I have to agree with that."

"Single moms are a lot to take on."

I loaded the basket into the company van I had borrowed. There wasn't anywhere for Theo's car seat in my Mustang, so I'd swapped out the ride for the day. I turned to Mary. "I know. I'm aware it's not just two people in the relationship. But he's a great kid. I like him a lot."

"Your mama is gonna have a field day with this."

"Let's not get ahead of ourselves here. I'll cross that bridge when I come to it."

She laughed, her shoulders shaking with mirth. She knew my mama well, having become friends with her and my sisters. Once Mama got wind of me dating a single mother, the phone lines were going to be burning up between Toronto and Littleburn.

Mary chuckled and patted my shoulder. "Enjoy the afternoon."

I slammed the hatch shut and kissed her cheek again. "I will. Thanks, Mary."

"Dinner Tuesday?"

"You know it." It was a regular thing for us—every second Tuesday. She'd make her pot roast, and I would tinker with anything that needed to be fixed. Some nights, we'd sit on her porch and talk. I enjoyed her company, hearing her stories, and I liked spending time with her.

I waved as I drove off, anxious to get to Gabby's. She was constantly on my mind, no matter how busy I was. The couple of texts we'd shared weren't enough. Even the unexpected visit I'd had didn't satisfy me.

Late Friday night, I'd taken a stroll, making sure her SUV was home safe.

The front door opened as I went by, and she headed to her car, stopping at the sight of me at the end of the driveway.

"Stefano?" she called out, her voice nervous.

"Hey, Tesoro," I assured her, heading up the driveway.

"What are you doing here?"

"Oh, couldn't sleep. Just taking a walk. I live about three blocks from here," I explained. "I was checking out the wrap on the SUV. Looks good. What are you doing out here?"

She opened the back door and held up a bag. "I forgot my shoes. There was a drunk in the bar tonight, and he dropped his full glass of beer on my feet. I had to borrow Lara's spare pair. I need to wash these."

"Ah."

"You all calmed down now?" she asked playfully. "Made up with your friends?"

"Yes." I had apologized and bought pizza. Everything was good, although I had a feeling that I'd be teased about it again.

I stepped closer. "We're still good for tomorrow, yes?"

"Yes. Theo is excited to see you."

I closed the distance between us, stopping in front of her. "And what about Theo's mama?"

Her dark eyes were wide in her face as she gazed up at me. "She's looking forward to seeing you too."

We stared at each other, the air around us growing warm. Bubbling with tension.

"Were you really just taking a walk?"

"I wanted to make sure you got home okay. I knew tonight was your later shift," I admitted. "I hate thinking of you driving home alone so late and not knowing if you're okay."

"Ziggy had those lights fixed—and now whoever works late gets walked to their car." She tilted her head. "Know anything about either of those things?"

Brett and I had changed the lights, using a customer's cherry picker to do so early in the morning before anyone was around. It was a simple enough job, but Ziggy admitted the expense of renting the cherry picker had held him back. Once that was done, I had spoken with him, suggesting he might want to look after his staff's safety a little more. I was glad he had taken my words seriously. I was sure the promise of some extra mechanic hours on his precious Camaro helped.

"Maybe," I confessed.

"Why?"

"Because you need someone to look out for you."

"And that someone is you?"

"Yes."

She lunged, dropping the shoes as she gripped my neck, pulling my mouth down to hers. I wrapped my arms around her waist, lifting her up and kissing her back, groaning with relief once our mouths fused.

My tongue sliding into her mouth made her whimper. The taste of her made me hard. She weaved her fingers into the hair at the back of my neck, twisting the short strands. I grasped her ass, pressing her into the side of the vehicle, grinding into her. Our tongues touched and stroked as I explored her hot mouth. Her breasts pressed against my chest, her nipples hard points on my skin. I slid my hands up and down her thighs, feeling the silky texture of her legs and the heat between them. Her breath became mine, our desire wrapping around us like a blanket, settling and forming a protective wall of heat. I kissed her as if my very life depended on it. Needing. Aching. Wanting. Mindless.

Until a car drove past and I recalled we were outside and acting like a couple of horny teenagers on a first date. Regretfully, I eased back, staring down at her. Her eyes were closed, her lips swollen and wet from mine. She was breathing heavily, her grip on my neck not easing.

"Tesoro," I murmured, tracing her mouth. "Gabriella, we need to stop."

Her eyes fluttered open, and the most adorable frown pursed her lips. "Oh."

"Another minute and I'm pretty sure we'd be inside the SUV, and I'd be inside you."

She peeked over her shoulder. "I'm good with that."

Laughing, I set her on her feet. "Don't tempt me."

She sighed. "How do you do this, Stefano?"

I picked up her bag, handing her the shoes. "Do what?"

"You befuddle my head. I see you, get close to you, and all my common sense disappears."

"You do the same for me." I pressed a chaste kiss to her forehead. *"Now go upstairs and go to bed. I'll see you tomorrow."*

I waited until she was upstairs and waved to me from the window. It took most of my walk home for my cock to soften. I could taste her on my tongue, smell her light fragrance on my hands.

I wasn't sure how much longer I would last before I wasn't able to stop and we ended up a mass of arms and legs, bare and naked, joined together in some inappropriate spot, unable to wait anymore.

Surprisingly, that thought didn't bother me at all.

I grinned thinking about it and had to adjust myself as I drove to get Gabby and Theo. I pressed on the accelerator a little harder, anxious to see them.

Theo was waiting on the stairway inside for me, flinging himself off the step into my arms.

"Hey, little man."

He was full of news. A new rock he'd found. How he'd helped his mom make cookies for today. How excited he was.

"Never been on a pic-a-nic, Stefo! Mom says we get to eat outside and I can play!"

"You sure can, buddy. There's a little pool there you can splash in too."

He squirmed from my arms. "I gotta get my suit! It has blue stripes," he called back to me. I chuckled and glanced over my shoulder, walking into Mrs. Scott's. She was busy doing one of her jigsaw puzzles. She had a table with a light set up over it, and she loved to spend hours piecing together the intricate pictures. I dropped a kiss to her white hair.

"How are you?"

She beamed up at me. "Good. This lightbulb you switched out makes all the difference."

"LED," I agreed. "Nothing like them." I knew the bright light would help her enjoy her puzzle time a little more.

"Your girl is on the phone." She indicated the kitchen.

I grinned at the words "my girl."

"I'll wait."

She smirked as she studied a piece of her puzzle and slid it into place. I picked up a piece and tapped it into the top corner.

"Hmmph. I've been looking for that one."

"Fresh eyes," I teased.

"So, a picnic."

"Yep."

She eyed me, her gaze mischievous. "Going all out, are you?"

"I'm trying."

She patted my hand. "Good."

"Maybe you can come next time."

"Oh, pssh, you don't want an old woman there."

"No, I don't. I want you."

She waved me off, but I saw her smile. "Sweet-talker."

Gabby came from the kitchen, a frown on her face. Instantly, I was alert.

"What's wrong?"

"There was another issue at Ziggy's. He has to shut down until Monday, so no shifts until then. I called Vanessa at Zeke's in case she needs anyone, but she says it's unlikely." She worried her lip then sighed. "Ziggy said he'd cover my wages for the night, so I guess there is that."

I knew her tips were what she was worried about. They made up a large portion of her income. I held out my hand, pleased when she took it. I squeezed her fingers. "At least there's that," I agreed. "And I don't have to have you back by four. So there's that too, right? We can do something fun tonight."

She smiled, although I saw the worry in her eyes. "I would love that."

Unable to resist, I brushed my mouth to hers. "It's okay, *Tesoro.* We'll figure it out. But let's enjoy today, okay?"

Theo bounded down the steps, holding up his blue-striped trunks. "Got them! Let's go, Stefo! I want to pic-a-nic!"

We all laughed. "Okay, little man. Let's go."

CHAPTER NINE

Stefano

Gabby sighed, lifting her face to the breeze. It moved her hair around, the wild curls swinging around her ears and the nape of her neck. In the sun, her dark hair glinted with red and gold, a kaleidoscope of color. It suited her. She was wearing a loose T-shirt and a lovely skirt that floated around her as she walked. It was trimmed in lace, covered in a pink floral pattern, and showed off her shapely calves. She looked pretty and sexy. She had pushed aside her usual worries, and we had talked easily in the van, listening to Theo's excited observations. The park was busy, which didn't surprise me, but we managed to get a great picnic table under the shade of a tree and close to the playground and splash pool. Within ten minutes, Theo had made friends with another kid, and they were busy on the swings and slides, laughing and talking like old friends. Gabby and I sat close on the bench, watching them.

"How easy it is for kids," she murmured. "All they do is smile, share a love of swinging on monkey bars, and bam, you're friends. No worries."

I slid my arm over her shoulders. "If you want to swing on my *monkey bar*, we can be friends, *Tesoro*."

She turned her head, looking at me. I winked lewdly, waggled my eyebrows, and it happened. She smiled, then giggled. The giggle turned into a chuckle, and then she was laughing. Out loud, clear and sweet. The sound made me laugh with her. She looked carefree and happy, the anxiety drained from her eyes, leaving them bright and joyful. I couldn't resist. I didn't want to.

I cupped the back of her neck and kissed her. It was long, slow, and intense. When I drew back, she smiled, touching her lips with her fingers.

I relaxed back against the bench, my arm slung over her shoulder. With a sigh, she laid her head against me. We both crossed our ankles and watched Theo. There was no need for words.

"This is the best fried chicken I ever ate." Theo's eyes were wide in his face. "Ever."

I had to agree. Mary made stellar fried chicken. It wasn't something I'd grown up with, so when I'd lived with her, it had always been one of my favorite meals. Her pasta was fairly abysmal, and my mama soon corrected that, but her fried chicken remained one of my most requested menu items. I was glad she had included it today.

Theo and Gabby had tucked into the picnic lunch with gusto. Egg salad sandwiches, chicken, and cut-up vegetables were devoured. The cookies Gabby made disappeared fast. The lemonade I had bought was cold and tart, and Theo declared it another favorite.

I wiped my mouth, replete. The afternoon was going well. Without a time constriction for Gabby to leave, we were relaxed and enjoying the warm weather and the park. Gabby was more tranquil than I could recall, and her laughter rang out more than once. Every time I heard it, I smiled, and I found myself saying and doing things I knew would make her laugh. Or smile. I loved her smile.

Theo gnawed on a chicken leg, his eyes on the playground. He'd been going nonstop since we arrived, but as the afternoon wore on, his choice of playmates was beginning to dwindle.

"Will you play with me, Stefo?"

"Absolutely. But I need a little *pisolino* first."

"What's that?"

I winked at Gabby. "A nap. Let the food settle."

"Settle?"

I patted my stomach. "Yeah, when you nap, the food all slips into place so you can eat more later."

His eyes became saucers. "Really?"

I nodded sagely. "Especially for picnics. Once you have a *pisolino*, you can play more and then get ice cream."

Gabby coughed into her hand, but I had Theo's attention.

"I love ice cream. So does Mom."

"Then I guess a *pisolino* is in order for all of us."

We cleaned up the lunch remnants. I walked over and deposited the trash, then headed back to my little man and his pretty mom. She had laid out the blanket I had brought and was sitting down, talking to Theo, who stood in front of her. She held his hand, and he looked down at her with such adoration, I felt my eyes sting. Their love for each other was blatant.

I settled with my back against the tree, smiling with delight when Theo curled himself against my knee, his tousled head the same colors as Gabby's in the sun. I lifted my arm in invitation, and Gabby settled into my side. Without thinking, I ran my fingers through Theo's hair, listening to his endless questions and answering them in ways that made Gabby's shoulders shake with mirth.

"What makes clouds?"

"They're marshmallows for the angels."

"How come they get dark and rain?"

"Someone forgot to lower the fire. When they turn on the hoses, the water has to go somewhere."

"What is thunder?"

"The male angels bellowing about the fire. The lightning is the female angels answering back."

He peered up at me. "Stefo, is that true?"

I ruffled his hair. "Maybe."

He chuckled. "Mom says it's because heaven is watering the earth."

"Well, there's that too."

His eyes fluttered, growing heavy. "I like your stories, too."

Then he was asleep.

Gabby peered up at me. "You're really good with him."

"He's easy to be good to. He's a great kid."

She ran a hand through his hair. "He is. He has always been so grown-up for his age. Sometimes, I worry about that."

"No, he's good. There's lots of little-boy mischief in there." I pressed a kiss to her head. "You're doing an amazing job, Gabby. Don't doubt yourself."

She reached up and clasped my hand lying on her shoulder, squeezing my fingers. For a moment, there was silence, and I felt her relax further into my side as she fell asleep. I glanced down at the two people I had known only a short time yet had made such a huge difference to my life. I leaned my head back, shutting my eyes and enjoying the warmth of the sun, the feel of Gabby snuggled into me, and the soft strands of Theo's hair under my hand. They were both relaxed enough to sleep, knowing I was there to watch over them.

It was a new job for me, yet one I had a feeling I wanted to claim for the rest of my life.

Theo's happy laughter rang out as I splashed him in the wading pool. We were the only ones in it, the park much quieter now than when we arrived. The cool water felt good on my skin as he splashed back, his movements uncoordinated but close enough, some of the water landed on me.

Gabby's eyes had grown huge in her face as I'd yanked my shirt over my head before joining Theo in the water.

"You're going in like that?" she sputtered.

I looked down, trying not to laugh. "How would you prefer I go in, *Tesoro?*" With a wink, I ran my finger under the waistband of my board shorts. "If I take these off, I'll be naked."

She swallowed. "Oh God," she whimpered.

I bent down, caging her between my arms. "Play your cards right, and I'll show you later." Then I kissed her and headed to Theo, who was impatiently waiting for me. I felt the heat of her stare burning into me. Every time I glanced up, her eyes were on me. Roaming over my chest, lingering on the way my shorts dragged low over my hip bones. The ardor of her stare warmed me, and more than once, I had to fight down my growing erection. Sitting down in the cold water helped a great deal.

The yearning I was feeling for her had been increasing all afternoon. Every glance, every smile, every touch was laden with desire. Even with Theo with us, the passion simmered just below the surface, ready to explode. I had never known this sort of draw to someone. The need to touch, to taste, to have, smoldered under my skin. I held myself in check, concentrating on Theo, on us as a unit, enjoying the day, but the need built, drip by drip, developing and morphing, taking on a life of its own every moment that passed.

By the time I carried Theo up the stairs, passed out from a day of sunshine, food, and too much ice cream, I was barely holding on. Everything was magnified. The sound of Gabby's voice was lower, throatier. Her scent seemed to swirl around me, ensnaring me. Her casual touches felt like more. Her lips were inviting, her glances beckoning. I wanted her more than I could ever recall wanting another woman.

I laid Theo on his bed, watching as Gabby pulled off his sandals and tugged his shirt over his head. She slipped past me, returning with a damp cloth that she gently wiped over his face and hands, smiling.

"At least that will get the sticky off. He can have a bath tomorrow."

She bent low, brushing his hair away and kissing his brow. She peeked up at me watching her. "He had an amazing day. Thank you."

"And you?"

She straightened, twisting the hem of her T-shirt with her fists. She worried her lip, then met my gaze. "I don't want the day to be over."

I held out my hand. "Then come with me, *Tesoro*."

In her room, I shut the bedroom door. "Can you hear him if he calls?"

She switched on a small monitor, and the sounds of his little-boy rumblings made me smile.

"Okay, good."

Our gazes locked and held. The air began to pulse with heat, and still, neither of us moved. Gabby's breathing picked up, her T-shirt suffering as she yanked and pulled on the hem.

"I think your shirt is bothering you. Maybe you should take it off."

"I'd rather you took off yours."

I tugged mine over my head, tossing it toward her with a smirk. I lifted my hands in supplication. "Anything else?"

I saw how her hands trembled as she pulled her shirt over her head. She wore a lacy camisole underneath, the soft pink feminine and alluring.

"You are so beautiful, Gabriella." My cock lengthened, my shorts beginning to feel obscenely tight.

"I like how you say my name."

I smiled, barely holding on.

She drew in a deep breath and popped a button on her skirt, the froth of lace and material pooling at her feet. As she stood in the light of early evening, her skin was like cream, the satin on the lingerie she wore moving like a whisper on her skin. I wanted to taste her.

"Are you, ah, really commando?"

"Why don't you come over here and find out?" I murmured. I needed her to make the first move. To be right there with me in this moment. I knew it was going to change everything.

I waited, my heart hammering, not sure what to expect. Then she moved. Fast. Crossing the room and lunging into my arms. I caught her, lifting her up as our mouths crashed. I turned, pushing her against the door I had closed. She wrapped her legs around my waist, drawing me in tight to her body. I groaned at the feel of her heat. I slid my tongue inside her mouth, exploring. Tasting. Sweet from the ice cream she licked, tang from the mint she chewed, perfect because it was her. Gabriella.

I slanted my head, kissing her harder. I couldn't get enough of her. She ground against me, grasping the back of my neck, her hard nipples rubbing on me through the silk of her camisole. I lifted her higher, sucking at her nipples, biting and teasing them as she gasped and let her head fall back to the door.

"Did you wear this for me?" I asked, tracing the lace, then running my hand down her side and under the soft fabric, feeling the smooth, warm skin underneath.

"Yes. I bought it just for you."

I covered her mouth again and carried her to the bed. I set her on the edge, breaking away. She stared at me, her eyes wide with desire, her chest lifting and falling in fast succession. Carefully, I lifted the camisole over her head. I wanted to tear it from her body, but I knew how hard she would have worked to buy it for me, and I didn't want to destroy her gift. I would buy her others I could tear off—this one was special.

She cast her gaze downward as I revealed her body. I slipped my fingers under her chin, forcing her to meet my eyes.

"You are so beautiful," I repeated. "Don't hide from me."

"I have marks—"

I interrupted her. "You. Are. Beautiful." I kissed her. "Sexy." I trailed my lips down her neck, kissing and licking as I went. "I want you so fucking much." I grabbed her hand, pulling it to my aching cock. "Feel this. Feel how beautiful you are to me."

She cupped me, and I groaned into her mouth. I rose, wrapping an arm around her waist, moving her toward the middle of the bed. I hovered over her, keeping my gaze locked with hers as I drew a hard nipple into my mouth. She gasped, arching up as I sucked and played with her breasts, alternating my mouth and fingers. She pulled on the drawstring, and I helped her pull away my shorts. I was impatient as I tugged on her tiny underwear, but I got them off without damage, hissing in satisfaction when I felt our bare bodies finally glide together. She was soft and supple and felt so right against my coarser skin.

She wrapped her hand around my cock, stroking and caressing. I slid my hand between her legs, the heat and wet of her like silk on my fingers. She whimpered as I teased her clit, stroking over it gently, the nub growing harder under my touch.

"You like that, *Tesoro*? You like me touching you?"

"More," she pleaded. "Oh God, Stefano. More, please."

I increased the pressure, pushing one finger inside, then adding another, keeping my thumb on her clit. She gasped, moving with me. I covered her mouth and kissed her. Sucked on her breasts. Laved her neck and nibbled on her ears. She grabbed at my back, dug her nails into my skin, stroked my dick in long, sure passes that made me grunt in pleasure. Her moans and whimpers grew closer together, and with a long shudder, she came, hard and pulsating around my fingers, drawing me deeper inside. My name fell from her lips, her long, airy sigh of pleasure filling my mouth.

I drew back, meeting her gaze. "That was the sexiest thing I have ever seen," I murmured. "And I want to see it again—this time with my cock deep inside you." I pushed up, grabbing for my shorts and the condoms I had slipped into the pocket earlier.

"You gonna let me?"

Her smile was all I needed.

GABBY

I felt euphoric, my body sated and relaxed, but still somehow needy.

Watching Stefano rip open a condom with his teeth, his gaze never leaving mine, I knew what I needed.

Him.

I needed his mouth back on mine, his teeth in my skin, and his cock—his glorious, thick, long cock—lodged inside me. I wanted to feel him moving. I wanted to see his face when he came.

Nothing prepared me for how it felt when he grasped my hips and pushed inside. Slow, inch by inch, until we were flush. Until I felt as if I would split apart from the girth of him. He flung back his head, and the sight of him, his neck cords pulled taut, his lip caught with his teeth as he sheathed himself inside me was the sexiest thing I had ever seen.

The animalistic noise he made was the most erotic sound I had ever heard.

He lowered his head, his intense, dark gaze clouded with lust, but determined.

"Hold on, *Tesoro.*"

So, I did.

He was exactly what I thought he'd be. Exactly what I needed.

He pulled back almost to the tip then thrust forward again, making me whimper. He began to move in long, powerful thrusts. In and out. Over and again. Hard. Strong. I tilted my hips, grasping on to the blanket for purchase as he plunged so hard we moved across the mattress. He grabbed my hip in one hand and leaned over me, bracing himself on the headboard. He kissed me, nuzzled my breasts, and talked. He murmured Italian phrases, moaned out my name, cursed dirty words.

"You feel so fucking good."

"Sei più bella di un angelo."

"Take my cock, yes, like that. Just like that."

"Siamo fatti l'uno per l'altro."

Most of what he said, I didn't understand, but I felt his adoration. It saturated his tone, and even his dirty words were infused with it. My body was awash with sensation. The feel of him inside me, hard and full. His skin, sweat-soaked and glistening, was like hot silk under my fingers. He balanced his weight on one arm, still pressing me into the mattress as we moved. His voice washed over me like a caress. His dark eyes, lit with fire, zeroed in on me, watching, ever focused, even as he lost himself to me. To us.

Another orgasm hit me, so intense and sudden, I thought I would shatter from the force of it. A scream lodged itself in my throat, and Stefano covered my mouth, swallowing my pleasure, riding it out until his body locked down and he shuddered, dropping his face to my neck, his voice muffled but his words reaching my ears.

"Gabriella, *ti adoro.*"

He collapsed, for one moment his heavy weight keeping me in place, then he lifted off me, our gazes locked. He drew one long finger down my cheek and pressed his mouth to mine in a series of light, sweet kisses. He slid from me, leaving me empty and aching for him. He got rid of the condom and slipped back into bed, pulling me close and curling himself around me. I tried not to giggle when I realized he was trying to fit on the bed and not fall off. I turned and snuggled against him, letting him bend his legs and mold himself to me.

"You were amazing," he murmured, his breath tickling my neck.

"You were pretty spectacular yourself."

He chuckled, kissing my shoulder, making me shiver. "We were spectacular together."

We were quiet for a few moments. He held me close, and I stroked his forearm with my finger.

"It's been a long time for me," I admitted.

"It has for me as well."

"How long?" I asked.

"Over two years."

"Can I ask why? Would you tell me?"

"I will, but not in your bed. Not after what just happened between us."

"Okay."

He rose from the bed and pulled on his shorts. Standing in my room, the light beginning to fade, the shadows playing over his muscular chest and large arms, he filled the space. He held out his hand. "Kitchen," he said simply.

I let him pull me from the bed, trying not to smile as I saw his cock begin to swell as he looked at me, naked in front of him. He made a low sound and handed me my robe. "Put this on. Now."

"Or?" I teased.

"No talking will be happening unless you count the groans you'll be making as I make you come. Again."

I took my robe and followed him to the kitchen.

I made coffee since that seemed to be his preferred beverage and waited until he took a long sip before speaking.

"We're not in bed anymore."

He met my eyes. "I'm going to keep this short. I don't like thinking about it, much less talking about it."

"All right."

"I've dated casually. Never anything serious until I met Leah. I thought she was pretty amazing." He huffed out a laugh. "Turned out to be anything but."

"I'm sorry," I offered, unsure what to say. He shook his head.

"I dated her for a month, and I even took her to meet my family. They didn't like her. She didn't like them." He lifted one eyebrow. "That should have been my first clue."

"Your family is important to you."

"Yes." He took another sip. "But I kept seeing her. Our relationship was odd, although I didn't see it at first. She had a weird work schedule that kept changing. We met when we could—often at my apartment over the garage where I worked in Toronto. I was fine with it—at the beginning."

"Was she married?" I guessed.

"No, but it turned out she had a whole other life. I saw her one day while I was out picking up parts. She was coming out of a restaurant with a group of people. I went over to say hello and surprise her—except it was me who got the surprise. She saw me coming and literally ran away. I had never seen her move so fast. She ran around the corner and disappeared, leaving me standing there like an idiot, the group of people she was with looking at me as if I were some sort of criminal."

"Why?"

He smiled, although it never reached his eyes. "She was ashamed of me. A lowly mechanic. Turns out, I was her dirty little secret. She had a boyfriend. A high-paying, steady nine-to-five job. Lots of rich friends. I was just a good, easy fuck."

"Oh, Stefano," I breathed out. "How horrible."

He lifted his shoulders in a dismissive shrug. "She tried to make light of it. Said I shocked her and she wasn't prepared, but it all came out when I didn't believe her. We fought and it got ugly, and I saw the real her. The one my family tried to warn me about. I told her to get out of my place and my life." He paused, and I saw the way the hurt flickered through his eyes. "She had a lot of not-nice things to say about me, and then she left." He drained his mug. "It didn't take me long to realize I was better off without her. A couple of months later, the garage had a fire, and Brett introduced me to Maxx and Charly. I moved here and started a new chapter in my life."

"And since then?"

"I'm not a monk. I dated a couple of women but nothing serious. I haven't slept with anyone for over two years." He frowned and scratched at his beard. "Maybe even longer, now that I think about it."

"I see."

He stood and poured another coffee and sat across from me. "How long for you, *Tesoro?*"

"Since the night I got pregnant with Theo."

He froze, his cup partway to his mouth. "Wow."

"So, it's been a long time."

"Why?"

"It's not exactly easy to meet someone when you're a single mom." I sighed. "Most men walk away when they hear a kid is involved, not that I've been looking. What happened between us is rare."

He reached for my hand and took it in his, stroking my palm. "I know. I'm not like other guys, Gabriella."

"I'm aware."

"What happened between you and Theo's dad?"

"He was never his *dad*," I snapped. Dad inferred caring. Love. Tenderness.

He held up his hands. "Sorry."

I knew I owed him an explanation. He deserved to know. But I was so worried he would decide it was too much. I was too much.

I wasn't ready to give him up just yet.

I stood and straddled his lap, cupping his face. "I'm sorry. I shouldn't have snapped."

"You need to tell me."

"I will," I promised. "But right now, all I want to do is kiss you."

"I won't be your secret."

"You're not. Oh God, you're everything, Stefano," I whispered, knowing I shouldn't, yet wanting him to know. He was amazing. Giving. The way he cared for me and for Theo was unlike anything I could have imagined. Even the way he checked to make sure I could hear Theo before he took me to bed. He was simply astonishing.

With a low growl, he pulled me to his mouth. His tongue stole in and licked me—hot, wet, and possessive. I undulated over him, feeling his erection kicking in. I pulled my lips away, kissing my way over to his ear.

"We're both safe, and I'm on the pill," I murmured, flicking my tongue over his lobe. "This time, I want to feel all of you."

He groaned and stood, taking me with him.

"This time," he growled against my mouth, "I'm going to make you come three times." He flung me on the bed, kicking off his shorts and cupping his heavy erection. "Maybe four."

And then he was on me, and everything else faded away.

CHAPTER TEN

Stefano

I was distracted on Sunday. I couldn't concentrate or think about anything except Gabriella. What it felt like to be inside her. How she looked as she orgasmed. The way she melted under my hands. The sensation of her skin gliding along mine. The taste of her mouth. Her subtle scent. Every single thing about her had become alive in my mind. I could hear her voice whispering my name. Moan in passion, whimper in desire. The way her eyes shut as she succumbed to pleasure. Burned into mine with an intense longing as I drove into her.

She was all I could see.

Even tossing the football around with my nephews, bouncing baby Cara on my knee, helping Sonny with his homework, she was there in the background.

"Stefano."

I looked up, meeting my mother's concerned gaze.

"You sick?"

"No."

"You no eating. What's the matter?" She frowned. "You no like my food no more?"

"It's amazing as usual, Mama. I was thinking about work." I picked up my fork, realizing I had barely taken a bite of her lasagna.

"Work," she repeated.

"Work," I stated emphatically.

My sister Gianna interrupted us, saving me from any more interrogation. "Mama's car is making an odd noise."

"What kind of odd noise?"

"Like something is loose. There's a high-pitched squeal."

"Why didn't you tell me sooner?" I demanded.

She frowned. "It just started."

I quickly finished my plate. "I'll take a look."

"You need to eat more," Mama protested, pushing my plate closer. "*Mangia.* Look at car after."

I didn't argue, knowing there was no point. I would lose. I ate another helping then headed to the garage, quickly finding the loose belt and tightening it. To stall, I checked out a few other things, ensuring the car was fine other than the belt. I added air to the tires and topped up the oil. No matter how often I told her to do so, she never remembered.

I walked into the house, wiping my hands, only to discover my siblings had deserted me. Mama waited at the table, a coffeepot in front of her, some of her delicious cookies on a plate. She knew I could never resist those.

With a sigh, I sat down, knowing what was coming and realizing I couldn't avoid it.

I picked up my coffee and took a sip of the dark brew.

"What's going on?" Mama asked. "Don't say nothing. I see trouble on your face."

I tried not to smile. When she'd had to find work when my dad died, using English as her primary language had been difficult for her. She had learned, and we had done our best to help her, but when upset, Mama lapsed into her old way of speaking. Short, stilted sentences, often mixed with Italian.

I met her eyes. Intelligent, warm, kind. They always had been. Today, they held a trace of worry.

"A woman?" she guessed before I could speak. "No that Leah. Say no, Stefano."

I shook my head. "No, Mama. Not Leah."

"But a girl?"

"I met someone," I confessed. "Someone special."

"You bring her here. I meet her."

"It's too soon," I protested.

"No. You like her. I see it."

I rubbed my face. "I'm worried you'll scare her."

"Scare her? What nonsense is this?"

"I think…" I sighed as I trailed off then tried again. "It's complicated, Mama."

"How so?" she asked. "You like her?"

"Yes."

"She like you?"

I thought about how much Gabby had liked me last night. Early this morning. How hard it had been to leave her.

"Yes."

"Then how complicated?"

"She has a son. He is five."

Her eyes grew round. "Stefano, *cuore mio*, you no dating married woman?"

I lifted her hand and kissed the knuckles. "No, Mama." I paused, unsure how much to tell her. "I think maybe the man she shared her life with hurt her. I think she's hiding."

She frowned. "He hurt her? *Stronzo*," she muttered. "*Bastardo*."

"She hasn't told me, but yes, I think so. She's skittish."

"Skittish?" she repeated.

"Worried. Afraid."

"No of you."

"No. Of her past. Telling me."

She was quiet for a moment, and I drank my coffee. I knew she had to mull it over.

"You bring her here. I meet her. She will see nothing to be frightened of. Family protect family." She met my eyes. "You make her your family, then she is part of this family, Stefano."

My heart swelled with love for this woman. She had always been open and understanding. She never let the old-world customs interfere with her life here. She accepted my brothers-in-law as her own sons, despite the fact that two of them weren't Italian, Catholic, or even particularly fond of pasta. She loved them because of the way they loved her daughters.

She taught them to love pasta because that horrified her more than the fact that they were a different nationality.

"Next Sunday, she comes here. We meet her."

"I'll ask."

She nodded. Then she pushed the plate closer. "*Mangia*, Stefano. You get too thin, *il mio bambino*."

I had to laugh. "I'm hardly your little baby anymore, Mama."

"You will always be. Now, eat. I send home food. You share with your friend…" She trailed off, lifting an eyebrow in question.

"Gabby."

"Gabriella? Italian?" she asked hopefully.

"No. But she loves pasta."

She nodded. "Good. I will make feast for her next week."

I took a cookie, remaining silent. I had to hope I could convince Gabby to accompany me next week. I had a feeling it wasn't going to be easy.

"Meet your mother?" Gabby whisper-yelled. "Why would she want to meet me?"

I stifled my smile, having expected her reaction.

"I told her about you and Theo, and she wants to meet you."

She frowned, glancing down at her hands. She was too far away, and I beckoned her with my hand. "Come here, *Tesoro*. Sit beside me." I patted the small space left on the love seat. "Here."

I had dropped by after dinner. Theo had just gotten out of the bath, so I sat with him, listening to his day, getting him to hold still as Gabby combed out his clean hair. He talked nonstop, asking questions when I told him I had lunch with my family.

"You have brothers?" he asked.

"Two," I confirmed. "Three sisters."

"What are their names?"

"Vince and Michael are my brothers. Gianna, Mila, Izzy are my sisters. I'm the youngest," I explained.

His eyes were wide. "I wanna be a big brother. Mom said not now." He grabbed my hand. "Maybe you could talk to her? It'd be fun being a big brother."

I looked over to Gabby, who was busy concentrating on Theo's head. A streak of color ran across her cheekbones. Our eyes met briefly, and I threw her a subtle wink.

"I'll see what I can do. It's not always, ah, easy. Sometimes it takes a lot of effort." I bit back my smile. "Lots and lots of hard work."

The color deepened on Gabby's cheeks.

"You told me you like hard work." Theo pointed out.

It was all I could do not to burst out laughing at the look on Gabby's face. I wanted to keep teasing her, but I couldn't. I leaned forward. "Having babies isn't as easy as wanting one, little man. Maybe one day you'll get your wish."

Luckily, he let it drop.

She sighed and came over to the love seat. Before she could sit, I caught her waist and pulled her to my lap. She gasped as I held her close. I kissed the end of her nose, rubbing mine along it affectionately. "Hi."

She frowned. "This is not sitting beside you."

"I improvised."

She squirmed, and I groaned in warning. "Gabriella."

She stopped, looking mischievous. "What?"

"Keep that up, and there'll be no more talking."

"What were we talking about?"

"You coming to lunch at my mother's place next week," I said dryly, knowing she knew exactly what we'd been discussing.

"Oh, right."

I tapped her nose. "Nice try."

She turned serious. "Why?"

"Why what?"

"Why are you taking me to meet your family?" She paused, her fingers worrying the edge of her shirt the way they always did when she was nervous. "You said you didn't take Leah to meet them for a month. We've barely been a couple for a week. Why would you want me to meet them?"

144

I studied her, letting her question sink in. I hadn't taken Leah to meet them that quickly. I wasn't even sure the day I'd taken her I was ready. Yet with Gabby and Theo, it was right. I knew it without question.

"Because you're important to me. Both of you are. More important than Leah could have ever been. I want you to meet my family."

"Stefano," she whispered. "It's so fast."

"I know."

"I need–I need to think it over."

"Okay." I had assumed, knowing Gabby, that she would. She would overthink it, come up with a thousand objections I would have to kiss away, and then on Sunday, I would take her to meet my family.

I traced my finger down her cheek. "Would you rather discuss that baby brother or sister for Theo? He was pretty determined."

She slapped away my hand in annoyance. "Do not encourage him. He's been on about it for a while, but ever since he saw Charly and her baby bump, he's been asking me daily. He's five."

"Your point?" I teased.

She rolled her eyes. "I am not explaining to my five-year-old how babies are made and why we can't just have one."

"What did you tell him?"

"That babies are expensive, and I don't have the money or time to look after one." Her cheeks colored again. "I also told him that it takes a mommy and a daddy to get a baby." Sadness drifted over her face. "That brought even more questions."

"About *his* dad?" I asked gently.

She tensed against me, and I ran my hand down her back. "Relax, Gabby. Everything is okay."

"I don't want to talk about it." She looked up at me, her eyes pleading.

I tamped down my frustration. I had hoped by telling her about Leah, she would trust me and tell me her background. I was sure what she had gone through was more intense, but I wanted her to know we all had scars from our past. But she wasn't ready.

"What *do* you want?"

She ran her fingers along my jaw. "You."

I was silent, letting her make the decision.

"I was thinking about you all day."

"Yeah?"

She nodded. "How you felt inside me. How you made me feel." She pressed her mouth to mine, flicking her tongue on my bottom lip. "How much I wanted you to make me feel that again," she whispered.

With a groan, I covered her mouth with mine. I kissed her like a starving man and she was the finest meal on earth. She shifted, straddling me, and all thoughts of her past, mine, my family, and everything else disappeared. All I could think about was her.

Impatiently, I tugged her shirt over her head, then brought her mouth back to mine. Her skin was velvet under my fingers as I stroked her back. She ground down against me, moaning as my erection hit her. Once more, our mouths broke apart, and my shirt came off. Her nipples rubbed against my chest, hard, and begged for my mouth and fingers. I somehow got her leggings off, and my pants were pushed down to my ankles. I kicked them off, slouching lower on the sofa as she rubbed against my cock, her need for me making me groan. I widened my legs, and she opened fully, gasping as I slid inside. I stilled at the feeling of her. The way she gripped me. How her muscles contracted around my cock, the silkiness of her desire, the heat of her need over-riding everything else.

"You feel so good, *Tesoro*. So fucking good."

She grasped my shoulders, lifting herself and sliding back down with a low moan.

"Ride me. Take what you need," I encouraged.

She circled her hips, lifting and lowering. I gripped her waist, guiding her, my passion building.

She bent back, her breasts lifting to my mouth. I sucked and licked, listening to her soft cries of pleasure, groaning out my own. When she began to tighten around me, I sped up, thrusting hard, and she dropped her head to my shoulder, shuddering with her orgasm. I thrust wildly, letting the pleasure overtake me, until I was spent.

I gathered her close, tugging an old blanket around us as she lay on my chest. I nuzzled her head, smiling.

"Okay, Gabriella?"

She peeked up with a smile. "Okay."

"That what you wanted?" I teased, tracing her mouth with my finger.

"For starters."

I lifted one eyebrow. "Starters."

She nodded. "Like an appetizer."

I chuckled.

"What?" she retorted. "You use baseball analogies—I like food."

"So, what you're saying is now you want the main course?"

Her eyes glowed. "And dessert."

"Well then, *Tesoro*. Brace yourself. Consider the bases loaded, and I plan on bringing them all home—safe."

She grinned. "Batter up!"

I stood, still lodged inside her. I planned to take her in the bedroom and not stop until she was passed out from pleasure.

"Up is right," I growled. "And it's all for you, Gabriella. All for you."

Her smile said it all.

CHAPTER ELEVEN

Stefano

I walked into the house I shared with Brett and headed to the kitchen. He was sitting at the kitchen table, a beer at his elbow as he studied a manual open on the table. He looked up, surprised, then frowned and peered behind me.

"I'm sorry, do I know you?"

I chuckled as I slid the pizza box onto the table. "Ha-ha."

"Seriously, you look like a guy who used to live here, but I haven't seen him in ages."

I grabbed a beer from the fridge, flipped up the lid on the pizza, and handed Brett a plate. "You saw me at the garage."

He laughed as he reached for a slice. "Someone who looked like you, except he was grinning all damn day like a Cheshire cat."

I chewed and swallowed, grunting as the rush of hot peppers and spicy sausage hit my taste buds. I chased down the heat with a long pull of cold beer.

"Whatever."

He folded a large slice in half and took a bite. "Damn," he muttered. "They were generous with the peppers."

I felt the flicker of heat under my skin. "Yep."

We ate in silence for a moment, then I met his eyes. "I haven't been around much," I admitted.

He shook his head. "I'm yanking your chain. I get it." He took another bite. "How's Gabby?"

"Complex. Frustrating." I huffed a long breath. "Amazing."

He snorted. "So, basically perfect."

"Pretty much." I wiped my mouth, then rose and grabbed a couple of bottles of water from the fridge. I handed Brett one. "She has a lot of baggage." I sipped the cold water. "Most of which she won't share."

He nodded. "Theo?"

"Yeah. There's history, and she's keeping it to herself."

"You haven't known her that long. Give her some time."

"I'm trying." I picked up another slice. "I'm taking her to meet Mama."

Brett whistled low in his throat. "Holy shit, that's a major step. She must be important."

"She is."

I'd met Brett when we worked together at a garage in Toronto. Despite our differences, we had become good friends. He came from a small town, raised by a widowed father who, to this day, treated him as if he was sixteen instead of thirty-five. Mr. Conner

BREAKING THE SPEED LIMIT

still ran the small general store in Littleburn. Brett had worked in the store his whole life and had been anxious to leave it behind. He'd discovered Toronto wasn't the place for him and returned to his hometown when the garage we worked at had a fire and shut down. Luckily, he got on with Maxx and had contacted me to come and check out the garage when a position opened up. I had never returned to Toronto except to visit my family. I'd lived with Mary, while Brett used the small place in the back of the garage until we found this house to rent in Lomand. My mother loved Brett, as did my siblings. He fit in well.

Growing up with just his father, he enjoyed the chaos that my large family brought with them. He was a regular at Sunday brunch. My mama treated him the way she treated me, and he liked her fussing. Once Rosa Borelli decided to take you under her wing, her love knew no bounds.

We ate in silence for a few moments, the pizza disappearing fast.

"Rosa is gonna have a field day with this," he observed, sounding just like Mary.

"I told her about Gabby. As soon as she heard about Theo, she was in. You know she can't resist kids. Add in a single mother I like?" I ran a hand through my hair. "Gabby doesn't stand a chance."

He regarded me. "You ready for that, Stefano? The instant family, the history—" he paused and drained his water, then lifted an eyebrow "—your *mama* getting involved?"

I thought about Gabby. How I felt when I was with her. My little man and how he made me smile. The urge to be with them as much as possible. It had taken everything in me not to show up at the bar where Gabby worked tonight. I wanted to sit and watch her. Make sure she was okay and no customers hassled her.

151

Except I knew she would kick my ass and inform me she could handle herself. Still, I simply wanted to be close to her. Watch her smile, see her laugh. I had never experienced anything like this before in my life.

"Yeah, I am."

He lifted his beer and waited until I did the same. We clinked bottles and he smiled. "Congrats, man. I hope it works out for you."

His smile didn't quite reach his eyes, and I studied him closer. "You okay, Brett?"

"I'm good."

"How are things with Cindy?"

He had met Cindy a few weeks ago, and I knew he'd been seeing her. He liked her, and the one time I'd met her, she seemed nice.

He picked at the label on his bottle. "Yeah, so, that's done."

"What happened?"

He met my eyes and shrugged.

"Oh God," I groaned. "Again?"

He grinned sheepishly. "What can I say?"

I let my head fall back as I laughed. Brett was a great guy. Too great. He was known for being nice. Helpful. And he had a habit of dating women who had just broken up with their significant others. And somehow, they always ended up returning to them. Brett, it appeared, was a great listener. He managed to land in the friend column every damn time.

"You need to change careers. Relationship counselor suits you."

He chuckled. "I think I'll stick to cars." He finished his beer. "And casual dating. I seem to be the best at that. Relationships and I don't mix."

"You'll find the right girl." I winked. "My sister gave you Lola's number. Call her. Maybe you should try the long-distance thing."

A strange look came over his face, but it passed quickly. "Not sure Toronto is long-distance, but maybe that's the answer," he agreed.

"You just need to meet the right one," I said again.

He laughed and stood, taking the empty pizza box with him. "If you managed to do it, then there's hope for me yet." He leaned on the counter. "You home for the night?"

I yawned and leaned back in my chair. "Until later, yeah."

"Heading out for another late-night walk?" he asked, lifting his eyebrow.

"Maybe."

He laughed. "There's a Jays game on."

"Awesome."

"Chase said they were starting up the baseball teams again. I signed us up. First game is Saturday afternoon. You in?"

"Absolutely." We all loved baseball, and the garage was a sponsor of the local team for Littleburn and Lomand. I loved playing the game and enjoyed the camaraderie. No one took it too seriously, and we always had a good time. "I assume Maxx passed this year?"

Brett shook his head. "Charly told him she wanted him out of the house. He's apparently too close all the time."

I laughed. "She loves him close. And if she thinks it's bad now, wait until the baby is born."

"He basically said that. She informed him Saturday afternoons will be pie day and girl time. He needs to be out of the house. I added his name, but we'll see what happens. He can be a spare."

I stood. "Makes sense. Now let's watch some baseball."

Saturday night, I was sitting on the front steps when Gabby got home. She eyed me warily with a shake of her head, walking up the driveway and standing in front of me.

"*Tesoro.*"

"Stefano. What are you doing here?"

"I was out for a walk. Got tired, so I thought I'd sit awhile."

"You got tired. Right by my driveway."

I nodded. "Convenient coincidence." I held out my hand. "Join me?"

She let me pull her down beside me, and I smiled as I felt the way she snuggled into my side. I slid my arm around her shoulders, tucking her even closer. I pressed a kiss to her hair.

"How was baseball?" she asked.

I chuckled. "Fine. Relaxed. We're not in it to win any championships." I dropped another kiss to her head.

"How was your night?"

"Quiet," she sighed. "They're still having issues in the kitchen, so it was closed. A lot of people left when they couldn't get food. The regulars were there, but it wasn't a great night."

"Sorry."

She shrugged. "It happens. I budget according to my hours and the lowest amount of tips I think I'll make in a night. Anything extra I consider bonuses."

"It's obvious where the extra goes, Gabby. Theo is well cared for." I hesitated. "It's you I worry about. You do without a lot."

She stiffened. "I'm fine."

"You're a great mother," I replied. "I'd just like to spoil you a little."

For a moment, there was silence. "You already have," she finally said. "The newer SUV, the way you are with Theo and Mrs. Scott. Your nightly walks." She paused. "The way you treat me."

"You deserve to be treated well."

"I'm not used to it," she admitted.

"I gathered that. I assume it has something to do with your ex?"

"Yes," she said shortly, her posture becoming tense.

"Did he hurt you, Gabriella?" I asked quietly.

"Not as badly as he could have," she whispered. "I got out."

I pulled her as tight to me as I could. "*Tesoro*, I'm sorry."

She slid her hand along my thigh. "It's over now."

"You have to trust me. Tell me."

Her hand slid higher. "I will. I promise."

I groaned as she cupped me through the denim. I was already half hard for her. Sitting this close, inhaling her soft fragrance. Feeling her against me.

"Take me upstairs," she whispered, pressing her lips to my throat. "I want you." She dragged her lips to my mouth, her breath washing over me. "Please."

Two minutes later, I was looming over her on the bed, her skin pale and soft in the dim light. I knew what she was doing. Distracting me. But she was a siren, and I couldn't resist her.

We would talk tomorrow. I would find out her past and help her deal with it. Then we could move forward. The three of us. Together.

I slipped out of her room in the early morning light. I tugged my shirt over my head as I crept down the hall, avoiding the spot in the middle that creaked so loudly. My mind was on Gabby. The feel of her under me. How she tasted. Sounded. Surrounded me. How she looked as she half woke when I slid from the bed, grumbling and reaching for me. I had shoved my pillow toward her, pressing my lips to her cheek.

"Sleep a bit more, Tesoro. *I'll be here at eleven."*

"Hmm," she mumbled. "You're warmer." She yawned, burrowing her head into the fluffy cushion. "And you smell better."

I had chuckled, kissing her again and smiling as she started to snore lightly. She needed some more sleep. I didn't let her get much last night.

Or a few other nights this week.

I was so deep into my thoughts, I didn't notice the little form sitting at the kitchen table.

"Stefo!" An excited whisper startled me.

I stopped in the doorway, smiling at Theo. I was busted. Again.

"Hey, little man."

"I looked for you on the sofa, but you weren't there."

"Oh, ah…" To my shock, I felt my cheeks warm at the thought of creeping out of Gabby's room and being caught by her son.

"Did you sleep with Mommy?"

My cheeks were now on fire.

"She has a big bed, so it would be more comfortable. She hogs the blankets, though, so you were probably cold." He looked upset. "You could borrow my Avengers blanket next time if you want." His face brightened. "Or I can sleep with Mommy and you can have my room."

I relaxed when I realized he was more concerned with the thought of me being uncomfortable sleeping than knowing what I did to his mother in her bed. I sat down with a relieved grin.

"I'm too tall for your bed, Theo." I ruffled his hair. "I'm too tall for any piece of furniture here, but I, ah, make do."

He nodded. "You get too tired to go home?"

"Um, yeah." I cleared my throat. "You want some cereal, bud?"

"Please."

I poured him a bowl and got one too. I figured since I'd been caught, there was no need to rush out. We ate for a few moments, the only sound the clinking of our spoons on the bowls and the crunch of the Frosted Flakes we chewed.

Theo rubbed his nose. "You kiss her lots." He pursed his lips. "Is that why you're tired and fall asleep in her bed?"

Cue the heat on my face. I'd had no idea I could feel embarrassment of this sort, but Theo had a knack for making it happen.

"I like to kiss your mom," I said carefully. "But we talk a lot and sometimes I get sleepy because I've been working all day, so I close my eyes and I fall asleep. Your mom lets me rest."

"If I fall asleep, she takes me to my room and tucks me in." His eyes widened. "She doesn't carry you, does she?"

I had to chuckle. "No, she, ah, nudges me awake, and I walk myself."

Or roll over and fall asleep. And often, I was the one nudging her. Repeatedly. But I kept that to myself.

He nodded. "You can stay anytime. I like having breakfast with you."

"Thanks, little man."

Gabby stumbled in, stopping when she saw us. Her eyes widened, and she glanced between us.

"Hey, *Tesoro*. Theo and I were talking about how I fell asleep last night and you let me stay."

Theo nodded. "He said he fits better on your bed than the little sofa, but it's still not big enough. You should get a bigger one for him, Mom." He chewed a mouthful of cereal. "He's got long legs."

I tried to stop the laughter building in my chest. Gabby looked as horrified as I felt having this conversation. I stood and rinsed my bowl in the sink. I pressed a kiss to Gabby's head. "Thanks for the hospitality," I teased. "I'll pick you up at eleven."

"Sure," she mumbled.

I headed toward the steps, muffling the laughter that threatened to explode as I heard Theo.

"Mommy, Stefo says he likes kissing you. But I think kissing makes him more tired, so he falls asleep. I'm not going to kiss girls if it makes me sleepy." There was a pause in which I heard Gabby's fast intake of air. "Do you like to kiss Stefo? Does it make you tired?"

"This conversation makes me tired," she muttered as the sounds of the coffeepot being moved reached my ears. There was no doubt she was going to want the caffeine. Theo's inquisition plus the fact that she would be meeting my family? She needed it.

I chuckled all the way home.

CHAPTER TWELVE

Stefano

Gabby looked lovely when I picked her up. Her wild hair was gathered away from her face, and she wore one of her pretty skirts and a blouse. Theo was in pants and a clean shirt, and he looked excited.

His mother looked as if she was going to throw up at any moment.

I helped strap Theo into his car seat, then opened the door for Gabby. I took the large bunch of flowers she held tight in her grip and placed them in the back seat.

"You didn't have to spend money on flowers," I assured her. "Not necessary."

"You said I couldn't bring food. I had to bring something to say thank you. It's only polite," she insisted.

I smiled and kissed her, brushing her ear with my lips. "Relax, *Tesoro*. My mama is going to love you. They all are."

I shut her door and crossed over to the driver's side, sliding in. I reached for her hand and squeezed it in reassurance. "Promise." Then I lifted it to my mouth and kissed the knuckles.

"Careful, Stefo," Theo said, sounding worried. "If you keep kissing Mommy, you'll fall asleep, and I don't know how to drive yet."

I laughed and threw him a wink over my shoulder. "It's all good, little man. I have to kiss your mommy a lot more to get sleepy."

"Ugh," was his reply. "I'm not kissing girls, then," he muttered, looking down at the toy in his hand. "Too much work."

"Good," Gabby and I said at the same time, then laughed.

"Worth it," I said, quietly smiling at her, sharing the joke.

She grinned and looked out the window, but the levity helped ease some of the tension from her expression.

We headed toward Toronto, Theo once again enthralled by the DVD I put in for him. He was engrossed in the show, and Gabby turned to check on him, meeting my eyes as she turned back.

"He's going to want one of those in the SUV," she observed.

"You can get them. They hang over the seat."

"We don't take a lot of long rides."

I nodded, taking a sip of the coffee we'd stopped to pick up. Theo was enjoying the chocolate milk I had gotten him.

"What will your family think about you pulling up in a van?" she asked. "Not your usual ride."

I smirked. "Mama will love it. She hates the motorcycle. She tolerates the Mustang but only because of the fact that it was once my father's. She would far prefer it if I drove something else."

"Your Mustang was your dad's?"

I nodded, changing lanes. "He took it as part payment for something he did for someone. My mom was furious, but he insisted it was a good deal." I flashed her a grin. "Or at least that's how I heard the story. He fixed it up and drove it until he couldn't anymore. Kids and a Mustang don't go so well together. He bought an old Chevy he used to drive us around in. He kept it and tinkered on it. He convinced my mom that it was worth nothing, so keeping it wasn't an issue. Truth was, he loved that car and didn't want to part with it. When I got old enough, I started fixing it up. My brothers weren't interested in cars the way I was, so they had never bothered."

"So it has a sentimental value to it. It's not just a toy."

"It's that too. But yes, I love it because it was my father's. I only drive it in the summer. I use the company truck most of the time or, like today, I borrow this. Maxx is cool with it."

She slipped her hand over mine. "I'm sorry I said what I did the day we met. About your car."

I had forgotten about her offhand remark about boys and their toys.

"You didn't know." I cast a quick sidelong look at her. "I wasn't exactly on my best behavior that day. You knocked me for a loop."

"Back at you."

I pulled off the exit, heading toward my family home. Gabby became quiet, her nerves kicking in again. Theo was glued to the screen, and I thought about the day I had met Gabby. The instant attraction. The way I had kissed her. How she had responded. I silently thanked the powers that be for flat tires, short skirts, and pretty girls who mouthed off to me. It was divine intervention that had me pull over to offer the stranger help.

She had changed my life.

And now, I was about to change hers.

I pulled up in front of my mother's house. The number of cars in the driveway and on the street let me know Gabby was about to be thrown into the Borelli family circle feetfirst.

I put the car in park and turned to her. "Ready?"

She swallowed, her eyes wide. "Okay."

I winked. "Let's go."

Mama waited at the door, not concealing her curiosity or enthusiasm. She barely let me introduce Gabby and Theo before she hugged them both, clucking over Theo and insisting Gabby call her Mama. "Everyone does," she claimed.

I held back my smile. Only family and Brett called her that.

She laughed in delight as Theo held out the flowers. "Nice to meet you, Mrs. Borelli. These are from Mommy and me—" he faltered, then recovered "—to say thank you for lunch." He paused. "I hope it's good. I'm hungry."

My mother fell in love that second. She cupped Theo's face, kissing his cheeks. "You call me Nonna Rosa. And it's good. Promise."

Then she took his hand, and he followed her into the house. I grinned at Gabby. "Welcome to the Borelli family crazy."

Inside, there was a frenzy. Theo was being hugged and introduced. He ate it up, his smile wide, not in the least shy. By the time Mama was done, he had headed off to play with the kids, then she turned and announced with a flourish, "Dis is Stefano's Gabriella!"

It was Gabby's turn to be exclaimed over. Hugged. Kissed. Complimented. My sisters were effusive. My brothers affectionate. Their spouses welcoming and amused, no doubt recalling their own welcomes to the family.

I couldn't help recall when I had brought Leah to meet them. They had all been reserved and polite. Not a single one of them liked her. But it was as if they knew how important Gabby and Theo were to me and responded. As if they could see her goodness and light.

It was great to witness.

A short while later, gathered around the table, Theo's eyes were huge. "Mommy," he whispered loudly. "I've never seen so much food!"

Mama laughed. "*Mangia. Mangia.* I make all for you."

"What does that mean?" he asked.

"Eat up," I told him. "Eat as much as you want."

His eyes grew even bigger. "All of it!" he crowed.

"Go for it, little man," I encouraged. "Try it all."

I helped him with the bowls and platters, giving him a taste of everything. He gobbled it up, asking for more pasta, cutlets, veal, and even the fish. Gabby got him to eat a mouthful of salad, but he waved more away.

"You make that, Mommy. I like the new stuff!" He turned to my mother. "I like this, Nonna Rosa! You're a really good cook."

"You have favorite?" she asked.

He furrowed his brow in thought. "The ziti and meatballs."

She nodded. "I make them when you come back. Every time."

He beamed and reached over, kissing her cheek. "Thank you!"

She patted his cheek. "*Bravo ragazzo.*"

"What's that?" he asked.

"Good boy. Your momma raise good boy. Like my Stefano."

"I like Stefo. He's my friend."

Mama smiled. "Good."

"I like having breakfast with him."

I felt my neck begin to warm. Gabby inhaled quickly, covering it up with her napkin. My mama lifted one eyebrow.

"Oh?" she asked.

I felt the weight of everyone's stares at the table, my siblings covering their chuckles.

He nodded. "He has sleepovers with Mommy. He kisses her too much, and they talk until he gets tired and falls asleep in her bed 'cause his legs are too long for the sofa. I offered him my Avengers blanket to stay warm because Mommy hogs the blanket."

Gabby made a low sound of distress. My eldest brother began to laugh. My sisters began to giggle. Mama looked at me. I met her eyes bravely, reminding myself I was a grown adult. I was allowed to sleep with anyone I wanted to.

"I hope Stefano is a good houseguest, Gabriella. He no make a nuisance of himself?"

"He's a perfect gentleman on the *rare* occasion he stays over," Gabby said, sounding desperate.

"Mommy," Theo protested. "He is there almost every night. Did you forget that?"

The entire table broke into laughter, and I had to join them. I was totally busted. Even Mama laughed, holding her napkin to her face and guffawing. Then she bent and kissed Theo.

"You funny boy. You go play with cousins until dessert."

He skipped away happy, not aware of the bomb he had just dropped. Mama watched him and looked at me. "Good boy," she reiterated. "Good family." She stood. "I like."

I draped my arm over Gabby's chair. "That's the biggest compliment she can pay. She likes you."

"She thinks I'm some sort of loose woman with you sleeping over all the time," she hissed into my ear.

"No," I replied, kissing the tender lobe, smiling at her shiver. "She thinks I'm head over heels." I kissed her again.

"And she's right."

After lunch, I played with the kids, and we kicked around the soccer ball, lifting our hands high when goals were scored and enjoying ourselves. My brothers and I had always loved soccer, and I liked carrying on the tradition with my nieces and nephews. Gabby stayed inside, insisting on helping to clean up. I hoped my sisters and Mama weren't giving her too hard a time.

I snuck in to check on her, surprised to find my sisters in the living room and Gabby and Mama alone at the kitchen table talking. Whatever Gabby was saying had my mom transfixed. She listened intently, then cupped Gabby's cheek and said something before standing and hugging her. Mama caught my eye and headed past me, stopping.

"She good for you. She need you. You bring her back next week. And I look after Theo one night and you take her to nice supper, yeah?"

"Sure, Mama. That'd be good."

She nodded. "Yes. Good." She leaned close. "I like. You keep."

I grinned. "I plan on it."

Theo fell asleep before we hit the highway later that afternoon. We'd had a nice time sitting outside, drinking coffee, and eating Italian cookies and cannoli. Theo had loved them, devouring three in succession, then running around to wear off the sugar and chocolate. Mama made the best cannoli in the city. Gabby ate two herself plus sampled the cookies and exclaimed over everything. Mama had beamed, her affection growing.

In the back seat was enough food to feed Gabby and Theo for a week—easily. Pasta, chicken, veal, bread, sweets. An extra lasagna Mama had "on hand." Some cold cuts she'd bought "by mistake."

"Make my Theo sandwiches," she insisted. "It go bad here, me all alone."

I tried not to scoff at her. She was rarely alone since some sibling or a spouse checked on her all the time. Someone was constantly at her place for meals, and the kids usually went to Nonna's daily. But I loved the fact that she wanted to spoil Gabby, so I stayed quiet.

"Your family is amazing," Gabby said, bringing me out of my thoughts.

"They loved you. All of them. Mama, especially."

She smiled.

"Would you be comfortable with us going out one night and Mama looking after Theo?"

"I only get one night off."

"We can make it work. Or wait until another time. But I would like to take you out on a proper date. Dinner at a nice place. There's a steak place I really like we could go to."

"I'd like that."

"Okay. We'll figure it out."

She reached for my hand, squeezing it. "You're pretty amazing yourself."

"So are you." I lifted her hand to my mouth and kissed it. "I had a great day, *Tesoro.*"

"Me too."

I glanced in the rearview mirror with a grin. "Even with Theo spilling our secrets?"

She bit her lip. "I'll talk to him about privacy."

I laughed. "Haven't you figured it out? With my family, there is none. My mother can sniff out a secret and have you telling her before you have even finished a coffee. She'll have him ratting us out every time."

"Hmm."

I winked. "Give it up, Gabby. We're in it now. My mama knows you stole my virtue. You'll have to make an honest man of me."

She laughed. "Your virtue was gone long before I got my hands on you, Stefano."

I held her hand to my chest. "But yours are the only ones I want touching me now."

She rolled her eyes and looked away, but she was smiling.

CHAPTER THIRTEEN

Gabby

On Monday night, there was another issue with the kitchen. Frustrated, Ziggy decided to shut down the bar completely until they could trace the problem with the gas line. When I called and told Stefano, he came right over. Together, we played with Theo, and I put him to bed, enjoying a few moments of unexpected time with him. Stefano sat on the floor of Theo's room, smiling as Theo drifted off to sleep as I read out loud from the book about the mechanic shop for kids that Stefano had bought him. Where he had found a book like that, I had no idea.

After, we sat on the love seat, and I sipped the wine Stefano poured us, reveling in the moment.

"Will the bar reopen tomorrow?"

I shook my head. "Ziggy thinks Thursday."

"So you have time off."

"What it means is that I have no income this week," I muttered, mentally going through my bank accounts and expenses. My emergency account was going to be drained quickly.

"Charly is exhausted," he announced.

I glanced over at him, realizing I had zoned out for a few moments. "Sorry?"

"She was dragging her ass everywhere today. She fell asleep at her desk twice. Maxx carried her home and tucked her into bed, refusing to let her come back." He held up his phone. "I just texted him and told him you were free. He wants you at the garage. So there's your wages looked after."

"Oh. That's awesome!"

He shifted closer to me, running a finger down my cheek. "What else can I do?"

I stared at him in wonder. "Um, nothing? I think you've done enough for me."

He smiled, his dark eyes dancing. "Come on, *Tesoro*, give me a challenge. There must be something you need." He slid closer. "Something you're *desperate* for," he whispered into my ear. "Theo is asleep. It's early. I'm here. Surely there is something I can do to you." He grinned. "I mean, *for* you."

I tried to look stern and failed. Stefano grinned, hauling me onto his lap. His lips covered mine, and he kissed me deeply, his passion evident. I whimpered into his mouth as he caressed the skin of my back, sliding his hand down to my ass and cupping the cheeks.

"Anything come to mind?" he murmured, tugging on my earlobe. "Anything at all?"

He twisted me, shifting until I straddled him. His erection was prominent, and he yanked me down on it, grinding against me. I gasped at the feel of him, hard and unyielding. Solid and filled with promise. He slid his hands under the loose sweatshirt I had changed into, stroking my tight nipples as he kissed up and down my neck. "Maybe now?" he breathed against my neck as I rocked into him.

"Please," I begged.

"There is something you want?"

"Yes," I gasped as his fingers slid against me. "*You*, inside me."

"Here?" He pressed, his fingers finding my clit.

"Oh God, yes."

"Right now?"

"Yes," I panted. "Now."

"You'll have to be quiet."

I fisted his shirt. "You'll have to be fast."

He grinned. "We're both going to get what we want, then."

In seconds, he was inside me, hot and thick. He gripped my hips, pulling me up and down, groaning low in his throat, kissing me hard to cover my moans. It was fast and hard. Dangerous, knowing Theo could wake up any second. Sexy, because I knew it was wrong. Perfect, because it was Stefano, and he would make sure it was all okay.

I shuddered as my orgasm rushed through me, my body shaking with the effect of it. Stefano dropped his head to my shoulder, encasing me in his arms as he shuddered and came. His breath was heavy on my skin, his arms a cage I didn't want to escape.

Seconds passed as we clung to each other, then he straightened, meeting my eyes.

"*Ti amo,*" he whispered. "*Ti amo.*"

I guessed at what most of his Italian words meant. Some were dirty, others were praise, and always, they were affectionate. But I knew what those words meant. I felt my eyes widen in alarm, but he smiled and touched my mouth.

"You're not ready, I know. But I wanted you to know how I was feeling. I'm here for you. With you. I'm not going anywhere, *Tesoro.* Whatever you need, whatever I can do, I'm here." He smiled, his eyes soft, his voice dripping with love. "You're not alone anymore. You never will be again."

He gathered me against him, pressing my head to his chest. Under my ear was the loud beat of his heart. Like the rest of him, it was strong, comforting. Steady. I closed my eyes and let it center me. His words were an echo in my head.

He loved me.

Stefano loved me. He asked for nothing in return but gave me his love freely.

I wanted to say it back. To tell him all the feelings I had about him. How safe he made me feel. How special. How much I adored the way he was with my son. How incredible he was.

But I was scared. Worried. He still didn't know about my past. The danger it could be to him, even though it seemed a lifetime ago. I lifted my head and met his eyes. They were gentle, understanding.

"Stefano—"

He shook his head, cutting me off. "I don't expect you to say it, Gabby. I just want you to know you're not alone. I'm here."

I felt tears spring to my eyes. He stood, holding me and trying to pull up his pants, cursing low in his throat. I began to chuckle, and he dropped a kiss to my head.

"Bed," he said. "We could both use the extra sleep."

"But——"

He kissed me. "We'll talk later. Mama is going to take Theo one night, and we're going on a date. Lots of adult conversation will happen then."

I let him carry me to bed. I was tired, and I needed time to process his words. What they meant to me.

What he meant.

The garage was busy. Stefano was right, and Charly looked exhausted. I checked on her during the day, even taking a break to make a big pot of soup and leaving it on the stove so she wouldn't have to worry about dinner. She was so organized and I was familiar with her systems, so I was able to step in easily. Dealing with the customers face-to-face was sort of like handling the bar patrons, only they were sober and usually had much larger bills. Business was booming, and a lot of regulars inquired about Charly and how she was feeling. After the first day, other meals were dropped off, and I knew how much the people around here cared about her. Maxx was touched, and Stefano and Brett took turns carrying casseroles and baked goods to the house. Maxx found every excuse he could to check on things in the house, and more than once, he came back grumpy because

Charly had kicked him out. I was sliding a pan into the freezer when I heard her one time.

"Holy moly!" she yelled. "How can I rest when you're in here every five minutes, Maxx?"

"It's not every five minutes, Red. I'm just making sure you're okay."

"I have my cell if I need you," she replied, her voice quieter. "I'm fine, just tired. Your damn kid is using me as a punching bag and tap-dancing on my kidneys! All I do is sleep and pee."

There were some hushed words, and I knew without a doubt he was talking to her stomach. She insisted his voice quieted their growing child more than anything. They were thrilled to be having a daughter this time, although she knew Maxx would be overprotective.

"Lord help us both. That child will be spoiled and locked up until she is thirty, I swear," she bemoaned with a wide grin. "Maxx will go gray overnight with worry." She laughed, rubbing her hands with glee. "I can hardly wait."

I wiped the counter and rinsed a couple mugs. Maxx came down the steps, looking troubled. I put a hand on his arm. "She's right, Maxx. Sometimes, the second baby is harder. She told me the doctor says everything is fine."

"She's here alone."

"If Mary stayed here with Thomas, Charly wouldn't rest. She has her cell. If that isn't enough, put the baby monitor in your room. If she needs you, she can call out. But let her sleep."

"That's a good idea."

"I'll come over later and sit here to make my calls. I'll make sure she eats and is okay."

He sighed and ran a hand through his hair. "Thanks, Gabby. I'd appreciate that."

I liked being at the garage. The constant stream of people and the banter. Seeing Stefano several times a day. Checking in on Charly. Listening and chatting to the guys, although I noticed they made sure to maintain a respectful distance, which made me chuckle.

Theo spent some time with Mrs. Scott, some with me and the men at the garage, and some time with Mary and Thomas. He loved being with people, and I realized how isolated we had been before Stefano came into our lives. Theo was more outgoing and happier than I had ever seen him.

Late Wednesday afternoon, Charly came in, looking better. She slid onto the seat beside me with a smile.

"How are you?" I asked.

"Good. The break has been good. I was hoping I could convince you to give me a few more hours. We'd pay you, of course."

"Sure. I can do that."

"The mornings are hard. Maybe you could come in and be here? Bring Theo—it would only be for a couple of extra hours every day. I can take my time before I start work."

"Sounds good."

"Great."

My phone rang, and I smiled at her as she got up and waddled toward Maxx. He watched her adoringly, holding out his hand when she got close. I had a feeling he'd take her home right away. I felt a sneeze coming, and I grabbed a Kleenex to cover my mouth as I answered the phone.

"Hello," I muttered, trying to hold back the sneeze.

I heard nothing, only the crackling of dead air.

I hung up and reached for a file. A short while later, my phone rang again. I checked the number, and it registered as local but no name.

"Hello."

Again, I only heard silence and a slight crackling noise in the background.

I hung up, rolling my eyes. Obviously, a scam artist. I blocked the number and forgot about it.

The days passed in a blur. I felt busy and productive.

Friday, Ziggy confirmed the bar would open on Monday, which meant I had the weekend off. I couldn't recall the last time I'd had that much time off from a job.

Charly shuffled in, sitting down as my phone rang. I rolled my eyes, not answering.

"Scammers?" she asked.

"I think so. The number changes, but no one is there when I answer." I frowned. "At least I think that's what they are."

She nodded. "I heard there's been a rash of them again. I hate it. I had a run of them about a month ago. I used to keep a bull-horn handy, but Maxx took it away."

I chuckled, her words helping me feel better.

"I hear you have a big date tonight."

I nodded. "Stefano and I are having dinner in Toronto at some place he really likes. I get to get dressed up. His mom is keeping Theo."

"For the whole night?" she winked slyly, waggling her eyebrows.

I laughed. "No, we'll pick him up and head home."

She shook her head, leaning closer. "You should have gotten a hotel. Hotel sex is the best sex. The first time I had sex with Maxx was in a hotel." She fanned herself. "Girl, talk about hot. The man had moves—and the thing he did with his tongue—"

Maxx stomped in, almost growling. "Stop talking about us having sex to the employees, Red." He leaned over, hitting the intercom button. "Or at least make sure the speaker is off. Everyone knows now."

I tried to hold back my laughter but failed. Maxx kissed Charly hard and stormed out of the office. She wasn't at all offended—in fact, she called after him.

"At least I said it was hot! You were smoking, big man!"

Then she looked at me and winked.

"You knew it was on."

"I needed to rile him up." She winked again. "I have needs he has to meet."

"You are terrible."

She grinned. "He's always too careful with me when I'm pregnant. A girl's gotta do what a girl's gotta do. I'm feeling better, and I need sex. Sex with Maxx."

She held out her hand, and I let her grip mine and hoist herself out of the chair.

"Now I'll go through the garage and stop partway. I'll frown a little, and he'll have me in his arms in a second. I'll get a ride home. Then maybe I'll get a different ride. You'll have to shift the appointments a little."

"Again, terrible. But I can do that." We shared a grin.

She shrugged and shuffled away. A few seconds later, I spied Maxx carrying her out of the garage. Charly met my eyes and gave me a thumbs-up. I laughed.

Stefano appeared a short time later, wiping his hands. He dropped a kiss to my shoulder, then sat down.

"Looking forward to dinner?" I asked.

"I am."

"The bar is closed until Monday."

He grinned. "Excellent. I get you all weekend. We can go to Mama's on Sunday and take Theo to the park."

"He'd like that."

"Great. I'll pick you up at six thirty. That enough time?"

"Yep."

He stood and winked. "Awesome." Then he leaned down close to my ear. "Charly's right. Hotel sex is awesome. Mama would be happy to keep Theo…"

"Stop," I chided gently.

"You, me, no noise restrictions," he whispered. "A huge bed, room service…" Again, he trailed off.

"Room service?" I squeaked.

He chuckled. "The idea of food got you? Not loud sex?"

"Um…"

"I already booked a room. There's a spa tub. And I took the day off tomorrow."

And with those words, he left the office.

I looked down at the papers in front of me, not seeing the words.

All I saw was him naked, in a tub. The steam swirling around his body as he held out his arms. His muscles would be on display, and his cock would be hard and waiting.

For me.

"Come to me, Tesoro," he would murmur.

I squeezed my thighs together.

Suddenly, I was looking even more forward to tonight than I had been.

CHAPTER FOURTEEN

Gabby

The restaurant was dim, the atmosphere intimate. The booths were round and surrounded by thick glass and wood, each one private and cozy. I sat beside Stefano, our thighs pressed together. I sipped the heady red wine he'd ordered, glancing at the menu.

"What looks good to you?" he asked, closing his and picking up his wine. He swirled the wine, inhaling it before taking a long, appreciative sip.

"It all does."

"They have a sharing platter. Appetizers, soup, a large steak, and sides." He grinned. "Two desserts."

"Sounds perfect."

"Medium rare, right?"

"Yes."

He ordered dinner and offered me the basket of bread. I bit into the dense, rich piece of the focaccia bread, the rosemary and garlic exploding on my tongue.

"How did you find this place? Is it your date go-to?" I teased lightly.

He chuckled, chewing and swallowing his bread.

"My family knows it well. The other half is more, ah, open than this part. Families, friends—that sort of casual vibe. Brett and I would come here on occasion and enjoy a good steak. My family books the private room at times." He lifted my hand and kissed it. "This is the first time I've brought a date here."

"Oh," I murmured.

"Did I mention how beautiful you are tonight?" he asked.

I glanced down at the deep green dress I was wearing. I had bought it on sale last year with an unexpected tip around the holidays. I had loved the simplicity of it and the way it looked on with the off-the-shoulder neckline and asymmetrical skirt. I had never worn it but had been grateful for the impulse buy as I slipped it on tonight. I wore my hair up, showing my neck, and Stefano was filled with effusive praise when he picked me up.

"You did. A few times."

He leaned close, dropping a kiss to my neck. "Stunning," he breathed out.

I shivered. He'd been looking at me as if I were the meal the entire time.

"Do you think Theo is okay with your mom?" I asked, trying to change the subject.

"He'll be fine. Mama has my number if there is an issue. She'll spoil him all night. She was making him ziti with extra meatballs. She baked cookies. She loves spending time with her grandkids."

My wineglass froze partway to my mouth. "Theo isn't—"

He cut me off. "She already adores him. He's family to her now."

I set down my glass. "Your entire family moves fast."

He shrugged, waiting until the salads were in front of us before he spoke again. "Mama knows what loss is. She has always encouraged us to grab life and live it." He pierced a forkful of lettuce. "She knows how I feel about you."

I was quiet as I ate my salad.

"You seem too good to be true sometimes, Stefano."

He wiped his mouth. "I'm hardly perfect, Gabby. But I try to be a good person. It's easy with you." He covered my hand with his, warm and strong. "You make it easy. You expect nothing and are always shocked by kindness." He paused. "I assume whatever you left behind you didn't include much of that?"

I set down my fork. "No."

He studied me. "I'm not going to push. When you're ready, I'll listen."

"Theo's father and I—it wasn't good. I left him. I had to protect Theo."

"Good."

"He wasn't happy about it," I confessed.

"I'm glad you're out of it. I'm glad you're here, with me."

The soup arrived, and Stefano changed the subject. I was grateful, not wanting to talk about this in a public place. I knew I had to tell him, but part of me was scared to. He might decide that I, that we, were too much to handle and walk away.

The thought hurt me.

My phone rang, and I glanced at it, shaking my head and ignoring it. He noticed my frustration and lifted an eyebrow in a silent question.

"I must be on some sort of list," I complained. "I keep getting hang-up or dead-air calls."

Stefano grunted. "I hate those. I was getting them so much I ended up changing numbers. Best not to answer."

"I don't."

"We can look into it, if you want."

I sat back in wonder. "You just want to help with everything, don't you?"

He shrugged. "When it comes to you, yes." He met my gaze. "Is that a problem?"

"I'm not used to it. I had to learn not to rely on anyone but myself."

"You don't have to anymore," he said gently. "It's just going to take some time for you to get used to that."

I wasn't sure how to tell him I was afraid to get used to it. Worried that he might change his mind. Terrified if I told him how much I loved him back, he might still choose to walk away.

I couldn't seem to find the words.

I wasn't sure if I would ever be brave enough.

But I had to try.

STEFANO

Gabby gasped as she looked at the huge spa tub in the bathroom. The gleaming marble was bright under the lights, the pile of fluffy towels and the robes laid out beside it inviting.

She had been quiet during the last half of dinner. Smiling and responding to my questions, eating her meal and commenting on how delicious it was, but I saw the small furrow between her brow that kept returning. Felt the occasional tremor of nerves that came over her every so often. Something was on her mind. I had to figure out how to get her to reveal her thoughts to me. To open up and trust me completely. Anything less was unacceptable.

I slipped my arm around her waist. "Like that, *Tesoro?*"

"You could fit three people in there easily!"

I chuckled and bit her earlobe. "Not into sharing, but I bet we could play around in the water. Figure out how to use all the space."

She giggled, the sound low and soft.

"Fill the tub," I murmured in her ear. "Then I'll give you something to compare with Charly when it comes to hotel sex."

She was laughing as she bent over the tub, her pretty green dress riding up and showing me her shapely thighs and the bottom curve of her spectacular ass.

I couldn't hold back my groan at the sight of the barely there lace covering her ass cheeks.

She peeked over her shoulder. "You like that, Stefano?"

"You're lucky I didn't know what you had on under there," I replied, palming my growing erection. "Dessert would have been a lot different with me under the table and having you on my tongue instead of eating the cake they brought us."

She turned, standing before me with a shy smile. She reached behind her, tugging down a zipper, her dress becoming a shimmering pool of forest green at her feet. Lacy lingerie met my eyes, the black a splash of ink against the paleness of her skin.

"You are so fucking beautiful," I growled. "Temptation on legs."

She advanced toward me, tossing her dress to the counter. "How about you get between my legs and show me?"

I pulled her into my arms. "Consider it done."

Our mouths met in a blistering kiss. Long, wet, hot. Moments passed as we shared oxygen, our breaths mingling, becoming one. My need for her that always seemed to simmer just below the surface of my skin exploded and grew. My already-hard cock became steel, my nerves on fire. I wanted her more than I had ever wanted another woman. I knew, without a doubt, she would hold me under her spell the rest of my life.

There was no one else on earth like my Gabriella. My *Tesoro*.

Our hands fumbled, desperate to remove the last of the clothing that kept us apart. My shirt ended up somewhere on the floor. Together, we tugged and yanked on my belt and zipper, my pants kicked away to join my shirt. I picked her up, sitting down in the water, both of us gasping as the heat surrounded us. Her breasts rubbed on my chest, her nipples hard and perfect on my skin. I gripped her full ass, settling her on my lap. The warmth of the water had nothing on the heat of her center that surrounded my cock. I groaned at the slickness of it that water couldn't disguise.

"This is going to be hard and fast," I warned.

"You can make it up later," she responded, moving over me, making me hiss.

I gripped her hips and brought her down flush on me, filling her completely. She cried out, grabbing the edge of the tub and flinging back her head. "Fuck," she gasped. "Yes, Stefano. Like that. Fuck me like that."

We moved like a wave. Rolling, cresting, never-ending, our bodies in perfect sync. The water splashed, the steam rose around us, and my body was awash with sensation. I loved how her wet body slid along mine. The heat and grip of her around my cock. The way her skin glistened with steam and sweat. The taste of her mouth moving with mine. The way her nipples reddened with my tongue and teeth on them.

The way she looked as she climaxed. Lost in the moment and nothing but ecstasy written on her face. My orgasm hit me as I watched her spiral into hers, and I held her close, chasing the pleasure, riding it out until it peaked and ebbed. Until she collapsed into me and we were both at peace.

The room was steamy and quiet as I lay back in the water, taking her with me. The only sound was our breathing and the occasional ripple of water as the faucet dripped. Lazily, I used my toes to turn on the tap and add some more water to the tub. I ran my fingers up and down her back, my cock still deep inside her.

"Do you plan on moving?" I murmured.

"I seem to be anchored at the moment," she replied, looking up at me, her eyes dancing.

"Good. Just checking. Round two will happen in due course."

She pressed a kiss to my neck, her lips lingering, her tongue tracing lazy circles on my skin. My dick didn't fail to notice and twitched a little, already stirring to life.

"Mmm," she mumbled. "I like that."

"Is that a fact?" I chuckled.

"The fact that you find me sexy enough to get hard again so soon after you fucked me? Yeah, it's sort of an ego boost for me," she confessed quietly.

I lifted her chin, bending to kiss her soft mouth. "Gabby, I'm hard for you all the time fully clothed. Being naked with you? You're going to be lucky to get any sleep tonight."

Her lips curled into a smile.

"Bring it on, Stefano. Bring it on."

We eventually got out of the tub and moved to the bed. Gabby lay in my embrace, her body pliant and soft in my arms. I'd had her again in the tub and once on the floor of the bathroom. We were both sated and relaxed. Her head fit under my chin perfectly, and she felt right beside me. She sighed, the sound low and sad in the room. I pressed a kiss to her head, wondering what she was thinking.

"Talk to me," I murmured.

"I met Wayne the day of the fire that killed my parents. He was one of the volunteer firefighters."

I was shocked at her words, that she was going to tell me her story now. I hadn't expected it, but I kept my voice calm.

"That's Theo's father?"

"Yes."

I tightened my grip to let her know I was listening, but I remained silent. Whatever it was that made her open up now, I was grateful. I wanted to know her story. To understand her fears.

"I wasn't in a good place. I felt lost. In shock. Wayne seemed so nice. He checked up on me, brought me dinner a few times, seemed to be a really decent guy. We started dating. Everyone told me how lucky I was—what a great guy he was."

"I see."

"I worked as an inventory control manager at a clothing warehouse. I liked what I did. I worked mostly on my own, checking stock and keeping track of items, replenishing as needed. We had various managers who decided which pieces were kept in stock at all times, which were specialty items, and sent me their lists. I had my own office, and most days, it was just me and the mounds of paperwork and numbers. I was off for a few weeks after the fire, and when I went back, I sort of kept to myself. I was always a bit of a loner, but it became obvious how much of one I was after —" she swallowed "—after the fire."

"You were in mourning."

"And depressed, I think."

I held her closer. "Understandably."

"Wayne was around more." She shifted. "I lost myself, Stefano. It was as if I stopped thinking. I went through the motions every day, but I wasn't there. Before I even realized it, a few months had passed and I was living with Wayne. Not long after that, he convinced me the commute to my job was too far, and I quit."

"He wasn't so great, was he?"

She shook her head and glanced at me in the dimness. "No. He was controlling, and he bullied me. He was thrilled when I let my friends drift away. I had no one but him. He dictated my every move. What I did. Where I went. And I gave him that control."

"Did he lay hands on you, *Tesoro?*"

"Yes, but not so anyone could see. He liked to use words. Belittle me. He was cruel in many ways. The angrier he got, the more he hurt me." She shivered as if a memory had frightened her. I held her closer.

"Six months into our relationship, I discovered I was pregnant with Theo. He used condoms, but they'd failed. He blamed me, of course."

"So you weren't happy about the pregnancy?"

"Strangely, I was. All I could think about was how much this baby would love me. Need me. Wayne backed off a little. I thought maybe we could make it work. The day Theo was born was one of the happiest of my life."

"Then…" I encouraged, keeping my voice low.

"I was happy, but it seemed to set Wayne off. If people came over, he acted like a proud dad, but only when they were there. Otherwise, he ignored Theo. He never held him. He raged all the time about how little sleep he got. Theo was a colicky baby, and he did cry a lot, which annoyed Wayne. He never fed him or changed him. It was my job, he informed me. My fault I got pregnant, so my responsibility to look after the mistake." She paused. "That's what he called his son. A mistake. I sat up most nights rocking him so Wayne could sleep. And things just got worse." She paused as if trying to find the right words. "When Theo was born, it was as if the fog I had been living in began to clear up. He was the most important thing in the world to me. I realized Wayne had no interest in being a father. He only wanted the image—to add to his already fake image of being a great guy."

"What happened, Gabby?"

"I told Wayne the truth. I didn't love him, and I didn't think he loved me. I wasn't happy, and he obviously didn't want to be a family the way I did. I told him it would be best if I left." She hesitated. "He shoved me so hard, I fell and hit my head." She took my hand, letting me feel the raised skin under her hair.

"I woke up in the hospital. Alone."

"Where was he?"

"Staying away. Theo was with a friend of his."

"I don't understand."

"He couldn't wake me up. He panicked and called his friend who lived down the street. He and his wife came. They called the ambulance, and she took Theo home with her. He told them and the paramedics he'd come home and found me on the floor."

"He lied."

"Yes. And everyone believed him. After all, it was Wayne—the great guy liked by everyone."

"What happened?"

"I was discharged quickly once I was stable. I went home, and Wayne was there with Theo. He looked scary. He refused to give me Theo." She swallowed, a long tremor running through her.

"Wayne told me if I ever said anything like that again, he would kill me. Then he told me if I tried to leave him, he would kill Theo first."

I held her tighter, horrified. "Baby," I breathed out. What a piece of shit this Wayne was.

She kept talking. "I knew I had to find a way out. But he was watching, so I had to be careful. One day, he told me to go to the store to get something he wanted. I was only gone ten minutes, but when I got back, he was standing beside the crib. He was holding Theo by the arms, yelling at him, furious because Theo was crying." Her voice became thick with tears. "I guess Theo woke up and I wasn't there, and Wayne had no clue what to do with him. If I hadn't come home then, I think he would have shaken him to death, Stefano. I knew I had to get out fast. I had to protect my son."

"How?"

"Two days later, Wayne was called to a fire. A big one. I knew he'd be gone for a few hours, and he always went out for drinks with some of the boys after. As soon as he was gone, I threw what I could carry in a suitcase, packed Theo into his stroller, and left. One friend who'd stayed by me, Margie, drove me as far out of town as she could go that night and not be missed. I took the next bus out of there and started running. I had what was in the suitcase, the money I stole from Wayne's dresser, and that was it. That was over four years ago. I've been on the run ever since."

I rolled her over and pulled her into my arms. She burrowed into my warmth, and I knew she was seeking my strength. The safety of my embrace. "You think he's still after you," I murmured. That explained her worries and fears.

"I don't know," she admitted. "I saw him once, but I got away before he found me. Another time, Margie warned me she heard he was looking again, and I ran. I thought I had gone far enough, but I bumped into someone we both knew, and I knew he would tell Wayne, so I packed up and left again. And that time, I went over two thousand kilometers. It's been two years, and I don't think he'd look that far or for that long. He was always an out-of-sight, out-of-mind sort of guy with things. I had no connection to Ontario or anyone here." She let out a long breath. "But it scares me that he might. I think he might actually kill me if he found me."

"I won't let him near you, *Tesoro*."

"What if—"

I cut her off. "He won't get near either of you. Your life has changed now, Gabby. You have me. Friends. A community. He can't get to you."

"I want to believe that."

"Then believe it. I'm here, and I'm not going anywhere. If it's been two years, he's probably given up. Like you said, you had no history here—especially the little town we're in. You've been careful, you left no trail for him to follow."

She relaxed a little in my arms.

"Why are you telling me now?" I asked.

She looked up, her lovely eyes anxious, worried, yet still so beautiful. "Because you said you loved me. You should know who the person you love is. The danger they bring."

I slid my fingers under her chin. "There is no danger for me. I can handle myself. And now that I know, I can look out for you too."

A tear ran down her cheek, another following in its path. I saw the emotions she was still too afraid to express. I saw her love. The worry and fear.

It would take time, but now I understood it. I wrapped her close. "Thank you for trusting me."

"I do trust you, Stefano. I thought..." She swallowed. "I thought you might not want to keep seeing me once you heard my story."

I shook my head. "Nothing could be further from the truth. I'm not going anywhere." I kissed her forehead. "I have you, Gabby. I have you."

CHAPTER FIFTEEN

Stefano

After telling me her story, Gabby fell asleep in my arms. There beside her, I thought about what she had been through. How strong she had to be. How incredibly brave and selfless a person she was.

How much she needed someone in this life she could depend on.

I wanted that person to be me.

It didn't matter if we were moving too fast. If anyone had a problem with it, I didn't care. She—we—felt right. I adored Theo, and I knew we were only going to get closer. The thought of being a stepdad didn't trouble me at all. In fact, I liked the idea. We could be a family. Maybe one day we could discuss the idea of adding to our family.

The thought of that made me smile, and I fell asleep with the idea in my head.

Gabby was quiet in the morning but calm. I didn't bring up her ex or what she had told me. I knew I needed to give her a little time before asking her more questions.

"Still up for taking little man on a trip to the zoo?" I asked her.

"He would love that so much," she agreed. "I've never been there."

"Then that's where we're going."

Later, we picked up Theo at my mama's place. She had coffee and a plate of treats waiting, and we visited with her for a while. When I told her we were taking Theo to the zoo, her eyes lit up. I was thrilled when Gabby asked her if she would like to come along. Mama was out of her chair in a second, hurrying into the house.

"I get ready!" she called over her shoulder. "Theo, bambino! Nonna coming to the zoo!"

Theo threw up his hands in happiness and headed our way, the soccer ball he'd been kicking around forgotten. He ran over, excited, throwing his arms around Gabby. I lifted my cell phone, taking a quick picture of the two of them. His joy, her smile as she held him. It was infectious.

The whole afternoon was great and only solidified the thoughts I'd had the night before. Gabby and Theo were meant to be mine. We fit so well together. I knew Mama saw it as well, the way she smiled and nodded in our direction.

It was a perfect weather day, not too hot, and although the place was crowded, we got to see lots of animals. Somehow, my mama managed to cram snacks into her bag, and between those, the ice cream, the hot dogs we ate for lunch, and the various other treats we indulged in, we arrived back to Mama's a happy but exhausted crew. We ate leftover ziti, and Theo was asleep before we left the driveway, even though it was still early. He had worn himself out. Gabby dozed beside me, her head on my shoulder, and I hated waking her up when we got to their place. Gabby tucked Theo into bed without waking him, only wiping his face and hands with a damp cloth. We had just sat on the sofa when my phone rang, and I answered it.

"Hey, Brett."

"We're a man down for the baseball game tonight. You available?"

"Um, I'm at Gabby's."

She shook her head, overhearing the conversation. "Go and play. I'm tired and plan on crashing early. You've been ignoring your friends enough."

"Are you sure?" I asked quietly.

She laughed. "I'll see you in the morning, Stefano. You're going to get sick of me. Go and play baseball."

Brett chuckled. "You heard her."

"Okay. I'll drop by the house and grab my stuff and be there soon."

"Awesome. We'll have a beer while we wait."

I hung up and stood, dragging Gabby to her feet. I walked to the door and paused, bending and pulling her close. I kissed her long and deep.

"Just for clarity, I'll never be sick of you. But I'll pick you up in the morning."

"Okay," she replied, breathless.

"Call me if you need me."

"Stop fussing."

"I love you," I muttered. "It comes with the territory."

She cupped my cheek. "That means more than you know. Thank you."

I left with a sense of satisfaction. She hadn't said it yet, but I knew she was feeling it. And soon, she would say the words.

Then we would go forward.

Except, the next morning, Gabby called early. The sun was barely up. I was lying in bed, thinking. About her. Theo. The future. How much I preferred waking up with her beside me. When my phone rang, I was startled to see her number.

"Gabby? What's wrong?" I answered.

"I have to cancel today. I'm not well," she responded, her voice raspy and rough.

I sat up, flinging off the blanket. "I'll come over."

"No. Spend the day with your family."

"I'll pick up Theo, and you can rest."

"I think your family has babysat enough this weekend, Stefano. We're fine."

Her words disturbed me. "My mama loved being with Theo, and he with her," I objected. "She didn't consider it a chore."

"No, he's staying home with me."

A catch in her voice caught my attention. There was almost a panicked tone to it.

"Gabby, are you sure you're okay?"

"Just too much sun and a touch of the stomach flu or something. I'll be fine. I just want to stay at home today."

"Okay," I soothed. "Can I bring you anything? Some breakfast or coffee? Tylenol?"

"No. I don't need anything."

Her words sounded odd, but I let it go. I didn't want to push her.

"I'll check in later."

She hung up, the lack of any goodbye bothering me more than I wanted to admit.

At lunch with my family, I was quiet. Distracted. Some underlying tone in Gabby's voice had triggered a niggling worry in my chest. She had sounded distant. More upset than sick. I tried to push aside my strange fear, but it sat in my mind, festering.

Mama was worried when I told her Gabby was a little under the weather. She packed up some food, including a container of minestrone soup. "This make her better," she assured me. "They come next week. You bring Theo to me again."

I forced a smile. "Sure, Mama."

"Oh, Stefano," she mused, shaking her head. "So like your father. Your love is sick, and you worried." She patted my cheek. "Go to her. Take her food. Let her rest. All will be good."

I drove to Gabby's, surprised when no one answered the door. I tried Mrs. Scott's doorbell but still received no response. Gabby's SUV wasn't in the driveway and, worried, I took out my phone and called her, frowning as it went to voice mail.

I hesitated, concerned. Had she become sicker and gone to the hospital? Where was Theo? I glanced up at the sky as a raindrop hit my cheek. As I'd headed home, the clouds had moved in, and it was starting to rain.

Why would Gabby be out in this weather if she was ill?

I decided to call Charly and ask her if she had heard from her just as Gabby's SUV pulled into the driveway. She stared at me through the window, and something in her gaze made my chest tighten. She climbed out of the vehicle and opened the hatch, pulling out some totes. I hurried down the steps toward her.

"Gabby, I was worried."

"Why aren't you at your mama's?" she asked, her tone almost annoyed.

"I was. As I said, I was worried. She gave me some food to bring you."

Her face softened. "That was kind."

Then she pushed past me, climbing the steps.

"Give me the totes," I offered.

"It's fine."

"Gabby—"

She cut me off. "I said it was fine, Stefano. I'm perfectly capable of carrying a few empty totes."

I blinked at the anger in her words and followed her upstairs. She set down the totes, crossing her arms, everything about her screaming for me to back off. I felt my impatience growing at her attitude, although I tried to tamp it down.

"Obviously, you're feeling better."

"Oh?" she snapped.

"Too sick to come to lunch but well enough to go shopping."

"I want to organize Theo's toys. I needed some bins."

"Where is Theo?"

"Playing with a friend."

I stepped toward her, reaching out my hand, horrified when she backed away, shaking her head, avoiding my touch.

"*Tesoro*, what is it? What's wrong?"

Dropping her arms, she squared her shoulders, meeting my gaze yet somehow looking right through me.

"I can't do this anymore, Stefano. I-I don't want to see you anymore."

I stared at her, aghast, certain I had heard her incorrectly. "You don't mean that."

"Yes, I do."

I stared into her eyes. They were calm, dead, showing no emotion. She was hiding herself from me. Something was wrong. Terribly wrong.

I reached for her hand. Her skin was clammy and cold. She was pale. "Talk to me, *Tesoro*. Tell me what's going on."

"I said I don't want to see you anymore."

"I heard what you said. Now, explain it. What the hell changed from last night to this morning?" I demanded.

She shook me off and stalked toward the door. "I came to my senses, that's what happened. What's going on is that you are *smothering* me. Constantly around me. I can barely breathe. I don't want this. Your family. Your friends. Everyone so sweet and nice and welcoming. It's too much. All of it. I can't do this." She sucked in a deep breath. "I don't *want* to do this. I don't want you in my life."

Her words sank in, tearing at my heart. I steeled myself, pushing down the hurt. I needed to stay focused. To figure this out.

"Are you sure about that?"

She held her head high, meeting my gaze. Hers was cold and vacant. "Yes."

"You know what I think?"

She tossed her head, defiant and determined. "I don't care what you think."

"Too bad, because I am going to tell you. I think you're scared. I think you feel something for me. More than you can handle. And instead of admitting that and talking to me, you're running away." I cocked my head. "You're good at that, aren't you, Gabriella? Running, hiding."

"*Get out.*"

"Don't do this. Talk to me. Let me in."

"I don't want to see you anymore, Stefano. I'll be respectful at the garage, but that's it. Don't come here anymore. Don't call me. Just stay out of my life."

Her words cut into my chest like blades. Hot, piercing, and deep.

"You're making a mistake."

She shook her head. "The only mistake I made was getting close to you. Letting yet another man take over my life. I don't want or need you to protect me or fight my battles."

"You don't mean that. I'm nothing like your ex." Then I frowned. "Is that what this is about? Your ex? Are you feeling upset or worried because you told me your story?"

"This has nothing to do with him," she lied.

I laughed, the sound bitter. "This has *everything* to do with him. You lie for shit, Gabby."

"I want you to leave. I don't owe you anything."

"What about what you owe yourself? Theo?"

She glared at me, her chest rising and falling rapidly in agitation. Outside, the storm gathered, the darkness matching the feeling surrounding me in that room.

"Are you forgetting how good we were together, Gabby? How your body reacted to me?"

She slid in the final knife. "The sex was good, but that itch has been scratched." She waved her hand as if dismissing it. Dismissing us. It reminded me of my ex and what she had thought of me, how she had used me, and it made me angry.

"So happy I serviced you well," I stated, sarcasm dripping from the words.

Our eyes locked again, mine probing, begging her to stop this. Her dark gaze remained impassive.

"I want you to leave now," she said, gripping the back of the chair. Her voice quavered.

I hesitated. I wanted to drag her into my arms. Make her talk to me. Tell me why she was doing this. Get her to stop. I took a step toward her, but she moved back, shaking her head.

"Don't touch me. I don't want you here. Leave."

"Theo…"

"Don't worry about my son. He isn't your concern. Neither am I." She indicated the door. "Get out. Leave me alone, Stefano. Just leave me alone."

I hurried down the steps, my body propelling me away from her.

But my heart remained, trapped in that room.

CHAPTER SIXTEEN

Stefano

Early Tuesday evening, the sounds of sirens screaming past the garage brought me out of my fog. I had been staring down at a design, listless and unseeing, for over an hour.

Gabby's words echoed in my head on repeat. They never stopped.

He isn't your concern. Neither am I.

The only mistake I made was getting close to you.

The sex was good, but that itch has been scratched.

Leave me alone, Stefano. Just leave me alone.

Her hurtful words had played on a constant loop in my head since I had left her. I had barely slept. I couldn't eat. I felt as if part of me was missing. I felt numb most of the time.

I told myself I was being ridiculous. I had only known her a short time. There was no way I had formed such a strong attachment to her—*to them*—that I should feel so devastated.

But I did.

Brett knew what had happened. I had confided in him when he got home and found me sitting on the sofa in the dim light. He looked shocked, switching on the table lamp.

"What the hell are you doing?"

I only shook my head.

"Stefano—what the hell is going on?"

"Gabby broke up with me. She told me to leave her alone."

He sat down heavily. "Shit. I'm sorry. What happened? Things seemed to be going so well."

"I have no idea."

"Take off your coat, man. You're dripping wet."

I glanced down, surprised. I was still wearing my coat. The material was soaked through, as were my jeans and my hair. My skin had goose bumps. I hadn't even noticed.

"Yeah," I agreed. "I need to do that." Still, I didn't move.

"C'mon, Stefano. Work with me, buddy."

Buddy. That was one of my names for Theo. The thought of not seeing him again, not spending time with my little man, hit me like a punch to the gut.

I looked up at Brett.

"I need to get her back. I need to figure out what happened and talk some sense into her."

He squeezed my shoulder. "I think you need to give her a little time."

I didn't want to give her time. I wanted her to talk to me. To tell me why she pulled back. What had frightened her off.

Except her words, "You're smothering me," came back, hitting me in the gut again.

I knew Gabby—how she overthought things. How skittish she was. Her trust issues. Maybe Brett was correct. Maybe with a little time, she'd cool down and talk to me. Tell me what was wrong and what had caused this reaction.

I felt a small flicker of hope.

And I held on to it with the force of a hurricane.

I'd tried to act normal at the garage the past couple of days, and when Charly had approached me on Monday, looking crestfallen and worried, I had shaken my head.

"Don't, Charly. Please."

Standing on her toes, she flung her arms around my neck and kissed my cheek. "I'm here if you want to talk."

I let her hug me, patting her arms. "Thanks."

She waddled away, not saying anything else, but I saw the tears in her eyes. Knowing she was hurting for me eased the pain a little.

But not much.

Everyone else carried on as if nothing was wrong. They talked around me, including me when they could, and ignoring the elephant in the room. I was grateful for that. Gabby hadn't been at the garage. Charly told me she had asked to work from home.

"I think she'll come back next week," she said, patting my arm. "Maybe you can talk then. Figure this out."

More sirens went past, and I stood, going outside. Brett was striding toward me, and I frowned at the serious look on his face.

"What's going on?"

"Ziggy's bar." He grasped my shoulder. "There's been a fire."

It was after six o'clock. Gabby would be working. Fear tore through me.

"Fuck," I snarled, pushing past him. Maxx's truck was at the front of the driveway, and I jumped in, knowing his keys would be in the ignition. I tore out of the driveway, the tires spinning, dust and gravel kicking up behind me. Cop cars were ahead of me, and I followed, keeping my foot on the gas.

Gabriella.

She had already lost her family to a fire, and now she was in another one?

The thought of her hurt, or worse, made my stomach tighten, and I gripped the steering wheel so tightly my knuckles were white.

It didn't matter what had occurred between us. I didn't care what words she had flung at me on Sunday. If she was scared, hurt, or in need, I would be there.

I pulled into the parking lot, slamming on the brakes. Ziggy's bar was fully consumed by flames. The fire shot high into the air, black smoke billowing around. Firefighters were frantically trying to douse the inferno. Cops and paramedics were working on people. I cast my gaze around frantically, seeing that Gabby's SUV was parked in her usual corner. I threw open the door of the truck and took off running. A cop tried to stop me, but I dodged him, yelling over my shoulder.

"My girl is in there!" I screamed and kept going. I saw Ziggy standing, a blanket draped over him. He was watching the chaos, a dazed look on his face. I veered toward him.

"Gabby!" I yelled when I reached him. "Where is Gabby?"

He blinked. "It was so fast. There was a huge noise, and the bar was…" He trailed off. "It's all gone."

I gripped his shoulders, shaking him. "Where. Is. Gabby?"

His gaze was blank. "I-I haven't seen her."

Terror filled me, and I turned and ran again, heading toward the flames. This time, two cops grabbed me.

"You can't go in there."

I struggled against their hold. "I have to. She's—she's in there! I have to find her."

One of them, I recognized, and I grabbed his arm. "Jeff—Gabby is in there! I have to get her."

He shook his head. "You can't. It's fully engulfed. We got everyone out that we could, Stefano. Ziggy is in such shock he can't tell me how many people were inside."

"No," I gasped. "No!"

Then I heard it. My name being called, and I spun. Gabby was stumbling toward me, a blanket wrapped around her shoulders. Her hair was wet, her face covered in soot, and she was holding a bloodied towel to her head.

She had never looked more beautiful.

I rushed toward her, enfolding her in my arms. She came easily, fitting against me. She was sobbing, gripping me close, trying to talk, but the words were jumbled and unintelligible. I didn't care. She was there in my arms. She was safe. I had her.

And I wasn't letting her go again.

I paced in the hospital waiting room, thinking of the other time I had been here. When Charly had been brought in, injured, I'd had to physically restrain Maxx in the waiting room. I had found his impatience amusing.

Now I understood.

"She's going to be fine," Charly assured me, pulling on my hand. She had arrived not long after I'd followed the ambulance here. Maxx was with her, and so was Brett, all present for moral support.

I yanked my hand through my hair. I had only been on the periphery of the burning building, and I smelled like smoke. I could only imagine how Gabby felt.

After I had grabbed her, a paramedic appeared, scolding her about leaving the gurney. I carried her back, watching as he refitted the oxygen mask over her face. Her hands showed a few burns, and the deep cut on her head wouldn't stop bleeding. I held her hand as they did what they could, then told her she had to be taken to the hospital. Her tear-filled, anxious eyes met my gaze.

"I'll be right there," I assured her.

"Theo," she rasped.

"I'll call Mrs. Scott. I'll tell her you're okay, and she'll stay with Theo. Everything is all right, Tesoro."

She tried to talk, the words "sorry" and "forgive" tumbling out between sobs. I leaned forward, pressing my lips to her forehead. "I'm right here," I repeated. "I'm not going anywhere."

Her gaze stayed locked on mine until the very last second. I stayed behind only long enough to make a call to Mrs. Scott, then to Brett.

Lara caught me before I stepped into the truck to follow the ambulance.

"She went back in," she said. "Gus was at the back of the kitchen. She went back to get him, and she dragged him out. She got hit on the head with a falling piece of wood." She shook her head. "She saved him."

Gabby risked herself.

Part of me was furious she would have risked her own life, yet I was so proud of her, my chest felt tight. Lara smiled and returned to Ziggy's side, snaking her arm around his waist. I hoped this close call would end the games they played.

Jeff came over to Lara. "How many people were inside?"

"Ten. Six staff and four customers."

His shoulders dropped in relief. "Then everyone is accounted for."

I was glad, but the only one I really cared about was on her way to the hospital. I had to get there.

Once I was at the hospital, I checked on Gus and found out he was doing fine. Everyone else was being treated and not in serious condition. Gabby had inhaled a lot of smoke, burned her hands, and had a bad cut on her head from the wood. The doctor told me it could have been much worse.

"If it was one of the rafters that came down, she's lucky," he informed me. "It must have glanced off something else before it hit her." He shook his head. "If it hadn't..." He let his voice trail off.

The thought made me want to throw up.

"When can I see her?"

"Soon. Let us finish examining her."

"Tell her I'm here."

He smiled. "She already knows. As soon as she heard your voice in the hall, she relaxed." He clapped me on the shoulder and walked away.

Despite his reassurances, I couldn't relax. I needed to see her for myself. To hold her. I had to admit I was apprehensive. She had told me I smothered her. She wanted nothing to do with me. Had her jumbled apologies been a reaction to what had occurred, or did she really want me around?

Until I knew, I couldn't calm down. Pacing was the only option.

Maxx smiled in understanding, not trying to stop me. Brett offered quiet words of support, then went to get everyone coffee.

Charly fell into step with me, linking her small hand with mine.

"She's going to be fine."

"I'll make sure of it."

She smiled at me, tilting her head back to meet my gaze. "I know you will. And everything that happened between you on the weekend will be in the past."

I stopped, looking down at her. "How do you know that?"

"Because I saw how she looked at you, Stefano. It's the same way I look at Maxx. The same way you look at her." She worried her bottom lip. "I saw her yesterday, and I have never seen such heartbreak in someone's eyes. Whatever her reasons for doing what she did or said, it killed her to do so."

"What if she tells me to go?"

"I hope she doesn't. If she does, give her time if you can."

"I'll give her anything she wants as long as she's in my life."

Charly tilted her head. "Mary once told me to be patient with Maxx. You need the same thing for Gabby."

Before I could respond, my name was called, and I hurried to the nurse who was waiting.

"You can see her now."

CHAPTER SEVENTEEN

Stefano

Gabby's eyes were shut as I slipped behind the curtain. She was pale, the streaks of soot on her arms and cheeks standing out like stains on her skin. There was a thick bandage on her forehead, the bruised skin showing under the edges. I could see the evidence of tears on her cheeks. Cannulas pumped oxygen into her nose. She gripped the thin sheet, her knuckles white, showing her distress. I approached the bed, laying my hand over hers.

"*Tesoro*," I murmured.

Her eyes flew open, fresh tears pouring from them. She reached for me at the same time I bent to pull her into my arms. I held her tight.

"I'm here, Gabby. Right here."

"I'm sorry," she rasped, her voice thick and rough-sounding. "Stefano, I'm so sorry."

"Shh," I soothed. "We can talk about that later."

"I didn't mean it… I didn't want to… I was scared…" she sobbed, coughing at the same time.

I stroked her hair, comforting her. "It's okay, *Tesoro*. It's okay. No talking. Rest your voice."

She pulled back. "I h-hurt you."

"You did. But you're here. Safe. And you're going to promise me not to do it again." I tightened my arms. "That you'll talk to me later. Tell me the truth."

She coughed again. "I will."

I grabbed the water beside her, and she sipped it gratefully. "My throat is sore."

"The doctor said you inhaled a lot of smoke." I lowered my voice. "You risked your life to save Gus."

"His mom is ill. If he died, she'd have no one. I knew he was there, right inside the back door." She grimaced. "I didn't expect the beam."

I slipped my fingers under her chin. "Never risk yourself again. Do you understand? You mean too much to me, Gabby. To Theo." I stroked her cheek. "*Sei tutto per me*."

The doctor came in and checked her vitals.

"Much better, Gabby. I want to monitor you a bit longer, then we can send you home as long as you have someone to look after you."

"She'll be coming home with me."

Gabby blinked but didn't say anything.

"Good. That's good. Just rest now." He patted her arm. "I think you're in good hands."

He left, and I adjusted her pillow. "You heard him. Rest."

"Theo," she whispered.

"Is with Mrs. Scott. You're coming to my place. Brett is going to pick him up and take him to the garage in the morning, and he'll have a blast all day. You are going to rest and recover, and then we're going to talk." I paused. "All right?"

"Can–can Brett go stay at my place tonight, too, or take him to Charly?"

I frowned, hearing the anxiety in her voice. "Gabby——"

"Please," she whispered.

"I'll arrange it."

She cupped my cheek, and I grimaced at the sight of the burns on her hands. "Thank you," she whispered.

I gently kissed her palm.

"You're welcome."

I sat down heavily at the kitchen table, accepting a cup of coffee from Brett. He had arrived home a short while ago after taking Theo to the garage. He'd spent the night at Gabby's, making sure Theo was okay. He showered and changed then made coffee and waited to talk. The dark brew was hot and strong—exactly what I needed.

"She asleep?" Brett asked.

"Yep."

"You look like you need to join her."

I grunted.

They'd allowed me to bring Gabby home late the night before. She had showered, then climbed into my bed without a fight, falling asleep right away. She had talked to Theo earlier, although only briefly since she kept coughing. I talked to him longer, listening to him chat about how much he missed me.

"I missed you too, buddy. I'll see you tomorrow."

"Can we have a pic-a-nic this weekend?"

"As long as your mom says it's okay, then yes."

"Are we going to Nonna Rosa's?"

I met Gabby's eyes. She dropped her gaze to the blanket, not giving me any indication of what to say. "I'll check, okay, little man? You be good for Mrs. Scott and Brett."

"I will!"

I didn't push Gabby. I had no idea where we stood aside from her apology. I would bring up my mother's place later. I hadn't been able to sleep, even with Gabby safely beside me. The weight of what had occurred, what might happen the next day, the worries about her state of mind, not wanting her to wake up and need something and not hear her, all kept me on edge. I dozed but never slept deeply. Gabby, though, seemed exhausted and had barely moved all night, only waking long enough every two hours for me to check on her as the doctor instructed. She nestled close as if needing me, even in her sleep, and I enjoyed having her tucked against me. She didn't stir when I slid from the bed a short while ago. I could let her sleep now without disturbing her rest.

"Stefano," Brett began.

I looked up from my mug. "What?"

He cleared his throat. "Gabby's things were all packed at her place. Well, most of them. It looked as if she was getting ready to leave."

I huffed out a long breath. "I'm not surprised. Something spooked her."

"Do you think she'd really leave?"

I shrugged. "I think she'd do anything she thought she had to do to protect Theo." I leaned my arms on the table, scrubbing my face. "The problem is, she doesn't realize she no longer has to do it alone. She doesn't have to run anymore."

"Can you convince her?" He met my gaze. "We'll all help. Everyone likes Gabby." He smiled. "I like how you are with her. You remind me of Maxx with Charly. Protective."

I nodded, taking a sip of coffee. "Not a bad example to follow."

"You've really fallen for her, haven't you?" he asked quietly.

"Yeah, I have. For both of them."

"Then tell me what you need. Whatever it is, I'm there."

"You're a good friend, Brett."

He shrugged. "So are you. We have each other's back. And others feel the same. Maxx. Charly. Mary. All the guys at the garage. Gabby will be well protected. You need to convince her of that."

I nodded grimly. "I know."

Brett stood. "I'll go to the garage, and we'll look after Theo. I can bring him home with me later. So, keep Gabby here. Let her rest, and you guys talk."

"I appreciate it."

He shrugged. "Not a problem. We all like Theo—he's a great kid." He paused. "Any reason why she was worried about Mrs. Scott being alone with Theo?"

"I have a theory."

He met my gaze. "The ex?"

I nodded in silence.

"I think that is the key to all of this. Talk to her. Call if you need anything." He stopped at the door. "And Mary is bringing supper later. Your mama wants you to call her. She is worried about Gabby."

"How the hell did my mama find out?" I groaned. "Charly?"

He grinned. "Mary, Charly—better than any social media platform out there. Ten minutes after something goes down, everyone who needs to know, does. Your sisters all know too." His grin became wider. "I expect a lot of pasta and meatballs to show up soon."

I waved him off. "Get out."

"Just saying. Gabby's freezer will be full."

"She's not going home until I know she's okay."

He picked up his keys. "Even better, our freezer will be full."

He left with a wave, and I finished my coffee. Hearing Gabby cough again, I filled another cup and carried it to my room. She was awake, sitting up against the headboard, looking tired, pale, and wan. I sat down on the mattress, handing her the cup.

"Extra cream just the way you like."

"Thank you," she murmured, her voice still sounding raw. She sipped the beverage. "Good," she hummed.

"How are you feeling?" I asked, brushing a curl from her face.

"I'm fine."

At my skeptical look, she offered me a smile. "I feel tired, and my head hurts, but really, I'm okay. My throat isn't as sore as it was. It sounds worse than it is." She tried to be funny. "Maybe I should get a gig with one of those 1-800 sex numbers for a while. Make the best of it."

"You can talk dirty to *me*, *Tesoro*," I informed her. "Nobody else."

She shook her head, sipping her coffee. "I owe you an apology. And an explanation."

"When you feel better."

Her eyes looked over my shoulder, her gaze unfocused. She was silent for a moment, then spoke.

"I want to do it now."

GABBY

Waking up in Stefano's bed this morning, surrounded by his scent, had been unexpected. Everything that happened the day before raced through my mind.

I had been in turmoil since breaking things off with Stefano on Sunday. My heart ached and I was anxious. I wanted to rewind time and take back my words. I knew how much I had hurt him —his confusion and pain had been evident in his eyes before he had walked away. But I felt as if I had no choice. I refused to put him in danger, and I knew he would only be hurt even more if I let him become more attached than he already was.

Than I already was to him.

When I'd arrived at the bar last night, I was already tense. Theo had been upset we hadn't gone to the garage and he hadn't seen "Stefo" for two days—a lifetime to him. He had thrown a temper tantrum, and I'd sent him to his room, shutting the door firmly. I was shocked since he had never once acted out before. I realized I had misjudged how attached he already was to Stefano and that this was going to be harder than I expected. The sight of the packed totes was familiar to him, and I knew he was anxious, not buying my fib about organizing the apartment. I didn't want to tell him the truth yet. To watch how upset he would be, knowing we were leaving a place we actually liked and felt normal in. Emotionally, leaving here would be the most difficult thing I had ever done.

I'd tried to talk to him before I left for work, to distract him, but he was still withdrawn.

It weighed on my mind, and I knew we had to go the next day. The implications of leaving were so huge, my heart ached. But with the bar open tonight and the baseball teams playing, the place would be busy, and I needed the tip money.

Simply the thought of doing so was emotionally draining.

At the bar, I went through the motions. I listened to Ziggy and Lara squabble over mundane things. Gus came in a little late, Ziggy telling him off that the kitchen wasn't open and people wanted to order food. I had rolled my eyes at his words. There were four people at the bar, and none had asked yet. He was simply taking out his annoyance with Lara on Gus.

"I'll get on it right away," Gus promised, heading to the back where two other staff members were prepping for later.

I went about my usual routine, making sure we were ready for a busy night. I polished glasses, wiped the tables, and made sure the fridges were well stocked.

It happened as I went down the hall toward the kitchen. I caught the smell of smoke and, without thinking, pushed open the door of the stock room. Acrid black smoke billowed out, and for a second, I was lost in the memory of the night the cottage burned down.

One word burst from my lips, loud and clear. "Fire!"

Behind me, Ziggy began to yell, pushing me out of the way and heading to the kitchen. Lara screamed for everyone to get out, and we all headed for the front, the old wooden bar already filling with smoke as the fire spread quickly.

Lara was on the phone as I stumbled out, a sudden explosion behind me throwing me to my knees. As I staggered upright, I realized Gus wasn't with us, and with no thought to the danger, I ran toward the back. He always spoke to his mother as he waited for the deep fryers to heat, and I prayed he was still just inside the back entrance.

I recalled finding him, dragging him out, half unconscious. The sudden pain lancing across my head and staggering under the blow as it hit me. The next thing I remembered was being out front, the building quickly being eaten by flames. The staff and the few customers milling around. I focused hard, counting the people. Ten. That meant everyone was safe. Then, the sounds of the sirens. Being led to an ambulance.

"You risked your life," Stefano said.

I blinked.

I had been talking out loud?

I'd thought I was just thinking.

Stefano lifted my hand, placing a gentle kiss on the reddened skin. "You said it all out loud, Gabby."

"I guess my head is still fuzzy."

"It's to be expected." He brushed his fingers over my bandage. "You could have been killed."

"I know." I caught his hand, holding it to my chest. "I kept thinking the same thing. But I had to try. Gus has always been kind to me. Ziggy was in such shock, he was useless. Lara was calling for help. The customers were dazed and had no idea. Gus needed someone to make sure he was okay."

"You were very brave." He frowned. "And foolish."

I ignored his last statement. I couldn't deny it, although I would do it again.

"Sitting in the ambulance, all I could think of was you, Stefano. How stupid I had been. How much I desperately wished I could take back those words. How much I wanted the chance to do so —" My voice caught. "And then I heard you. You were there. Despite how awful I was to you, you were there."

"I had to get to you."

"Please forgive me," I pleaded. "I'm so sorry—"

He stopped me. "You are forgiven, *Tesoro*. You're here and safe. That is all that matters."

"I need to tell you."

"When you're ready."

"I am ready now."

He studied my face and nodded. "How about something to eat, and some tea and honey for your throat first?"

"You always take care of me."

He stood and pressed a kiss to my forehead. "I always will."

"Could I have another shower? I still smell like smoke."

He held out his hand. "Yes. I'll make you breakfast while you shower."

I let him help me from the bed, and he wrapped his arms around me. "Whatever you have to tell me, I'll listen, Gabby. We'll face it together, okay?"

I accepted his comfort and his warmth.

Together. That wasn't a word I was used to.

But then again, maybe it was time to try it.

CHAPTER EIGHTEEN

Gabby

Stefano handed me a cup of tea. The honey and lemon did soothe my throat, and I liked the flavor. I settled on the sofa with him beside me, his presence warm and comforting. The house he and Brett rented was small and cozy. Two bedrooms, an eat-in kitchen, and a large living room. It was filled with masculine furniture—heavy pieces that spoke of strength. The walls were cream, the floors hardwood, and it was decorated simply. Stefano's room held a lot of family pictures, and a few more were scattered around the house. I had only seen Brett's room from the hallway.

I cleared my throat, meeting Stefano's patient gaze. I knew if I told him I didn't want to talk about it, he would let it go. But I had done that enough. Used sex to distract him. It was time to tell him the truth. After my close call yesterday, I knew beyond a doubt I cared for him deeply. He needed to know the truth.

I reached for his hand, and he closed his larger one around mine, holding it loosely so he didn't hurt the burns.

"I told you about the friend who helped me leave. Margie?"

He nodded.

"We keep in touch. Wayne has never figured out it was her who helped me. He had no idea we were close. If she hears anything, she lets me know."

At his inquiring look, I explained. "Margie's a bartender at the place he and his friends hang out. She hears stuff and calls me."

"That could be dangerous for her."

"That's what I told her. But she insisted it wasn't. They don't pay her any attention. She's older, married, and Wayne had no idea we were even friends. She was certain she was invisible to them."

I stopped to take a drink of the tea and clear my throat.

"But something happened," he guessed.

I nodded. "She called me Saturday night. Somehow, Wayne found out I was in Ontario. She heard him telling the guys he'd tracked me down and that I was somewhere outside Toronto. He said he was coming for me as soon as he was certain of my location."

"How do you think he found you?"

"She doesn't know. But he seemed so confident, she thought I should know. Then she heard him tell the guys he'd gotten my cell number." I shuddered. "She was worried because her purse had gone missing, then showed up exactly where she'd left it. She wondered if he'd somehow gotten his hands on it. I thought she was worried for nothing, but now—" I swallowed "—the calls I've been getting I thought were scammers. I think it was him. I think he somehow was tracing my location."

Stefano frowned. "He'd need help for that."

"He had friends who were into computers and illegal stuff. I-I think he could do it." I gripped his hands, ignoring the flash of pain.

"She could be right, then."

"Yes."

"But she's being careful?"

"She says she's fine. That he would never try anything anyway. Her husband is a big guy and a cop. Her son is a firefighter who knows Wayne and has never liked him." I fidgeted, feeling the fear building. "She said she was watching him and his buddies as closely as she can. I begged her to be careful." I worried my lip.

"She heard him say I had someone new. And that he was going to make sure everyone involved suffered." A sob escaped my mouth. "I don't know how he knows that—"

My words were cut off as Stefano dragged me into his arms.

"Hush, *Tesoro*. None of that is going to happen."

"I-I can't risk it. I can't risk you," I sobbed. "I wanted to run right away, but I knew I had to plan it. She promised to keep an eye on him. He has a pattern and is at the bar every second day. If he goes missing, she is going to call. I figured I had a few days to get ready and go. Get a couple more shifts at Ziggy's so we had some extra money."

My explanations obviously made no sense to Stefano.

He pulled back, shaking his head, cupping my face. "When will you get this? What do I have to do, Gabby? You aren't alone in this anymore. If he comes after you, he'll come through me, through Brett and Maxx. God forbid, through Charly. He will never get to you."

"I got too close to too many people this time. They're going to get hurt just by being nice to me," I whispered in horror. "I *have* to go. Don't you see that?"

He cupped my face, shaking his head. His dark eyes were fierce and determined. "You aren't going anywhere. No one is going to get hurt except him. He isn't getting near anyone."

My crying caused me to start coughing.

He stood, left the room, then returned, handing me another mug of sweet tea.

"Drink."

I sipped, the cough abating. Then kept talking. "I have to disappear. Stay ahead of him." I met Stefano's eyes. "He wants Theo back. I can't let that happen. I can't let him get his hands on my son. I will keep running before I allow that to happen." My throat became constricted, and I couldn't talk anymore. Stefano pressed the mug to my lips.

"Drink."

He waited until I swallowed, then took the mug and set it on the coffee table. He grasped my hands, chafing at the cold fingers, careful not to touch the burned skin. "He won't."

"Legally, he has rights."

"He lost those rights the day he hurt you and showed his true self."

"Which he never showed anyone but me," I replied.

"And you're certain the calls came from him?"

"I am now."

"Why? What haven't you told me?"

"I got a text in the middle of the night Saturday. It came from an unknown number, but I know it's him."

"What did it say?"

"Gotcha." I swallowed the nausea that was building as I thought about the terror that single word evoked. The only thing that kept me from running right then was that I knew he was still in BC since he'd been at the bar that night. "He used to say that to me before he exploded. When he'd have me trapped in a corner and I couldn't get out."

"Why didn't you tell me, *Tesoro*? Why did you think you had to run?"

"I know Wayne. I know his temper. He was always nasty and possessive. If he found me and you were there, he'd be after you too. And your family. Mrs. Scott. Anyone he thought helped me. They are too wonderful for me to put in danger. I thought if I let you go, kept you safe, that was all that mattered. And I thought if I had to leave, it would be easier to give you up now."

"And if he has somehow tapped into your phone, he could still find you. That's how he knows you're still here. Did you think of that?"

"Yes," I whispered. "I planned to leave the phone behind."

"Which meant I couldn't find you either," he said, sounding horrified. "Gabby, how could…" He trailed off.

Unable to meet his eyes, I focused my gaze to the floor. "Yes."

He grasped my chin, lifting my head. "No." He shook his head, his tone firm. "You aren't leaving. All that matters is keeping you and Theo here and safe. And I'm not letting you face this on your own. You're done running."

"But he'll—"

He cut me off. "Don't you get it, Gabby? Leaving me doesn't help anyone. It doesn't protect me from being hurt. In fact, it hurts in a whole new way. I would be stuck here, lost and in pain without you. Anxious because I couldn't find you. If Wayne already knows about me, you being gone accomplishes nothing. He'd still be after me, and I would lose even more."

His words sank in, and I stared at him, horrified. The pain was evident in his voice. It saturated the words.

"I had never thought about it like that. I just thought leaving was the answer," I admitted.

"Well, it's not. So, stop. I will keep you and Theo safe. We all will. You aren't alone anymore. Trust me. Lean on me. I won't let you down."

"Why–why would you want to risk yourself for me? I don't understand."

His face softened, his voice becoming gentle. "Because I love you, Gabriella."

"Still? After what I said, after—"

He cut me off with a kiss.

"*Sempre*. Always."

STEFANO

She was asleep in my arms, having broken down completely and cried until she exhausted herself. It was all I could do to sit and hold her. I wanted to hunt down that piece of shit. Beat him into the ground for what he had done. The way he had treated her. Causing her to live in fear for years, constantly on the run and looking over her shoulder.

No wonder she was so skittish. The fact that she even allowed herself to trust me was a small miracle.

I ran my hand up and down her arm. She was wearing one of my T-shirts and a pair of my old sweats. Both were too large, but I liked seeing my clothes on her. In the sunlight, I noticed a couple faded scars I might not have thought about before. Now, knowing her story, I knew what, or who, put them on her skin.

That bastard had a lot to answer for.

She had told me more before she broke down. Her fears. The terror she lived with. How she fought to find herself again. How scared she was when she realized she had developed deeper feelings for me than she should have allowed herself.

"I came on so strong, Tesoro," I confessed. "I wish I hadn't."

"No, you were perfect," she replied, cupping my face. "You treated me like a woman. A desirable, sexy woman. I haven't felt that way in a very long time. And you made me feel safe, Stefano. Even when you kissed me that first night, I felt your gentleness. You didn't frighten me. Even that day when you were jealous, you didn't scare me." She frowned. "Which, now that I think about it, is strange. Somehow, my soul knew you were different." Her voice became lower, pleading with me to understand. To believe her. "I didn't want to leave you, Stefano. I wanted to stay here with you. But I didn't think I should. I

had to protect you and the people you love. If they were hurt because of me, you wouldn't be able to forgive me."

"He isn't getting near my family or you. I adore you, Gabby. And Theo. I'll do everything in my power to protect you."

My words circled in my head. I was going to require some help. I needed a plan, and I needed some advice.

Luckily, I knew exactly where to get both.

She woke up with a start, her eyes wide and her body tense. "It's all right," I soothed her. "I'm right here."

"Theo," she gasped, anxious.

"Is perfectly safe with Brett, Maxx, and Charly. So is Mrs. Scott. She's staying with Mary for the day."

She breathed out a long sigh of relief.

"You know for sure he's still in BC?"

"Yes. He was yesterday. Margie said he was at the bar."

"Okay. My mom is staying with my brother for a while. You can go to work with me, and we have lots of volunteers to look after Theo when he's not with us at the garage. You won't be alone for a moment."

I knelt before her. "And no more running. Your totes are not needed."

"You know about my totes?"

"Brett saw them. He told me."

She gripped my wrist. "I didn't want to. I was dreading it. Leaving. Running like a thief in the night. Stealing the SUV that Maxx gave me. I planned on sending him money to pay for it a little at a time, but I was still stealing it. But I couldn't get away without it," she babbled. "I'd hoped he would understand. I didn't know how I was going to live without everyone. Charly and Maxx. Mrs. Scott. Mary." Her eyes filled with tears. "You. The thought of leaving you killed me, Stefano. But I had to put you and Theo above that. The two of you were more important. I would keep him safe, and you would have everyone else to help you."

I pressed my forehead to hers. "Your thinking is fucked up, *Tesoro*. I need you above everyone else. And Theo. I love you both. Everyone else falls to a distant second. And just so we are clear? You aren't going anywhere. Ever. You're staying here with me. We're going to face this together, so stop thinking of yourself as alone. You're not."

She flung her arms around my neck, holding me tight. I buried my face into her neck, the faint scent of smoke still clinging to her. Reminding me of how close I'd come to losing her for good. I held her firm in my embrace, waiting until I felt her relax and calm before releasing her.

"You up to going to see Maxx and Charly? We have a plan, but we need you on board."

Despite the tremor that went through her, she nodded. "Yes."

"Okay."

She frowned. "I should change, but my clothes—"

I interrupted her. "I'll take you to your place. You can change there."

"Okay."

CHAPTER NINETEEN

Gabby

Stefano didn't say a word as we climbed the steps to my apartment. He glanced around, his lips tightening at the sight of the totes I had packed and the emptiness of the rooms. Two were Theo's toys. Another two of his clothes. One for mine. The other was filled with the things I couldn't bear to leave behind, and the last one, I'd planned to fill with the food I could take with me. The rest I would drop at the shelter in town for those who could use it. Six totes were all I could fit in the SUV. I had measured. The sight of the totes had also caused Theo anxiety. Although I'd told him I was just organizing the place, I was sure he didn't believe me. This had happened too many times, and because we'd stayed here so long, I had more to sort. More to leave behind. It had been breaking my heart.

"I, ah, will go and change," I muttered.

"Take your time." Stefano lifted two totes.

"What are you doing?"

He ignored me, disappearing through the door and heading downstairs. I recognized his stubborn look and, with a sigh, headed to the bathroom. I had a fast shower, washing my hair again to get rid of the fire smell. I didn't want to upset Theo even more than he would be already.

When I walked into the living room, all the totes were gone, and somehow, I wasn't surprised to find them piled in the truck bed when I got outside

I sensed Stefano's anger, and I held my tongue. Still, he reached for my hand, drawing soothing circles on the back of it as we headed to the garage.

When we arrived, Theo burst from the open garage door, flinging his arms around me. I fell to my knees as he approached and caught him, hugging him hard. I had worried needlessly, as he was not upset in the least. He was full of news of the garage, helping Brett, riding on Maxx's big shoulders, having fun, and feeling Charly's tummy move. I had to tamp down the swell of emotion as I listened to him. These wonderful people had taken care of my son so well, he had no idea anything was wrong.

He smiled up at me. "Brett says you're a hero!" Then he frowned. "But he says you got a boo-boo being one." He touched the bandage on my head. "Does it hurt?"

"If you kiss it better for me, it will go away," I assured him.

I lowered my head, and he touched his mouth to the bandage, holding my face in his little hands with a gentle touch that made the tears threaten all over again. I hadn't cried this much in years, and now it felt as if I couldn't stop.

Stefano hunched down beside us. "What a good boy you are, helping your mommy."

Theo beamed at him, then launched himself into Stefano's embrace. "I missed you, Stefo! When we played the tote game, I thought I wouldn't see you anymore." He screwed up his face. "I don't like that game."

Stefano glanced my way then shook his head. "You'll never have to play it again. Promise. I'm not going anywhere, little man. Neither are you."

He stood, taking Theo with him and holding out his hand to me. "Right, Mommy?"

I stood and smiled. "Right," I whispered. "Not anymore."

Stefano grinned. "Not anymore," he repeated.

I was greeted enthusiastically by all the mechanics. I was hugged by Brett and Maxx. Charly waddled out of the office, hugging me so hard I thought she'd break me in two.

"You scared us," she admonished. "No more burning buildings or making decisions based on fear, do you understand?"

"Um..."

"It's okay, Charly. We're all going to talk," Maxx said, draping a big arm around her and pulling her close. He rubbed her swollen belly tenderly. "Don't be getting all upset. My little one doesn't like it."

"I don't want to upset anyone," I protested. "That's why I was going—"

Maxx cut me off, shaking his head. "That's why you're going to go with my wife to the house and wait for us. You understand me,

Gabby?"

"I'm closing up the garage, and little bud and I are going to get a burger. I promised him if he helped me load up the deliveries today, I'd take him to my favorite place," Chase said, coming over. He smiled at me reassuringly. "My favorite place is Mary's house, and she's got her homemade burgers and fries waiting for us." He leaned down, giving Theo a high five. "I bet she makes her malted milkshakes for us too."

Charly linked her arm with mine. "Everything is taken care of. You come with me. The boys will be along shortly."

I had no other option but to let her lead me away. I glanced over my shoulder. My son was surrounded by men ready to protect him. I was being taken care of by people who considered me their friend. Part of their family. I looked again, meeting Stefano's intense gaze.

I was loved by a man so determined to keep me safe, he'd rallied these people together to help him.

For the first time in a very long while, I felt the stirring of hope.

In the house, Charly sat down, rubbing her stomach. She blew out a long breath, the red hair hanging over her forehead lifting.

"That takes a lot of effort these days." She grinned. "Walking. Who knew?"

"Where is Thomas?"

"With his auntie Kelly. They'll be back any moment, I'm sure."

At my quizzical look, she smiled. "My friend Kelly is a photographer's assistant. She travels all over the world, but she was here for Thomas's birth, and she came for this one. She visits when she can." A frown passed over her face. "She travels too much, I think. I want her to find what I have—a place of her own. A family of her own."

"Some of us want different things." I heard a dry voice laced with patience behind me. I turned and met the eyes of a woman, carrying Thomas, who was obviously Kelly. She smiled at me, and I returned it.

She was extraordinarily pretty. Tiny like Charly, with short black hair that clung to her head like a helmet and gleamed in the sunlight. In contrast, her light blue eyes stood out in her face, framed by the inky hair. She was fit, the muscles in her arms tight as she held a sleeping Thomas.

"You must be Gabby. Hello." Then she indicated the sleeping toddler. "Someone had too much fun and wore themselves out," she stated wryly. "I'll put him down. Coffee wouldn't be amiss if there was any."

I stood. "I'll make a pot."

"Great."

She headed upstairs, and I filled the machine, switching it on. I got Charly a glass of water and filled a plate with cookies. She reached for one gratefully. "I'm starving."

"I'll make you a sandwich."

She beamed in thanks. "I'm starving all the time, no matter how much I eat. This one is so different from Thomas." She chuckled. "I have a feeling she is going to give us a run for our money.

Maxx is already over the moon about having a girl, as well as fretting about it. It's amusing to watch him some days."

"I'll show you amusing, woman," Maxx rumbled as he walked in.

Charly grinned, not at all worried about him hearing her.

"Eating again, Red?" he asked with a dry chuckle. "My girl seems to need sustenance all the time."

"She's gonna be a fireball," Charly groused, biting into the sandwich I'd slid in front of her.

"Like her mommy," Maxx said. He crossed over, bending low to kiss her, his large hands resting on the swell beneath her loose shirt. He whispered something to her that made her smile and cup his cheek. The mutual adoration made me smile, and I looked up, meeting Stefano's tender gaze. He walked over, pulling out the chair beside me, tugging mine close.

"Okay, *Tesoro?*"

I nodded.

Brett walked in, grabbing the coffeepot and a handful of mugs, carrying them to the table.

"We'll need one more," Charly said. "Kelly will be down in a moment. She's just putting Thomas down."

A strange look passed over Brett's face. "Kelly is here?"

Charly nodded, looking happy. "She arrived a short time ago, surprising me. She's here until this one is finished baking and decides to show up." She beamed at him. "I wasn't even sure if she would make it."

He returned her smile, stood, and grabbed another mug. "Great. You need the help."

A moment later, Kelly appeared in the room. Stefano greeted her easily, offering her a hug. She teased him, then turned to Brett.

"Hey, Brett. You're looking good."

He eyed her, and I had to drop my gaze. The look that passed over his face before he schooled his expression had been one of pure lust, and her return gaze hadn't hidden much either. But he smiled and handed her a mug of coffee. I wondered if I was the only one who caught the heated exchange between them and filed that question away to ask Stefano later.

She took the mug and indicated the porch. "I'll give you some privacy."

Maxx waved his hand. "I think, unless Gabby objects, you should sit in on this. You'll be around for a while, so you should know what's going on."

I nodded in silence. Stefano slipped his arm around my shoulders, pulling me against him. He pressed a kiss to my forehead. "Relax, *Tesoro*," he whispered. "Relax."

I huffed out a sigh, and he tightened his arm.

"Gabby's ex is after her," he said simply. "She's been running and hiding since Theo was a baby. He's violent, abusive, and wants his hands on them."

"Not happening." Charly smacked the table, looking fierce.

"Nope," he agreed. "Not with everyone on alert."

I shook my head, feeling guilty.

"What?" Maxx asked, his tone gentle.

"I shouldn't put you all at risk. Charly—"

He cut me off. "Gabby, you know me. Do you think if I thought for one second my family would be in danger, I would allow this?"

I bit my lip, trying not to get upset.

Maxx leaned forward. "Our plan is simple. He wants you? He needs to show his face. And once he does and sees the fortress around you, he's going to give it up. He isn't getting near you or Theo. There is nothing I hate more than a man who preys on a woman. Especially the mother of his child. If he's a danger to you and your welfare, he'll be stopped."

"But he'll know where I am."

"Exactly. And he'll know the entire community knows who he is. What he's done. That we're watching."

I blinked.

Stefano picked up my hand and kissed it. "Brett is staying at your place and keeping an eye on the house. Mrs. Scott is going to stay at Mary's house. You and Theo will stay with me at our place. You'll drive to work with me. Neither of you will be alone. You'll have someone with you all the time."

"Theo can spend some time with me too," Charly piped up. "I love him. He can keep me and Thomas company. You can keep the office running." She smiled ruefully. "With the bar gone, you can give me more time." She huffed a huge sigh of air. "I have a feeling our girl is going to show up soon. I'll need all the hours you can give me."

"I can help wherever needed," Kelly assured me.

"Why?" I asked. "Why are you all being so amazing?"

"Because we care," Maxx stated simply. "Stefano is part of my family. Therefore, so are you. You're in trouble, and we're going to help."

"I have nothing to give you back."

Maxx leaned forward, resting his massive arms on the table. "That's not how this works, but yes, you do."

"What?" I asked.

"You're going to help my wife. I consider that more valuable than anything else. And I want your promise. That you'll trust us. Stay." He gripped Stefano's shoulder. "He needs you the way I need Charly." He met my eyes. "No more running."

"No," I whispered.

"I couldn't figure out why he texted her and let her know he'd found her," Stefano mused. "Then I realized he wanted her to run. To be alone where he could find her easily."

"I don't understand how." Charly frowned.

"He has somehow grabbed on to her phone signal. He can trace where she is. I think he was banking on scaring her enough to leave. That's why he hasn't shown up yet. He's waiting."

"I had planned on leaving my cell phone behind," I reminded him.

For a moment, Stefano's expression was dark, then he shook his head. "He was counting on the fact that you wouldn't do that."

I barked out a laugh. "He always told me how stupid I was. He'd never think I'd be smart enough to figure out something like that."

He leaned close. "He was wrong. On every count. You are smart. Beautiful. Strong. And staying. You hear me?"

"Yes."

Ignoring the fact that we had witnesses, he kissed me hard. "Good."

Then he faced the group. "Let's nail this down."

Maxx and Brett nodded, both looking fierce.

I had to admit, them knowing the truth was liberating. Their insistence we were safe made me feel better. They would not only look out for me and Theo, but also Stefano.

Maybe this would work.

Maybe, just maybe, I could stop running.

CHAPTER TWENTY

Gabby

L ater that night, I tucked Theo into the big bed in Brett's room.

"I'll leave the light on, so if you wake up, you know where you are," I said, sitting on the edge of the mattress, my leg tucked up under me. I was tired, my head ached, and I looked forward to being able to sit and be quiet. To think. The day had been filled with emotions and plans. I had listened and tried to keep up, although at times it became too much. Stefano watched me closely, then announced we were leaving when he saw me rub my tired eyes. I'd hugged everyone who was still gathered around the table, whispering my gratitude.

We picked up Theo at Mary's. He was full, happy, and excited about staying at Stefano's. We agreed to talk to him together once we were at the house and were alone. I didn't want to frighten him, but we had to explain what was going on.

Stefano walked in, carrying a book and sitting across from me on the other side of the bed.

Theo smiled, his little face happy. He patted my hand. "I like it here, Mom."

"You didn't like our apartment? I thought you were happy there, Theo?" I asked.

"I was. But Stefo is here, so I like it better." He tapped the mattress, looking at Stefano. "This is a big bed, so you could sleep here if you want," he offered.

Stefano cleared his throat. "I have my own room here, little man."

"Oh." His eyes grew round. "Mom, if you're gonna sleep here, you hafta bring your own blanket, okay?"

I tried not to laugh, and from across the bed, Stefano chuckled.

"Um, little man, your mom is gonna sleep with me."

"How come?"

Stefano brought one leg up, resting it on the bed and facing Theo. "There are two reasons. One, your mom has a bump on her head, and she has to be watched. So, I'll do that."

"But you're okay, right?" Theo's anxious gaze met mine, and I nodded.

"Yes, it's just a precaution, Teddy Bear."

"Mom," he hissed. "Five. I'm five."

"Right. It's just a precaution, Theo."

"Okay. What's number two?" Then Theo began to chortle, slapping the bed. "I said number two. Like poop, you know, Mom?" He looked at Stefano. "Mom doesn't like me to say poop. She calls it number two. But I said it—like a poop joke. It's funny!"

Stefano's lips twitched, and I had to turn my head. What was it about boys and bathroom humor? It seemed to amuse them no matter how old they were.

Stefano let out a guffaw, and for a moment, the two of them laughed as if Theo had made the best joke in the world.

"Can we get back to the subject at hand, boys?" I asked dryly, secretly loving the shared camaraderie between them.

"Right. Okay," Stefano muttered, wiping his eyes. "The second reason is I like sleeping with your mom. She smells good, and I like to cuddle with her."

"She hogs the blankets," Theo said, shaking his head in warning. "You'll get cold."

"I'll risk it."

Theo sighed. "Fine. But if you hafta kick her out, I'll share. Because, you know, she's my mom."

"Good man."

Theo glanced behind me at the totes piled up. "Mom, are we staying here forever? Is that why we played pack the totes?"

I took his hand. "No, baby, you were right. We were gonna move—"

"No!" He interrupted me. "I don't want to! Stefo, tell her no!"

I held up my hand. "It's okay. We're not going anywhere."

He flopped back to the pillow. "Promise?"

I looked at Stefano, somehow at a loss. He tilted his chin in encouragement, and I leaned closer to Theo.

"Remember I told you about the man—your father?"

He nodded, looking solemn. "He's not nice," he whispered.

"I thought he was coming to take us away, so I was going to leave and hide with you. But Stefano asked us to stay here with him."

He looked at Stefano. "You won't let him take us away?"

"No, little man. No one will let that happen. But we need your help, okay?"

"Okay."

"You have to stick close to your mom and me. The guys at the garage. Don't talk to strangers, and don't go with anyone unless it's one of us. Your mom. Me. Brett. Maxx or Charly. Chase."

"What about Mary or Mrs. Scott?"

"They're good too."

"And that lady I met today?"

"Kelly?" I asked.

He nodded. "I don't remember her name, but she smelled good and she showed me some nice pictures."

"Yes, Kelly is okay. So are the other mechanics. But no one else. If you see a stranger, run and get someone you know. If they come to you, yell. You have to promise us that."

"I will."

Stefano ruffled his hair. "That's my smart boy."

"Should I be scared?" Theo asked, his bottom lip beginning to tremble.

"No," Stefano said firmly. "You have nothing to be scared of. I won't let anything happen to you. No one will. You're safe with me."

I tried not to cry as I watched Theo stretch out his arms and Stefano enfold him in his embrace. He murmured something to Theo, who nodded and patted Stefano's wide shoulders. His hand looked tiny on the massive expanse, yet I knew there wasn't a safer place in the world for my son. Stefano cradled him as if he was holding something precious, and I realized that, to him, that was exactly what Theo was. What we both were.

I met Stefano's gaze over the top of Theo's head. He nodded imperceptibly, telling me without words we were both safe. Loved. I nodded back in understanding.

He dropped a kiss to Theo's head. "Okay, little man? You understand?"

Theo nodded, satisfied. "You'll take care of the bad man. And I get to stay here with you."

"Yep."

"Okay."

Theo yawned. "Can you read to me now, Stefo?"

"Absolutely."

Stefano looked at me. "I ran the tub pretty hot, so the water should be good now. You go soak, and I'll tuck in our little man, okay?"

I bent and kissed Theo's cheek. He flung his arms around my neck. "I love you, Mom."

I brushed the hair off his head. "I love you," I murmured.

I stood, pausing at the door, looking behind me. Stefano had stretched out, his back against the headboard, the book open on his lap. Beside him, Theo had cuddled down, clutching his blanket with one hand, his other resting on Stefano's leg, as if touching him made him feel safer.

"Stefo?" he asked, sounding drowsy.

"Yeah, little man?"

"I really don't have to play the tote game again?"

"Nope. Never. You and your mom are staying right here, with me."

Theo lifted his hand, and Stefano took it, encasing it in his much larger palm.

"Stefo?"

"Hmm?"

"I have a wish."

"You want to tell me what it is, or is it a secret wish?" Stefano asked quietly.

"I wish *you* could be my dad. I love you like I love my mom."

My eyes filled with tears at his simple words.

Stefano's voice was tight as he replied, his gaze never leaving mine.

"I love you too. And I love your mom. I'm gonna work on that, little man. Okay? You keep wishing."

Theo smiled, although his eyes never opened. "Okay."

Stefano kept looking at me, a silent promise in his eyes. He blew me a kiss, mouthing "See you soon," and indicating for me to go to the tub.

I walked down the hall and slid into the waiting bath. As Stefano predicted, the water was perfect. The old claw-foot tub was deep, and I sank under the water gratefully after I took a couple of Tylenol for the persistent dull ache in my head. Given all that had transpired the past few days, I should be a bundle of nerves. On edge and anxious. But here, in this room filled with steam and the scent of lavender, all I felt was calm. Right. Stefano's words had not only calmed Theo but me as well.

Stefano was right. I was no longer alone. Whatever tomorrow held, whatever happened next week, I wouldn't have to face it on my own. I could rest easy knowing Stefano was close, keeping us safe.

Stefano had lit a candle, and the flickering light cast shadows onto the walls, making the space cozy. I let my eyes drift shut, and I floated. My body relaxed, and I enjoyed the peacefulness surrounding me. The door opened, and I heard Stefano's low chuckle.

"Head up, *Tesoro*."

I lifted my head, and he tucked a towel behind it, running his hand over my forehead. "Little man is down for the count. He barely lasted two pages."

"Hmm," I murmured. "Thank you for making him feel better."

I felt his lips against my cheek. "Anytime. Anything." I heard him settle on the floor next to the tub.

"What is the tote game?" he asked after a moment. "Obviously, it has to do with you leaving, but I don't exactly know what it entails."

I sighed. "I get him to separate his toys. Put his favorites in the bin so I'm sure to take them when we leave. I didn't realize how clever he was and he figured out my 'organizing' meant that we'd be leaving."

"Not this time," he said roughly. "Never again."

"No," I agreed. "He loves being close to you."

"The feeling is mutual. I love that kid."

"I know. I heard."

"It's going to happen, *Tesoro*. We're going to be a family one day. We won't talk about it tonight, but soon."

Something in my chest loosened, and I felt myself relax. "Okay, soon."

He passed his hand over my head again. "It's been a long day."

"It has."

"I think you're going to drift off soon."

I smiled, not speaking. He continued to run his hand over my head. "I don't want you to fall asleep in the tub," he said, a trace of worry in his voice.

"I won't. I'm just enjoying the tranquility."

He stood. "Okay. I'm going to make a few calls. I'll be back to check on you shortly. Don't slip under the water."

"Okay."

He let out some water, replacing it with hot, swirling it around my legs, then he left, pulling the door behind him. I basked in the unexpected moment. The bathtub in my apartment was shallow —fine for Theo but not for soaking. And normally, I would be at work in the evening. Not home to put Theo to bed, not soaking in a warm tub. Often the little free time I had was spent going over the budget, trying to figure out how to cut corners, wondering what the next day or week would bring. Trying to find a way to give Theo what he needed. And doing it all alone.

There was never a sexy, sweet man waiting for me. Worrying about me. Wanting to help in any way he could.

But tonight was different. Tonight, I was safe. *We* were safe. Tomorrow would be the first day of a different life. I would work in the garage, helping Charly and Maxx. Theo would be close. Stefano would be there. We would be together again at the end of the day.

I had almost lost that. Stefano was right. I was so used to reacting from fright and worry. To doing everything on my own. I had lost sight of the fact that things had changed, and for the first time since Theo was born, I had a support system around me. People who cared.

A man who really loved me. Loved my son. Wanted to be a family.

And it was time to let him know I returned his feelings.

Stefano was stretched out on his bed, leaning against the headboard, talking to someone on the phone. He looked so sexy, his chest bare, sleep pants covering his legs. He had one leg up, the knee bent, his hand resting on it as he spoke. He smiled when I walked in, sliding his knee down and patting his thigh. I climbed onto the mattress, curling up beside him, resting my head on his soft flannel-covered leg. He immediately combed his fingers through my curls. I knew he loved my hair—he touched and played with it every chance he got. I found his ministrations very soothing, and his touch felt good on my aching skull.

"Great, Maxx. No, I think we've got everything covered. How's Charly?"

He listened for a moment and chuckled. "Sounds about right. Busting your chops. Any more contractions?" He slipped his hand to my neck, rubbing the sore muscles.

"If it changes, call. We can come stay with Thomas if they start back up again. Gabby can help Kelly, so you don't have to worry."

He talked for another few moments, then hung up.

"Charly's having contractions?" I asked, rolling over to look up at him.

"Braxton-Hicks," he said. "But Maxx is pretty sure the real thing is gonna happen soon. She's dropped, and, as he says, Charly is extra cranky and demanding. Busting his chops every five minutes. And being stubborn, insisting she can do everything like normal."

He chuckled. "Not that that is anything new. But he's worried in case she goes into labor quickly. Kelly is great, but she doesn't have a lot of practice with babies for the long-term. Helping Charly while she's there is one thing—left on her own…well, let's just say, Maxx is a bit uptight. I told him, between you and Mary, they're covered. I can have you there in ten minutes."

"Absolutely."

He probed the area around the cut on my head, his touch light and gentle. "How does it feel?"

"Okay. It hurts to touch it."

"Then don't touch it."

"Ha-ha. So funny."

He frowned, tracing the edge of the bandage. "I hate seeing you in pain."

I captured his hand. "I'm fine. It'll heal."

He nodded, a shadow passing over his face.

"When I thought I'd lost you, when I couldn't find you…" He trailed off and swallowed. "The feeling churning in my gut, the despair that threatened just at the thought—" He met my gaze, his tormented. "*Jesus*, Gabby, it was like nothing I had ever felt. I never want to feel that again."

I pressed his palm to my face. "I'm right here, Stefano. I'm fine."

"And you're going to stay fine," he said fiercely. "Nothing is going to happen to you. It can't. I just found you, and nothing and no one is taking you or Theo away." He paused. "And you're not going anywhere without me."

"No," I agreed.

"Promise me, *Tesoro*. If you get frightened, when that instinct to run kicks in, tell me. I'll hold you until it goes away. I'll fight whatever demons are haunting you. Trust me enough to do that."

I took in a deep breath. "I do, Stefano." My throat felt constricted, my voice tight. "You have to trust the person you love."

It took a moment for my words to sink in. He stopped stroking my head, his mouth opening slightly.

"What did you say?"

"I love you, Stefano. You mean so much to me. How it happened, when it happened, I don't know, but it's real." I swallowed. "*Ti amo.*"

He bent, hauling me into his arms, holding me close.

He whispered words. Phrases. Not all of which I understood. He pressed kisses to my cheeks, against the skin of my neck, the end of my nose, and finally covered my mouth with his, kissing me. I felt his love, his affection soaking into my skin with each caress. Every touch branded me as his. Every word that fell from his lips was a benediction, a celebration of us.

"Say it again, *Tesoro.*"

"I love you, Stefano Borelli. I love you with all my heart."

He sighed. "Those are my favorite words in the entire world."

"They're all for you."

He kissed me again. "Good."

CHAPTER TWENTY-ONE

Gabby

I woke up the next morning feeling differently. It was the first time in years I hadn't woken up panicked or worried. Even with the thought of Wayne finding me, I was more relaxed than I could remember being for a long time.

A lot of it had to do with the man I woke up beside. When Stefano was asleep, his face was relaxed and peaceful. He had one arm around me, holding me close, his head next to mine on my pillow. His strength and warmth surrounded me. His dark hair was messy, his beard thick. I ran my fingers over his jaw, smiling when he pursed his lips as if I were tickling him. I slid my hand down his torso, feeling the sinewy muscles and the dusting of hair on his chest. I ghosted his navel, feeling his erection pressing against me.

"Keep that up, *Tesoro*, and you'll be sorry," he rumbled, pulling me closer.

"Touching you?" I whispered. "I like touching you."

"Teasing me like that."

I dropped my hand, wrapping it around his cock. "Like this?"

"Jesus," he muttered as I pumped him slowly. "Gabby, Theo will wake up soon."

"I think someone beat him to the punch," I murmured. "You feel pretty up to me."

He groaned, then hissed low in his throat as I slid under the blanket, replacing my hand with my mouth. He was hot, thick, and musky. I tongued the underside, cupping his balls, then teased the crown, smiling at his low curses and pleas. I slowly swallowed around him, taking in as much of him as I could, and began to suck. I alternated between long, teasing pulls, flicks of my tongue, and deep suction, all while listening to his mutterings, the slap of his hand on the mattress, and seeing the way he arched his back, driving his hips forward, begging me for more.

"Shift up," he demanded. "Let me touch you."

Not releasing him, I spun and immediately felt his hand on me. Stroking, seeking, teasing. His thumb pressed against my clit as he sank two fingers into me, pumping in time to my mouth sucking on him.

"Jesus, you're soaked for me."

I whimpered low in my throat, making him moan my name. I hummed again, knowing how much he liked the vibration. He moved his hand faster.

"*Tesoro*," he groaned. "I can't take much more."

I hummed around him again, speeding up. I wanted him to fall. To let go and take for a change. He gave all the time. I wanted to do this for him. I was already so close, I could feel the tremors racing through me. He knew exactly how to touch me. How to take me to the edge fast. I stiffened around him, sucking deeper as he swelled and released, his hips undulating, his breathing hard as he came. My orgasm burst, and we were a mass of shivering limbs, low groans, and shared ecstasy. His free hand found mine, and he squeezed my fingers, holding it to his chest as he gasped my name, then stilled. I pulled back, dropping to the mattress, my head on his thigh, trying to catch my breath. For a moment, neither of us moved. I began to roll over when it happened.

His bedroom door opened. We both froze.

"Stefo, have you seen my mom? I'm hungry."

Stefano sat up fast, dragging the blanket higher, covering my legs and feet. The fluffy duvet was yanked over top of me as well.

Panic was evident in his voice. "I think your mom is, ah, in the bathroom, little man. You go to the kitchen, and I'll come get your breakfast."

"I just saw her feet. Why is she under the blankets?"

I couldn't help it. I began to laugh. I had to push my face into the mattress and try to stifle my amusement. Stefano slid his hand under the blanket, pinching my leg to stop my laughter, but it somehow only made the situation funnier.

"Oh, right. She came back. She was really cold. I tucked her in. She's—ah, she's asleep. So, we need to *be quiet*." He emphasized the words, pressing on my leg.

"Huh. Do you have cereal?"

"Pretty sure I do. Yep. You go check."

"Stefo, are you okay?"

"Um, yep. I'm good. Go, buddy. I'll be right there."

"You're breathing funny, and it looks like you're sweating. Maybe you got a cold. You should ask my mom to take your temperature."

"I just did," I whispered, the laughter beginning to escape again. "He was pretty hot."

Stefano pinched me again, but this time, I heard the amusement in his voice.

"Good plan."

Theo's voice got closer. "I could stay with you until Mom wakes up."

"No, it's good. You go look in the cupboards. If you don't find what you want, I'll go get McDonald's," Stefano said, sounding desperate.

"Oh, I like McDonald's better."

"Great. Go get dressed, and we'll go."

The sound of Theo's hurried footsteps met my ears, and I began to chuckle. The blankets were thrown back, and Stefano loomed over me. "You found that funny?"

"I found *you* funny. All panicked that Theo might join me under the covers and ask what I was doing."

He scrubbed his face. "I need a lock on the door." He swung himself off the bed. "I don't think I could have recovered if he'd found you." He pointed a finger at me. "And you weren't helping."

He dragged on his jeans, muttering about kids and boundaries. Women and early morning blow jobs without locks.

He tugged a shirt over his head, combing his fingers through the mess of hair on his head.

I sat up, letting the blankets fall away. "At least you weren't stuffed under a pile of blankets being suffocated and pinched."

He stared at me, then lunged. I was under him in seconds as he kissed me. "I'm going to stuff you with something else later until you scream my name. You are too goddamn sexy for your own good." He kissed me again, then pushed away.

"I gotta take our boy and get food."

Our boy. Hearing him say that made my heart smile. "Do I get an Egg McMuffin?"

He rolled his eyes, heading for the door. "Maybe."

"Stefano," I called out, waiting until he stopped and looked at me. "I love you."

A wide smile broke out on his face. "Egg McMuffin, it is."

Later at the garage, Charly shuffled in, not even trying to disguise her inability to move well. She sat down with a long sigh.

"How you doing?" I asked.

"I think I'll be in labor soon. My back is aching like crazy."

I smiled in sympathy. "Can I do anything?"

She shook her head. "It feels better if I walk around. You okay?"

I nodded. "Everything is great," I assured her. "If I can't find something, one of the guys usually knows where it is."

"Like the bathroom?" she asked with a smirk.

"What?"

"Theo tells me Stefano forgot you were in the bed this morning." She lifted one eyebrow. "He said you were asleep under the blankets with your head buried." She leaned forward. "The question is, buried where exactly, Gabby?" She paused. "He told me Stefano was all sweaty and hot too. He's worried he has a cold."

I burst out laughing, and she joined me. "Oh my God, you should have heard Stefano's voice," I whispered. "Two octaves higher than usual. Completely panicked. Bribing Theo with an Egg McMuffin to leave the room. It was hilarious."

Charly chuckled. "I can only imagine."

"He was adorably flustered."

"Despite everything going on, I've never seen him so happy," she said.

"Despite everything, I've never been so happy," I admitted. "He is so good to Theo. To me."

"He is one of the good ones."

Brett walked down the hall, poking his head into the office. "Ladies, you're doing okay?"

We both assured him we were fine, and he kept walking.

"There's another good man," I observed.

"The best."

"Is there, ah, something between him and Kelly?"

Charly sighed, pushing her hair off her shoulders. It was loose today, the red bright under the lights.

"I don't know. Neither of them will admit it, but I get the feeling there's something."

"He looked at her yesterday like he wanted to eat her."

Charly nodded. "She disappeared last night right around the same time he did. When she reappeared, she looked, ah, *worked over*, if you know what I mean. But she insisted she was out for a walk. He never came back to the house." She leaned closer. "I think they were ravishing each other in the stock room."

I waggled my eyebrows. "I noticed a few things out of place this morning. Like they'd been shoved aside in haste."

"Oh." She grinned. "Maxx and I have done our fair share of stock-room demolition." She winked. "He's a big guy. He takes up a lot of airspace. And he needs room for his maneuvers."

"His maneuvers?" I repeated.

She nodded slowly. "He has a lot of maneuvers." She rubbed her stomach. "Which is how I ended up pregnant again." She stood and began to waddle away, stopping to look over her shoulder. "We'll keep our eyes peeled for any shenanigans between those two."

"Right."

She moved away, barely making it three steps before Maxx appeared in front of her. He bent low to her eye level, talking quietly, and she nodded, letting him lift her into his arms without an argument. She gazed up at him in utter adoration, all the snark and sassiness gone. She was simply a woman in love with her husband and letting him care for her.

Until he announced he was taking the rest of the afternoon off and spending it watching over her.

"Holy moly, big guy! I don't need you hanging over me, jumping at every noise or grunt I make. You can forget that idea and get your ass back to the garage."

Her voice faded away as he carried her out of the garage, and I chuckled. He loved riling her up as much as she loved to get under his skin. They were perfect for each other.

"Hey." Stefano appeared, leaning on the doorframe. He was wearing a set of overalls, the logo emblazoned on the front. His hair was disheveled, and he was sporting a wide grin. "You got a minute?"

"Sure."

He held out his hand. "Come see."

I let him lead me over to the other side of the garage where he worked. "I just finished this bike," he explained.

I walked around the motorcycle, stunned at the intricacy of his design and the detail. He was so talented. "Stefano, it's beautiful. Really stunning."

He grinned, looking pleased. "I hope the customer thinks so."

"The roses look real."

"The lady who owns it, Nina, is an award-winning gardener. She wanted her love of flowers represented on the bike." He showed me the trail of vines and flowers woven over the fenders. "A change of pace from skulls and crests."

"I love the color."

"Burgundy-gray pearl. I mixed it myself. It's unique."

"Who did the upholstery?"

"Chase did it," he said, surprising me. "He's been taking courses. Teaching himself. He did this without me knowing, then showed it to me and Maxx. We showed it to the client. She was blown away."

I ran my hand over the tufted gray leather. "It's gorgeous."

"I'm making her a helmet to match. I'll work on that tomorrow. She'll pick up the bike next week."

"Has Maxx seen it?"

"He loved it."

"I can see why." I smiled at him. "You're so talented, *Amore*."

He froze. "What did you call me?"

"*Amore*," I repeated. "My love."

"I know what it means," he rasped, dragging me to his chest and kissing me. "Do you know what it does to me to hear you call me that?"

"You like it?"

"I love it. I love you," he added.

"Me too," I whispered.

"You know I'm never going to let you go back to your apartment, right?"

I laughed, tugging on his overall strap, somehow not surprised by his words. "It's been a day. Another week, you might change your mind."

"Never. I want you and Theo with me."

"What about poor Brett?"

265

"He told me this morning he and Chase are thinking of rooming together. We'll find a house with a good yard for little man, some expansion, and Brett and Chase can stay in our current house."

"Expansion?" I repeated.

"A little brother or sister for Theo." He paused. "To start."

I blinked.

"Am I overwhelming you again?"

"You want kids with me?" I whispered.

"I want it all with you, *Tesoro*. Kids, a wedding, a lifetime."

"But Wayne…"

"Will be out of your life very soon. Then we're going to figure out our future. Yours, mine, and Theo's. Together. Got it?"

My head spun, but in the very best of ways.

I smiled at him. "Okay, *Amore*. Okay."

CHAPTER TWENTY-TWO

Gabby

A couple of days later, as I was entering the last invoice into the computer, Chase came into the office, sitting down and waiting until I hit save.

"What's up?" I asked.

"I was wondering if it would be okay if I took Theo with me on my errands. Get him out of the garage for a while—a change of scenery, you know?"

"Oh, ah—"

He cut me off. "I'm a great driver—never had an accident. He'd be perfectly safe with me."

"Oh, it's not that," I said, unsure of my next words.

His shoulders slumped. "It's because of my past, isn't it? I mean, I don't blame you. But, honest, I've changed. I'm not a trouble-maker anymore. The guys will vouch for me. Even Maxx will tell you I'm reliable now, and he, of all people, had the biggest reason to never trust me again. I can go—"

I held up my hand, stopping him.

"It has nothing to do with your past, Chase. I don't know your history. I know you know some of it, but I'm not sure if you know my whole story. My past is catching up to me right now. My ex is after Theo and me. I don't want you to get caught up in this. That's all. I would hate for you to be bothered by it."

He sat back, crossing his leg over his knee. He brushed his light-brown hair off his forehead. His kind eyes glittered under his heavy eyebrows. He was clean-shaven and lean, although I knew his heavy denim overalls hid the fact that he was muscular. He worked out with the guys regularly, and his job entailed a lot of manual labor. He was a good-looking young man, pleasant and helpful, always ready with a smile. I knew Stefano and Brett treated him like a little brother and were very fond of him. Other than that, I knew very little about Chase Donner.

"I know about your ex. Stefano and Maxx told me. Everyone was warned to be on high alert, but I know more, because, well, because I'm closer to them. All of us are happy to be involved, Gabby. We like you. We like Theo. I'm not as big as Maxx or even Stefano, but if your ex showed up and Theo were with me, I would make sure he was safe."

"Oh," I said.

He sat forward, resting his arms on his thighs. "Now, before you say yes, you should know about me. I was a troublemaker when I was younger. My brother Wes was a bad influence on me, and it became worse as I grew up. My father ignored us and used his money and power to pay off whatever trouble we got into. Wes got crueler, his antics becoming more serious and nasty. For a while, I followed in his footsteps. Then one day, I met a girl. She made me want to be different. Be better."

"Love does that," I offered quietly.

He nodded. "Suddenly, I could see Wes in a different light. But he had a huge hold on me, and he didn't want to let go. I was torn between the girl I fell for and the brother I loved." His face darkened, and he clasped his hands together. "Until the day Wes went too far. What I thought was going to be a harmless prank put Charly in the hospital."

My eyebrows flew up in shock.

"I was so horrified by his callousness, I went to the police and confessed. My father washed his hands of both of us and turned his back. I went to jail on a lesser charge. Minimum security and I got out early on good behavior." He swallowed. "I told the police everything I knew about Wes and his illegal activities. He went to jail for a long time."

"That was very brave."

He shrugged. "It was the right thing to do. I was tired of always being compared to him, to all the terrible things he did. I hoped he'd change and learn his lesson. That he'd forgive me and we'd forge a relationship when he got out of prison." He sighed, sitting back and scrubbing his face. "I took advantage of every opportunity in prison. Counseling. Programs. School. Wes refused to try anything and became even angrier. Bitter."

"Is he still in jail?"

He dropped his head, shaking it slowly. "He died in prison," he said, his voice low and raspy. "Picked a fight with the wrong guy."

I laid my hand on his knee. "I'm sorry."

He looked up. "He never forgave me. I went to see him, and he told me what he thought of me then walked away. I never saw him again."

"Have you made peace with your father?"

"He, ah, died too—not very long ago. We never reconnected, even though I tried several times."

I wanted to fling my arms around him and cradle him the same way I did Theo when he was hurt. The pain was evident in Chase's eyes; it dripped from his voice.

"Chase—"

He held up his hand. "I'm not telling you for sympathy, Gabby. I've come to terms with it—well, mostly."

"And your girl?" I asked.

He smiled ruefully. "She moved away while I was in prison. It was too much for her. She's married now with a kid, and I'm happy for her. Someday, I hope for the same thing. She helped me change, and I will always be grateful to her for that."

He met my eyes. "That's my past, Gabby. I came here to make amends. Charly forgave me, and eventually, so did Maxx. I stayed because I got so much more than forgiveness from them. They gave me a place to belong and a new family. So, if you think you can trust me to look after Theo, I would love to take him with me. I would watch over him and enjoy the company."

I studied his honest expression. "I think you should be proud of how far you've come. I have no problem with you and Theo spending some time together. I know he'd love it." I paused. "Stefano showed me your work yesterday."

"Oh yeah?"

I nodded. "You need to sit down and talk to Maxx and him about it. You're talented."

"I will when I'm ready."

"Do you think you still need to prove yourself? Is that why you're still doing errands?"

He chuckled. "You and Charly are smart women, aren't you? For a long time, yes. I wasn't sure I could ever atone. But Brett and Stefano started teaching me more about cars and engines. Maxx joined in. And then I found I loved the hands-on side. It took a lot for me to show Stefano. I was blown away by his enthusiasm. Maxx's too. I will keep working and perfecting my craft and, hopefully one day soon, be part of the team that creates."

Stefano spoke from the doorway.

"That day is coming sooner than you think, Chase. We believe in you."

Chase looked over his shoulder, startled. "Thanks."

"So I hear from my little man the two of you are off on a road trip?"

Chase glanced at me, and I nodded. "They are."

Chase's smile was wide. "Awesome. We have to go to Osbourne to get those parts for the bike Maxx is rebuilding. I'm going to take him to that barbecue joint there."

Stefano grinned. "Lucky kid." He pulled out his wallet and slipped some money into Chase's hand. "Bring us back some brisket and ribs. Some burnt ends if they have any left."

"Will do." He stood. "We'll be gone the whole afternoon. Back around five, I think."

"Make sure he drinks water. Don't let him talk you into a lot of candy," I warned.

"Promise."

"You'll have to remind him to hit the head when you stop," Stefano advised. "Otherwise, there'll be roadside watering or wet pants. He tends to forget."

Chase laughed and high-fived Stefano on the way past him.

He sat down in the chair Chase had vacated. "I heard him telling you about Wes."

"Quite the story."

He nodded. "I noticed the kid omitted the fact that his father left everything to him in the will."

"Well, I suppose that was a little personal to share."

He leaned forward. "The kid is a millionaire. He refuses to touch the money, though. He works and scrapes by on his salary. To him, it's blood money. His father always gave money instead of himself. That was what Chase really wanted. He has a management company that donates chunks of it, but he says they make him more than he gives away."

"He might change his mind one day and want some of the money."

"That's what Maxx told him. The kid was just going to give it all away in a lump sum. We sat him down and convinced him to do it another way."

"He's not really a kid," I pointed out.

He winked. "I know, but he is to me. He's like my little brother. If I didn't call him kid, he'd be upset."

I laughed at his drollness. "I see."

"Maxx is sure Charly is going into labor today. He says she is restless as hell and keeps rearranging the nursery."

"I'll go see her once I finish this."

He bent forward, kissing me. "I like having you here."

I smiled. "I like being here."

"Good." He stood. "Make sure your cell is with you."

"I will."

He dropped another kiss onto my mouth and headed back to work. I leaned back, watching him walk away. He was as sexy from the back as he was the front—his back and shoulders broad, his T-shirt stretched tight across the muscles. His jeans hugged his ass and the backs of his thighs, and they emphasized his long legs.

I enjoyed the show.

I finished the entries, checked the schedule, pleased to see everything was going smoothly. There was a query about tires, and I frowned, recalling some new ones Maxx had gotten while they were on sale and stored in the barn, knowing this customer would be needing them soon. I would check on my way back from seeing Charly.

I headed to the house, trying not to laugh when I spied Kelly storming out of the barn, and I went in the same direction. Brett leaned against the doorway, his hair disheveled and his overalls half done up, watching her. Kelly's short hair was mussed, she had a towel draped over her shoulders, and she looked furious. She turned and flipped Brett the bird before walking into the house, slamming the door behind her. Brett pushed off the doorframe and sauntered my way, trying to look nonchalant.

"Never correct a lady's form when she is doing yoga," he quipped. "Apparently it ruins their zen."

"Um, Brett?"

"Yeah?"

"Her, ah, *zen*, is all over your neck." I indicated the lipstick smudges. "She got a little on your ear as well. And you missed a few buttons on the overalls."

He brushed a hand over his neck, inspecting his palm. "Well, shit. Busted, I guess."

"Your secret is safe with me."

"Thanks, Gabby. It's complicated."

"It always is." I paused. "Where does Maxx keep the extra tires he's ordered in the barn?"

"To the right of the workout area—behind the tarp. They're stacked and organized on pallets."

"Great."

I waved and headed to the house. Charly was at the table, looking amused. Kelly was pouring a cup of coffee, her movements jerky and rushed. She was muttering under her breath.

I sat down beside Charly. "Lover's spat," I whispered.

"She has a love bite on her neck," Charly observed.

"Brett has lipstick all over his."

"I can hear you," Kelly snapped.

"Good," Charly said, slapping the table. "Tell us what the hell is going on. Don't say '*nothing*' either. It's bull pucky. I am about to go into labor, and I am incapable of listening to bull pucky. Spill."

Kelly sat down, crossing her legs, her foot swinging in agitation. Charly was right. There was a love bite at the base of her neck. A good one. Obviously, nice guy Brett had a passionate side.

"It is nothing. Brett and I have some history. Of the sex nature. Nothing else. Today, he tried to suggest otherwise. We argued." She shook her head. "He ruined a perfectly great sex opportunity to get all emo." She slammed her hand on the table. "I have no interest in settling down. I am not my mother, and I will never be beholden to a man. I'm going to travel, see the world, take great pictures, and have as much meaningless, passionate sex as possible!"

I blinked at her tirade. For a moment, no one said anything. Then Charly spoke.

"How's that working out for you, Kelly?"

Kelly stood. "I would tell you to fuck off, Charly, but you're about to go into labor, so I'll let you off this time."

"By all means, brush me off," Charly retorted. "Run upstairs and hide. But we're going to talk about this before you leave."

Kelly sniffed and marched upstairs.

"I think someone is in deeper than she wanted to be," Charly said. "She has so many issues to work through, but if she faced them, I think she'd find that—"

She stopped talking, her hand flying to her stomach. She glanced down. "Shit. Just like last time. My water just broke." She met my eyes. "The baby is coming. Maxx. I need Maxx."

"On it."

CHAPTER TWENTY-THREE

Gabby

I opened the patio door and ran for the garage. Inside, I found Maxx and shouted his name. He didn't hesitate, dropping his tools and running past me. I chased after him, and behind me, I heard Stefano and Brett following.

In the house, Charly's head rested on the table, and she was panting and counting. Maxx dropped to his knees beside her.

"Red? Talk to me."

Charly lifted her head. "She's coming fast, Maxx. Just like Thomas."

Maxx stood. "Her bag is in the nursery."

Kelly raced down the steps, holding it up. "I heard—I got it!"

Maxx lifted Charly into his arms, concern reflected in his expression. "I got you, Red. We're heading for the hospital."

Brett spoke up. "Give me ten, and I'll drive you." He was covered in oil and grease, having just started an engine rebuild when I'd run into the garage. "I just need to get the grease off my hands and get out of these overalls."

"Can't wait," Charly gasped.

Stefano met my eyes, then grabbed the bag when I nodded in understanding. He hated to leave, but this was important. I would be safe here.

"I'll drive. Brett, you stay and man the garage until I get back. Kelly, you have Thomas?"

"Yes."

"I'll help," I said, catching Stefano's eye. "I'll stay in the house too."

"Okay, great. Everything is handled."

"Mary," Charly gasped out, another contraction catching her breath.

"I'll call her and let her know," I assured her.

Brett reached for his phone. "I'm calling Riley. I know he's on patrol today. I'll tell him to expect you to be breaking every speed limit there is."

Maxx nodded. "Good plan."

And then they were gone.

A short time later, Kelly sat down, running a hand over her short hair.

I handed her a coffee. "How you doing?"

She smiled ruefully. "I have no idea how Charly does this. Thomas is such a good baby, and I'm exhausted. He's everywhere—he moves so fast and is into everything. I can't keep up. Even Theo—how do you do it on your own?" Then she stared at me as if suddenly realizing something. "How the hell is Charly going to handle two?"

I laughed. "You sorta grow with them and adapt as they change. Charly is amazing, though. She'll rock it."

"A baby and a toddler," Kelly mused. "I can't even fathom it."

I took a sip of coffee. "You don't want children?" I asked casually.

She frowned, chewing the inside of her cheek. "I don't really know. I like kids, but I've never been one to stay in one place very long. Not much of a life for a child." Her face darkened. "Then again, trapped one place isn't always great either."

There was a story there, but I didn't want to push. "You must see a lot of beautiful places in your travels. Charly says you're a photographer's assistant?"

She nodded. "Carl goes all over the world, and I travel with him a lot. He's taught me so much, but I still have a lot to learn. I hope one day to be the one taking the photos and telling my assistant what to do."

"Do you have any of your photos?"

She pulled her laptop close and tapped on the keyboard, spinning it so I could see the screen. I scrolled through some photos in amazement. "Kelly, these are gorgeous. I mean, really gorgeous. You should be working for yourself, not as an assistant."

"I keep telling her that," Brett said, walking in. "She needs to break away from Carl and go on her own. I think she's better than he is."

Kelly glared at him as he poured a coffee and sat down. "Carl will tell me when I'm ready."

He took a sip, meeting her eyes. "Carl is a dick."

She curled her hands on the table in anger. "Takes one to know one."

He sat back, crossing his feet, not looking at all bothered by her anger. "You like my dick."

I cleared my throat. "Okay, then. I'm going to check on Thomas. No word from Maxx or Stefano?"

Brett and Kelly stopped exchanging furious looks.

"Stefano texted. He's hanging with Maxx while they get Charly settled. The contractions slowed down, but it's definitely happening." Brett barked out a laugh. "Stefano was sure he was going to be pulling over to help Maxx deliver this baby. He was sort of grateful he didn't have to. He's not sure he'd have gotten over that."

"Neither would Maxx," Kelly and I said at the same time, then laughed, the sound breaking the tension in the room.

Brett chuckled, glancing at his phone. "Chase will be here soon. He has barbecue for everyone."

"I hope Stefano makes it back for some. He was looking forward to it."

"We'll save him some. Chase says he and Theo had a wonderful day."

"Awesome."

"Theo is a great kid."

I smiled. "He loves being here with you guys."

"We like having him. He asks the best questions, especially for a five-year-old. I think the kid has found his calling."

I had to laugh. "By the time he grows up, he'll know more about cars than some people forget."

Brett grinned. "He'll be running the show."

I wondered about the future. What it held in store for Stefano and me. Theo. Could we find our way out of this and be a family? In my mind, I saw Stefano teaching Theo all he knew. Theo growing up to be like him. Kind, smart, thoughtful. Talented.

God, I wanted that.

I stood, stopping my thoughts. "While we're waiting, I need to go check on those tires in the barn."

Brett began to stand. "I can do it."

I waved my hand. "No, I'm good," I assured him, hoping while I was gone, the two of them could clear the air. "I'll be fast."

"Take a flashlight so you can read the numbers on the tires," he advised. "It's not well lit back there. There's one on the shelf by the side door."

"Great." I grabbed the flashlight and headed to the barn. It was still light out, although some clouds were moving in. I hoped Chase and Stefano would make it back before the rain came.

On my way to the barn, my phone buzzed. It was Margie, checking in, telling me that Wayne had been at the bar the night before. I knew she was still upset about her phone, but it wasn't her fault. I texted back to say thanks and slid it back into my pocket. I would call her later.

In the barn, I pushed aside the heavy tarp, not surprised to see the tires stacked—neat and organized, no doubt under Charly's direction. Even with the overhead light on, it was dim, and I was grateful Brett had advised bringing the flashlight. I walked through the three rows, checking the numbers until I found a complete set of four. The customer would be pleased. I would call him tomorrow and tell him we had them in stock and arrange an appointment for him. I turned, surprised to see the tarp I had pulled away back in place. It must have slipped back from the mooring.

Except then the overhead light went out. It startled me so much, I dropped the heavy flashlight. Flustered, I bent to grab it, cursing when it slipped from my hand and the batteries fell out, leaving me partially blind in the dull light.

A shiver ran down my spine, and panic seeped into my body. I shook my head, refusing to let my imagination run away with me.

I was in Maxx's barn. The house was a hundred feet away. All I had to do was scream, and Brett would be here in a flash. I wasn't in any danger. Wayne was still thousands of miles away. I was fine. Still, when my hand fell on the heavy metal flashlight lying on the ground, I gripped it, as well as a piece of discarded metal I found.

Then I heard it. The barn door slowly rolling closed. My grip on the piece of metal tightened.

I was wrong. I wasn't alone.

For a moment, I huddled close to the ground, trying to tamp down my panic.

"Hiding won't do you any good. I know exactly where you are."

I shut my eyes at the sound of the voice reaching me in the semi-darkness. I knew it far too well.

The animosity and cruelness of Wayne's tone made me nauseous.

How did he get here? He was at the bar the night before.

How did he find me?

I knew I needed to buy myself time. If I didn't return in a few moments, I knew Brett would come looking for me—as long as he wasn't locked in a passionate interlude with Kelly. I prayed to God they were still fighting.

I straightened, careful to keep hold of the dead flashlight and the piece of metal.

"How did you find me?"

His laughter was disdainful. "Everyone leaves traces now, Gabby."

I inched toward the tarp and away from his voice. There had to be another way out.

"Traces?" I asked, confused.

His chuckle was pure evil. "Your driver's license. Health card. When you applied for new ones, it left a trace. I have friends who helped me find it."

"Obviously, your friends have the same morals you do. None."

"And thanks to your stupid friend Margie leaving her phone in her purse, it was easy to grab and download her contacts. Process of elimination was all that was left, and I found you and traced you here."

"You mean, your friends did," I replied, letting sarcasm coat my tone. "You're not that smart."

"Don't make me angrier, Gabby. It only makes it worse. You know that."

I repressed a shiver, concentrating on an escape route. Annoyed Wayne used to punish me with words and slaps. Angry Wayne liked to hear me cry. And I could feel his fury. I couldn't let him get his hands on me.

I was almost at the tarp. I could throw something and distract him and crawl under. I'd start screaming then.

"You were in BC last night."

"I was on a plane early this morning. I've been watching you and your friends all afternoon."

I shut my eyes. Stefano was going to be so angry.

"Go away, Wayne. Leave, and I won't tell anyone you were here."

"You won't be telling anyone. I came to get my son, and you're coming with us."

"He's not your son," I spat. "Donating sperm doesn't make you a father."

I reached the tarp, tossing the piece of metal over my shoulder and hearing it hit something. I hoped it would distract him, make him go in that direction, thinking it was me.

I dropped and scrambled under the tarp, the light brighter on the other side. Except the second I was on my feet, Wayne grabbed me, his arm around my neck, his fetid breath on my face.

"Gotcha," he whispered.

CHAPTER TWENTY-FOUR

Gabby

"Where's my son?" Wayne's voice was low and angry in my ear.

"He's not here."

His grip tightened. "Stop lying."

I struggled against his hold, feeling the weight of the flashlight in my hand. It was my only chance.

"He's—he's not here," I gasped.

"I saw him with a man. That your new guy, Gabby?" he hissed. "You think you can walk out on me and find a new life? Take my son and leave?"

"You didn't want him," I protested, grateful when his arm slipped a little, much-needed oxygen filling my lungs. "Or me," I added.

"You're correct there. But he's the right age now. Trainable. I saw him," he snarled. "He's a momma's boy. I'll beat that out of him fast enough."

Rage tore through me at his words. I would die before I let him so much as look at my son. I didn't care what happened to me. All that mattered was Theo. Keeping him safe.

I raised my foot and stomped down as hard as I could. Wayne roared, and I broke away, grabbing at the flashlight. I turned and swung, catching his head. He howled in rage, and I ran for the barn door, screaming. I managed to get it to slide open when I heard it. The sound of a gun being cocked. I stopped, turning to look.

Wayne stood, bleeding and furious, holding a gun pointed at me. Outside I heard shouts, and to my horror, I saw Chase and Theo in front of Chase's truck, having just pulled up. Brett tore out of the house, stopping when he saw me standing by the barn door.

He hurried toward the barn, stopping when I held up my hand.

"Tell Theo to come here," Wayne demanded.

"No."

"I said, tell my kid to come here. Right now. Or he can watch his mother die."

I shook my head, stopping Brett and Chase from coming forward. I looked at Theo, his face confused. I smiled and blew him a kiss, pretending everything was fine. "Go inside, Teddy Bear."

Shutting the door fast, I spun on my heel, facing Wayne. "Shoot me, then."

"You've always liked to make things hard on yourself, haven't you?" he snarled. "All of this is your fault."

"Oh yes, I forced you to treat me the way you did." I shook my head. "You were always a horrible man. I was too blind to see it until it was too late."

"I'm taking my son, and we're leaving."

"No, you're not." I laughed at his insane thoughts. "You're not going anywhere but jail, no matter what. Whether you shoot me or not. You didn't think this through very well, Wayne. You may have fooled everyone back in BC, but the people here all know who and what you are. You will never get to Theo, even if you do shoot me." I shrugged, feigning a nonchalance I wasn't feeling, knowing it would anger him. "I doubt you're man enough to do that anyway."

Something, some slight movement behind Wayne, caught my attention.

Someone else was in the barn. I wasn't alone.

I returned my stare to his face, not letting him know I had noticed anything.

I felt another layer of fear hit me as I met his gaze. Even in the dim light, I noticed how different his eyes looked. Black. Soulless. Crazy. He was glowering, furious and malicious at my words.

I had never talked back to him, and he didn't like it. But I needed his attention focused on me—nowhere else.

"Why are you doing this? You didn't want me. You didn't want us."

His hatred was evident when he spoke. "You left me. Ran away. Humiliated me in front of people who respected me. Made them doubt me. Now you're going to come back and apologize. Tell them you were wrong. Show *me* how wrong you were."

"No." I shook my head. "I would rather die than go anywhere with you."

"I can arrange that. I'm going to be a father to my kid."

"You couldn't be a father to Theo if you tried," I mocked, seeing the shadow behind him creeping closer, silent and deadly.

"You never knew when to keep your mouth shut. You always were stupid."

"I would disagree with you, but then again, I let you into my life."

"Open the damn door and get my son."

"*No*. Go ahead and shoot me. But you're not getting him. Ever. You'll be in jail for murder, and he'll be raised by the people outside this barn. Brought up to be a good man—loving and caring. Kind. Nothing like you," I added, goading him. "I am never going with you, and neither is Theo."

Behind him, there was more movement. Slow, hidden in the shadows, but someone was there.

"No one else is raising my son."

I crossed my arms, tapping my foot. He used to hate that. I did it to distract him.

"You never have and never will raise *my* son. And just so you know, asshole? You didn't break me. You thought you did. I let you think you did. But I got away and made a life for myself. For us. A good one, surrounded by amazing people. You're nothing but a bully and a liar. Anyone who didn't see it before will see it now. So, go ahead and shoot me. *I. Still. Win.*"

The gun rose, but his hand was shaky. Blood seeped from the cut on his head I'd given him with the flashlight. He wasn't quite steady on his feet. He was sweating and not completely in control.

"You bitch," he seethed.

It came out of nowhere. A piece of wood was swung through the air, hitting Wayne's head with a low thud. His expression changed from rage to confusion and pain, his eyes rolled back in his head, and he dropped. Lifeless and still, he lay on the ground, the gun kicked away. I lifted my eyes and met Stefano's tortured gaze.

"Jesus, *Tesoro*, why are you always trying to get yourself killed?"

Then I was in his arms. Wrapped in safety. In love.

"It's over," he murmured. "It's all over."

I burrowed into his warmth, knowing he was right.

I was finally done running.

The next few moments were a flurry of activity. Stefano called for Brett, who came in, looking around in horror.

"Tie him up. Call the police. Tell them no sirens. I don't want to scare Theo."

"Where is he?" I asked, my voice shaky. "Where is Theo?"

"Inside with Kelly. She told him you'd seen a mouse and screamed but you were fine."

Chase came into the barn, carrying a coil of rope. "I'll help." He met my eyes. "Gabby, you okay?"

I nodded, trying desperately to stop the shivers racing through my body.

"Why did you goad him?" Stefano groaned into my hair, his arms still locked around me.

"I knew it would distract him, make him angry, and he would focus on me, not whoever was sneaking up behind him." I shuddered. "How did you get in here?"

"There's an old chicken coop door on the back. When my nieces and nephews come to visit, we play hide-and-seek. I use it a lot."

I eased back, looking up at him. "How did you know?"

"I was on my way back from the hospital. I saw a van pulled off the road close to the driveway. Given everything, I was suspicious. I stopped to check and saw it was a rental. Idiot left the doors unlocked, and I looked at the rental agreement. His name was on it. Maxx left his cell behind in the rush earlier and I gave him mine, so I couldn't call. I cut through the field and heard you scream in the barn. I knew that fucker was here. I snuck in."

"Thank God," I whispered.

"Okay, the asshole's trussed up and not going anywhere. I'll wait for the police. You two head in and see Theo. I'm not sure he entirely bought the mouse thing," Brett announced. "I heard him telling Kelly you were braver than that."

Stefano cupped my face. "Are you okay?"

I gripped his wrists. "Yes."

"Can you do this? Be calm for Theo? Act like everything is normal?"

I nodded.

He bent and pressed his lips to mine. The feel of his mouth on me grounded me. His touch soothed.

"I'll be right beside you, *Tesoro*."

I tightened my hold on him. "That's why I can do this."

On the ground, Wayne groaned. "My head. It hurts."

Chase kicked his foot. "Shut up. Just shut up, or your head will be the least of your worries."

With a deep breath, I hunched beside Wayne's prone figure. "Enjoy being in jail, Wayne. I'll be raising my son with the example of a good, strong, real man to look up to. One he is proud to call Dad. Think about that while you're rotting in a cell. Just so you know—neither of us will be thinking of you at all."

Stefano took my hand and, together, we walked away.

Theo looked relieved when we walked in, throwing himself into my arms.

"Mom, you screamed—like a girl! It scared me!"

I held him tight. Stefano glanced over his shoulder and shut the door. I knew the police had arrived, and he didn't want Theo to see the police car.

I shuffled us over to the table, sitting so he couldn't see outside.

"I am a girl, Theo," I reminded him, trying to stay calm.

"But you've seen a mouse before. We held them at the petting zoo."

"It wasn't a mouse," I said.

He looked up at me, triumphant. "I knew it. Was it a rat?"

I shivered. Unknowingly, he'd described his father to a tee. "Yes. A big one."

"I thought I saw a man behind you when you shut the door. Why did you shut the door?"

Stefano spoke up, sitting beside me. "That was me, little man. I was trying to help your mom keep the rat inside. She shut the door so he didn't escape or head toward you."

Theo's eyes were huge. "Was it really big?"

"The biggest one I've ever seen. He's in a crate now. They're coming to pick him up."

"Can I see?"

"No!" I cried out without thought.

Theo frowned. "Okay, Mom." He looked at Stefano. "I just asked."

"I think it's sick," Stefano explained. "Your mom doesn't want to risk you. That's her job, little man."

Theo nodded.

"Besides," Stefano continued, "you brought barbecue, and I'm starving. So is your mom."

That distracted Theo. "We had macaroni and cheese with brisket in it earlier. I ate my whole bowl, it was so good. But I'm hungry again."

Stefano clapped his hands. "Good. Let's eat."

It was the hardest thing to do—sit and eat, pretending everything was okay. Faking how delicious everything was when in reality it tasted like sawdust. Brett and Chase appeared shortly, washing their hands and sitting down.

Stefano looked at them, his eyebrow raised. "Animal control take away the rat, boys?"

"Yep. They, ah, need to talk to you and Gabby later."

"Okay."

"How is Charly?" I asked, needing to think of something else.

Stefano grinned. "I checked Maxx's phone. Baby Vivian was born about an hour ago. Mommy and daughter are doing great."

Everyone smiled around the table, thrilled for Maxx and Charly. Grateful they were out of the house when this all took place.

"We'll have to go see them tomorrow."

"Can I take a present for the baby?" Theo asked.

"Of course," I agreed. "We'll go pick out something in the morning."

"I need to swing by the hospital and take Maxx his phone and get mine," Stefano said. "And I'm a little tired. Would you mind heading out early, Gabby?"

I shot him a grateful smile, knowing he was saying that for my benefit. "Of course. It's fine."

"Mary is on her way," Kelly said. "She's so upset she was in Guelph today at that quilting show when Charly went into labor, but she's headed back now. I'll be fine with her here." She shook her head. "She wanted to drop everything and rush back, but I told her no. We were fine until this evening."

"I'll stay until she arrives," Brett offered, leaning his arm over the back of his chair. "I'm going to finish up that car Maxx was working on."

"I'll keep you company," Chase insisted.

"Then we all have our jobs," Stefano said, standing. "Dinner was great. Thanks, Chase."

He nodded. "Anytime. I had a great day with my little buddy here."

Theo high-fived him. "We talked about cars and motorcycles all the way there. And the parts guy showed me some stuff. It was so cool."

"Good." I ran a hand over his head. "I'm glad you had a good day."

He grinned. "The best."

STEFANO

I looked in on Theo. He was passed out, one arm flung out, the other holding his favorite stuffed teddy. He'd fallen asleep in the truck, and we didn't wake him. Gabby sat on his mattress, staring at him in silence for a long time. I hated to tear her away, but the police had shown up to talk to us.

"*Tesoro*," I murmured.

"Coming," she replied. She stood and bent, kissing Theo's head.

I held her hand on the way to the kitchen, feeling the tremors she was trying to hide.

She awed me with her strength as she gave her statement. It helped I knew the officers—both were customers at the garage. Todd and Barry knew all of us there. They knew the gist of everything, but Gabby filled in the blanks. After she finished telling what had occurred in the barn plus the background, she sat back, her tension evident.

"Where is he?" she asked.

Todd finished the cup of coffee she'd poured him, setting it on the table. "In jail. He has a massive headache and says he's going to press charges for assault, but I somehow think you have no worries on that end." He shook his head. "He had rope and gags in his rented van. The idiot had a list of what he wanted to do. How he planned to kidnap both of you. As he tried to defend himself, his story only incriminated him more. He refused a lawyer. There is no doubt he's going to jail for a long time. The list of charges we have against him is pretty serious. And he is insisting he wants to be tried in BC, not here."

"He thinks he'll get a friendly jury," Barry added with a smirk. "He's wrong."

"I'll feel better once he's out of this province."

"We'll help you with paperwork and a restraining order so he doesn't try to contact you or have anyone do so on his behalf. You and Theo are safe now, Gabby. He's behind bars, and he's going to remain there a long time."

"Did he really think he'd get away with this?"

The two men exchanged glances. "I don't think his thought process was very clear. We found drugs in his possession. Hard ones. Pretty sure they were floating in his system too." Todd paused. "He had himself a little side business. As I said, his list of charges is long."

The odd look in his eyes Gabby had commented on now made sense. The idiot was high and stupid. Not a good combination.

They stood. "You'll have to come to the station and sign some papers. Both of you."

"Tomorrow okay?" I asked, eyeing Gabby. I wasn't sure how much more she could take tonight.

"Yep. Anytime is fine."

After they left, Gabby disappeared, and I heard the shower come on. I rinsed out the coffee cups and checked on the doors, making sure they were all locked, knowing Gabby would need to feel extra safe tonight. I was surprised to hear the shower still running, and I peeked in, my heart breaking at the sight in front of me.

Gabby was facing the wall, her face buried in a towel. Her shoulders were shaking with the force of her sobs, her distress evident.

I discarded my clothes, stepping in behind her. She gasped as I pulled her back to me, wrapping my arms around her.

"I'm right here, *Tesoro*. You're not alone."

She turned and flung her arms around me, crying.

I ran my hand up and down her back in long, soothing passes. "It's okay, Gabby. Let it out. It's over, my beautiful girl. My *Tesoro*. He will never come near you again."

Her sobs grew harder, her entire body shaking.

"I didn't want to die," she confessed. "But I couldn't let him near Theo. Or Brett and Chase." She clutched me harder. "I didn't want to leave you."

"You were so brave, *Tesoro*. You told him off and let him know what you thought of him. You needed that. I was as proud of you as I was scared. Never put yourself in that position again. I can't lose you."

"I love you," she whispered over and over. "I love you, Stefano. *Amore.*"

"Shh," I hushed. "I know. I love you too. And tomorrow, we'll start new, yes? Go see Maxx and Charly. Take Theo to the park. A day of just us."

I rocked her in the steamy shower, letting her get it out. She needed the release. I needed to hold her.

Eventually, she nodded against my chest, her sobs beginning to ease off. "We have to go to the police station."

"We'll do that first and get it done. Theo can have breakfast with Mary and Kelly. Then it's over."

A long shudder passed through her body, and she relaxed against me. "It's over."

"Your past can't hurt you anymore, Gabby. It's time to start focusing on the future. Our future."

She looked up, her eyes red-rimmed and exhausted, but still so beautiful she made my chest ache.

"Our future," she repeated.

"You, me, and Theo. Yes?"

She sighed, a long, weary puff of air. She rested her head back on my skin.

"Yes."

CHAPTER TWENTY-FIVE

Stefano

"Oh my God, she is so beautiful," Gabby said, looking down in wonder at Vivian. Maxx and Charly watched her, both proud and pleased with her observation. "Her hair is already red!"

"I know," Maxx said, happy. "She looks like her mom."

Gabby traced her finger over Vivian's plump cheek. "Do you think her eyes will go dark?"

"I hope so," Charly said. "She'd look so pretty with dark eyes."

Gabby laughed. "I think she'll be pretty, regardless."

"What does Thomas think?"

Charly wrinkled her nose in amusement. "He liked her but thought she slept too much. He wasn't impressed that she didn't seem overly interested in his trucks he brought to show her."

I chuckled. "He'll get over it."

"Do you want to hold her?" Gabby asked.

I held out my arms. "Sure."

She carefully slipped the small bundle into my embrace, and I sat down, looking at her tiny face. She was a beauty. "You're going to have your hands full, my friend," I muttered, glancing at Maxx. "She is gonna give you a run for your money."

He smiled, his eyes filled with love as he looked at his daughter. "I know."

Theo peeked over my arm, his eyes filled with curiosity. "She's so tiny."

"I know," I agreed, shifting slightly so he could look closer. "You going to give her your gift?"

He pulled a large stuffed bunny from the bag, holding it up. "I got you this," he said shyly. "I thought you'd like the pink floppy ears."

Maxx ruffled his hair. "She'll love it. That was very thoughtful of you, Theo. Thank you."

"You can hold her if you want," Charly offered.

Theo's eyes grew round. "Can I?"

"Sure."

I settled him in the chair, and Maxx tucked a pillow on his lap. We showed him how to hold her head, and I slipped her into his arms, crouching beside the chair in case. He stared at her in wonder. "Are babies all this small?"

"They come a bit larger, but yeah, they are pretty tiny," I informed him.

He whispered something to her, then looked up. "I want one. Okay, Stefo?"

Maxx covered his mouth to stifle the chuckle, and I grimaced. "We'll talk about it later, little man."

He shook his head. "She's cute and small. She can live in my dresser for a while, and I'll help. She's so little she won't be a problem. You and Mom can get me one."

I scratched my chin, unsure how to respond. Seeing Gabby hold her had done something to me. The thought of her swollen with my child, of holding my daughter in my arms, made my chest ache with a longing I had never admitted to myself. Thinking of Theo being a big brother made me grin. I glanced over, meeting Gabby's slightly amused, somewhat panicked gaze.

"They're a lot of work even if they're small," Charly said. "And they cry a lot."

"She's not crying now," Theo insisted.

"They can't live in a dresser," I added.

He frowned, gazing down in rapture. "I'd let her have my room. And my toys." He looked up, his eyes pleading. "Please, Stefo?"

"I'll talk to your mom."

Maxx chuckled. "This oughta be good."

Gabby came over, bending down and talking to Theo, rolling her eyes at me.

I stepped away with Maxx, closer to Charly.

He leaned in, his voice low. "Everything go okay this morning?"

"Yeah. Statements signed. He's been transported to Toronto. He's, ah, going through withdrawal and had to be restrained. He had enough drugs in his system they're shocked he could walk, never mind attempt a kidnapping."

"Shame. I hope they tied the fucker down tight."

"Me too."

"Your woman is brave," Charly said softly.

"Foolish, but yes, brave."

"She was protecting her child. I can understand that."

"I hope it's the last time she is in that position." I shook my head. "I can't take more fires, vindictive exes, or her running."

Charly grinned. "I suppose not—you have to concentrate on making Theo a baby now. That should keep you busy."

I had to laugh. Gabby hadn't been impressed with my response, but we would talk about it later. I had some ideas I wanted to discuss with her.

We left shortly after. Charly was looking tired, and I knew Maxx was hoping to take her home later that day. She would rest once she got home. I drove us back to my house, and we sat outside in the backyard, enjoying the sun and fresh air the rain last night had brought with it.

"Does your mom know what happened?" Gabby asked suddenly.

"Yes."

"She must dislike me now."

"Why on earth would you think that?"

Gabby didn't look at me. "I've caused an awful lot of problems for you. Upset you. Put you in danger."

I slid my chair closer. "Hey." I waited until she met my eyes. "The only thing she is upset about is that you put *yourself* in danger. She wants to go find your ex and 'give him a little taste of his own medicine,'" I said, using Mama's voice and hand gestures. Gabby's lips quirked a little at my actions. "She adores you and Theo." I tucked a wild curl behind her ear. "She knows I love you, and she just wants us happy."

"Do I make you happy?"

"Very much so," I growled. "When you're not running or risking your life. No more, *Tesoro*. Promise me no more."

"Never," she vowed. "I love you, Stefano. I-I want a life with you here, if that's what you want."

I studied her. "I want that and much more."

"More?" she repeated.

"I want to marry you, *Tesoro*," I said honestly. "Buy a house together and build a life. Make that baby for Theo. Take you to Mama's on Sundays."

She blinked. "You're going fast again, Stefano."

I winked. "Breaking the speed limit. You gonna join me or give me a ticket?"

For a moment, she said nothing. Then she smiled. "I'm right beside you."

I pulled her close. "*Ti amo*, Gabby. My *tesoro*. My life."

She snuggled close. "*Amore*," she sighed.

GABBY

Stefano laughed loudly at the antics of the kids on Sunday. They tended to gang up on him, and Theo joined in happily. Right now, he was under a mass of small, wriggling bodies, being tickled until he agreed to ice cream. Little did they know, he'd already planned that but was soaking up the attention.

Rosa sat beside me, watching, her hands busy as ever as she snapped green beans for dinner. The house smelled incredible, the scent of roasting meat and fragrant tomato sauce making my mouth water. I was starving again. I was constantly hungry the past couple of days, and I suspected it was the stress that had disappeared.

Stefano received a call the night after Wayne's arrest. He'd had a seizure that landed him in the hospital from the drug withdrawal. Another followed, and his heart gave out. He was dead.

I looked at Stefano in disbelief. "He's gone?" I asked.

He crouched beside the chair. "You never have to fear him again. Or worry about Theo."

I let the news filter through my brain for a moment. "Is it wrong I feel nothing? No remorse or sadness?"

He stroked my cheek. "No. The man you thought he was didn't exist. The man he became was created of his own choices. You don't have to feel as if you have to grieve that."

And I didn't. I realized I had no good memories of Wayne. The short time before I'd seen his real nature had been eradicated by all the terrible things he had done. I no longer had to worry about him looking for me. Coming after me.

I was free.

Rosa handed me a plate of cookies, interrupting my thoughts. "You sad, Gabriella?"

"No."

"You look sad."

I shook my head. "Thoughtful. Thinking."

She patted my hand. "No more thinking about past." She indicated the mountain of kids laughing and wrestling with Stefano. "Your future. There."

"I love him."

She smiled. "I know. You give him baby soon, and he be happy."

"Pardon me?"

"You hungry. You cry. You smile at same time. I was same when I carried Stefano. It's good. You marry him. Give baby family."

She stood and winked. "I keep to myself until you tell him. He be very happy." Then she frowned. "No more hero. *Capisci?*"

I was dumbstruck as I watched her walk away.

Pregnant?

She thought I was pregnant?

She was wrong—

I found myself counting backward, realizing I was late.

Holy shit.

Rosa could be right. I had to take a test. I had no idea how to do that with the way Stefano was watching me right now. If I left the room, he followed, his anxiety still evident.

Then I got an idea and sent off a text.

By tomorrow, I would know.

But if it was positive, how was I going to tell Stefano?

Monday, I went to visit Charly. Maxx was happy to see me, and he headed to the garage, taking Thomas with him. Thomas was a quiet toddler, speaking rarely, but happy and sweet. When he did talk, he didn't mince words and came right to the point.

"Bibby no like my twuck."

This was, it seemed, unacceptable to him. I hunched down, smiling at him. "She's too little."

He sighed. "I gib to her. She not take."

I stood, laughing. "One day, you'll complain that she takes everything. Trust me."

He frowned, then began to giggle as Maxx put him on his massive shoulders. "Come on, my boy. We'll leave the girls to it."

As soon as he was out the door, I looked at Kelly. "Did you get it?"

"It's in my bathroom. I went two towns over. I saw no one I knew."

Charly grinned at me. "This is so exciting."

"For you," I replied dryly.

Ten minutes later, I sat beside her, shell-shocked, staring at the lines.

"Oh my God. Rosa was right."

"She knew before I did, too," Charly mused. "She's good."

"I'm pregnant," I whispered. "Stefano is still freaked out over the fire and Wayne. Not to mention the whole gun and 'go ahead and shoot me' thing. When he finds out it happened while I was carrying his baby, he is going to go mental."

"Prepare yourself for the Italian caveman." Charly chortled, clearly enjoying herself. "When are you going to tell him?"

"I have no idea," I muttered, reaching for the coffee Kelly had given me.

Charly clucked her tongue. "You need to limit your caffeine."

"Oh God. I need this one. I haven't had any today."

"Just one."

I sipped the brew gratefully.

"What have you told Theo?" she asked, and I knew she was referring to Wayne.

I sighed. "We sat with him and told him the bad man had died. That we never had to be afraid again. Stefano was so good with him and answered all his questions. He accepted it easily and went to bed happy. He said he wasn't afraid anymore because of 'Stefo.'" I smiled. "He loves him so much. He's everything Wayne would never have been. Theo hasn't asked another question about him."

Charly rubbed my arm. "So then, this baby is a good thing, isn't it? You know what an amazing dad Stefano will be."

I thought about the night after we'd visited Charly in the hospital. We were lying in bed, the dark of the night all around us,

Theo asleep down the hall. I was wrapped in Stefano's embrace. His quiet confession about his reaction to seeing me holding Vivian. That he truly hoped one day it would be his child I was embracing. I had told him what seeing him hold a baby did for me. The tender expression on his face as he looked at her. The patience he had with Theo as he showed him how to hold her. The utterly adorable panic that crossed his face when Theo asked him to get him one.

"He will be ecstatic," I agreed.

She lifted Vivian to her shoulder, stroking up and down her back. "And you?"

"Excited. Scared. My last pregnancy was so hard."

"Physically?"

I shrugged. "Wayne was nasty. I wasn't allowed to show much of any kind of emotion. If I wasn't feeling well, I had to keep it to myself. If I was happy, same thing."

"Hey," Charly called. "This is Stefano. He'll be exactly like Maxx. Loving, supportive, ready to bring you ice cream at three in the morning. He loves you, Gabby. Totally. And he is as far from that other asshole as you can get. I promise you." She reached over and squeezed my hand. "Trust him. Trust *in* him. He won't let you down."

Her words struck a chord inside me. She was right. It was Stefano.

"I do trust him."

She squealed, the sound muffled by her hand. "Holy moly, we're gonna have a wedding and a baby soon. This is gonna be so much fun!"

Kelly rolled her eyes and stood. "I'm going for a walk."

"Is that a euphemism for hooking up with Brett in the stock room?" Charly asked dryly. "Try not to knock over the oil cans this time."

Kelly flipped her the bird before walking out.

Charly winked. "She didn't deny it."

I had to laugh. "No, she didn't."

We left the garage, and I frowned as Stefano pulled up in front of Mrs. Scott's place.

"Kicking me out now?" I asked, teasing, even as it hit me I could move back to my apartment now that the danger had passed. Life could return to normal—or at least as normal as it would be from now on. I had a lot of plans to make.

Stefano chuckled and lifted my hand, kissing it. "No, Mrs. Scott has a lightbulb that went out, and she wants to see you and Theo for a bit."

"Ah, okay," I said, secretly relieved.

Inside, we were greeted with hugs and kisses. Stefano changed the lightbulb, and we visited a bit. I was surprised when Mary showed up, bringing dinner. We ate fried chicken and salad, enjoying some time together. Neither woman brought up what happened in front of Theo, but their hugs had been fierce, and the words whispered in my ear let me know how much they cared.

After dinner, Stefano stood and extended his hand. "Let's go for a walk, *Tesoro*. I know Mary and Mrs. Scott want some time with Theo."

"We have strawberry shortcake and a surprise for him," Mrs. Scott added.

At those words, any protest Theo might have had at being left behind died. He loved strawberry shortcake—never mind the lure of a surprise.

I took Stefano's hand, and we walked down the street, turning the corner. We didn't talk, enjoying the fresh air and light breeze. I let him lead me since he seemed to have a destination in mind. He stopped in front of a house, gazing at it. I followed his stare, admiring the two-story structure, the picket fence, and the garden. It was large and pretty with the stonework and ivy growing on it. A double garage was set back from the house at the end of a long driveway.

"I have to drop something off here," he said.

"Okay," I replied, following him as he tugged me up the driveway. "Lovely house."

"Yeah, it is."

He didn't stop at the front door, instead opening it and stepping in. I was confused by his behavior but followed. Inside, I stopped, unsure.

"Stefano, it's empty."

He met my gaze. "For now."

I looked around, suddenly understanding. "What have you done?" I gasped.

"Arranged for a viewing," he replied.

"Stefano—"

He cut me off. "Look around with me. Please."

I was in love before we got to the second floor. Wide-planked wooden floors, a fireplace, a huge, updated eat-in kitchen, plus an office were on the main floor. The rooms were bright and filled with light. Upstairs were three large bedrooms, the master having the benefit of an en suite added to it. The attic was a blank canvas, ready to be finished. Downstairs was lots of storage and, as Stefano insisted, a prerequisite wine cellar and cold room.

"All Italian homes have one." He grinned.

We ended up back in the living room. I ran my hand over the mantel, admiring the intricate molding.

"I'm glad they didn't change this when they updated."

"No, the owner was very sympathetic when he did the renos. A new gas insert but the old-fashioned look."

I nodded, my gaze straying to the backyard that could be accessed through a set of French doors here and off the kitchen. There was a planned deck, Stefano told me, plus a great garage.

"Can you see Theo playing in the yard?" Stefano asked me.

I turned to him. "You want to buy this house?"

"I want us to buy this house." My eyes widened in shock as he sank to one knee and offered me a box. "I want us to live here together as a family. Marry me, *Tesoro*. Please."

His simple words filled my heart. His love-filled gaze broke me.

"I'm pregnant," I burst out, then began to cry.

His jaw went slack. He stood, towering over me, his gaze a mixture of emotion. He cupped my face, holding my cheeks tenderly. "Pregnant," he whispered.

I nodded. "I found out today. It's early, but I'm pregnant. I was on birth control, but it failed, I guess. I don't know how—"

His chuckle broke into my ramblings. "The usual way, I suspect." He bent and kissed the end of my nose. "You know I can't keep my hands off you."

He slid one hand down, resting it on my stomach. "A bambino," he murmured. "Mine."

"Are you—are you happy?" I hiccupped.

He returned his hand to my face, shaking his head. "*Tesoro*, I told you I wanted everything with you. A life, a family. Do you really think I would greet this news with anything but joy?" He frowned. "How are you feeling about it?"

"Happy, excited, scared," I replied, covering his wrists with my hands. "I want this baby, Stefano. I want a life with you."

"You have no reason to be scared. This time, *this life*, will be different, Gabriella," he whispered. "I swear."

"I know."

"Then say yes. Accept my ring and marry me. Soon."

I drew in a deep breath. "Yes."

He crashed his mouth to mine, kissing me deeply. He lifted me off the floor, swinging me around, laughing.

Setting me on my feet, he opened the lid of the box and slid the ring on my finger. An oval-shaped diamond was surrounded by smaller ones, the effect stunning. More tiny diamonds studded the intricate band. It glimmered and shone in the light, casting its brilliance on the walls.

"It's beautiful," I whispered.

"I knew you would love it as soon as I saw it. I've had it a couple of weeks."

"Breaking the speed limit again," I said.

"Smashing it," he agreed.

"Does anyone know?"

He grinned, lifting one shoulder. "Only Brett. I kept this all to myself, otherwise. Even the house. Speaking of which…" He trailed off, slipping his phone from his pocket and calling someone.

"Trevor? Hey. Yeah, she loved it. Finish the offer. I need possession as soon as possible."

He hung up, looking pleased with himself.

"Pretty sure I just bought us this house, *Tesoro*."

I flung my arms around his neck, the tears coming once more. He held me tight, slowly rocking us.

"Everything is going to be good now. I promise," he crooned. "You have nothing left to fear."

"I know."

He pulled back, wiping my cheeks. "Nothing will hurt you again."

"I know," I repeated.

Then his eyes grew round. "Holy shit, you were pregnant when—"

"I didn't know," I whispered. "I had no idea."

He looked horrified, and I stroked along his tense jaw. "I'm fine. It's over. I don't want to let him into this moment. Please."

"Not happening again," he growled. "Any of it. I'm not letting you out of my sight."

That made me laugh. Charly had been right. "Okay," I agreed easily.

"I'm serious. I'm going to watch over you like a hawk. Between Theo and me, you're going to take it easy and be safe. Understand? Anything you need. Anything you want. You ask, it's yours."

His words were all I needed. I knew without a doubt this pregnancy, my life, would be vastly different. Because of him.

"I'm so glad you asked me to marry you before you knew I was pregnant," I confessed. "To know you wanted me with you before you knew I was carrying your child just makes it all the sweeter."

He smiled and kissed me. "I've always wanted you. Right from the first time I saw your luscious ass bent over the back of your car, I've been yours, *Tesoro*."

I grinned. "Is that a fact?"

"It is."

Suddenly, he looked mischievous. "Theo is going to be ecstatic when we tell him about the baby."

I groaned. "He'll think you did it to please him."

"I'll let him."

"He'll ask for other things."

"No, he's a good boy. The baby will make him happy." He winked. "At least until Christmas."

He became serious. "I want to adopt Theo. If you'll let me. I want him to have my name and to know he's as important as this baby. As any of our children."

"He'd love that. So would I."

"I have a friend who is a lawyer. He said we could since, ah, his father isn't around to object."

"Then we'll talk to Theo about it. I think he'll be thrilled."

"The night he told me he wanted me to be his dad…" He paused. "I liked the sound of it. A lot."

"Really?"

"Yes. I want that."

"I want it too."

"Good. Then I'll make the call."

I looked around. "I can't believe this is going to be our home."

"Close to Mrs. Scott. To all the things that are familiar to you and Theo. I can walk to Brett's place."

"And he's okay with you going?"

"He knew where this was headed, and it was only a matter of time. He and Chase are gonna do the roommate thing. That'll open up the apartment for the next apprentice, or it can be a guest place for Maxx and Charly."

"What about Kelly? There's something going on between her and Brett."

"I figured as much, but he doesn't talk about it. I think her lifestyle precludes anything serious."

"Things can change." I pointed out.

He nodded, looking thoughtful. Then he caught my hand and kissed my ring. "Enough about them. Let's plan our future."

My heart ached with love for this man. For his strength and love. His tenderness and patience. His overbearing ways that surrounded me with warmth. I loved him for the way he loved me back. Loved my child.

"Yes."

EPILOGUE

A year later

GABBY

The sun warmed my skin, the heat soaking in as I sat, enjoying a few rare moments of silence. My daughter nuzzled into my neck, contented and sleepy. I sipped the lemonade, enjoying the tartness, thinking about the last year.

Stefano's offer was accepted, and two weeks later, we had possession of the house. We organized some painting parties, and with many hands, the walls were all fresh and inviting. Neither Charly nor I were allowed to paint, but we provided lots of food and we supervised. Rosa was with us, cooking up a storm. Chase insisted the reason we had so many people wanting to help was her lasagna. I had to agree.

The guys spent a week building the deck that Stefano had envisioned on the back. It stretched the length of the house, with two levels. He'd set up a large smoker and a barbecue outside the kitchen end, and Brett and Stefano spent a lot of time experimenting with the smoker, their faithful little sidekick Theo never far away. They were Theo's two favorite people, and the feelings were returned to him fully. Chase was around a lot, and he and Theo were best buds as well. Maxx, Charly, and the kids were frequent guests, as well as Stefano's family.

My family now too.

We were surrounded by love.

Drowsy and content in the sun, I smiled as I recalled our wedding day.

I had never seen Stefano in a suit until that day.

He stood, tall and proud. Intense as hell, waiting for me, his toes tapping in impatience. My breath caught as I looked at him—the way the deep navy suit jacket hugged his shoulders, skimmed over his broad back. He smiled at me, wiping a tear from his eye as I walked toward him, holding hands with Theo. It was only the three of us at the flower-covered altar. Theo wore pants and a vest, proud of his tie that matched Stefano's.

Stefano's gaze took in my lacy, summer dress that hung off my shoulders. I loved the feminine feel and the soft pink color. Charly had woven some ribbons and pearls into my curls, and I added strappy sandals I knew Stefano would love. His eyes were lit with fire as he lazily eyed me up and down, his expression passionate, his approval evident. He held out his hand, and I hurried the last few steps to meet him. He bent and kissed me, his lips warm on mine.

"Beautiful, Tesoro. You take my breath away."

Everyone laughed as Rosa huffed. "Stefano, no yet. Be patient."

He chuckled and threw her a wink. "I've waited long enough, Mama."

"Oh Dio," she sighed, looking heavenward.

Our ceremony was brief and simple. We exchanged vows, rings, and Stefano included Theo in his heartfelt declaration, stating he vowed to love and cherish us both. Theo held up his arms, and Stefano bent and lifted him, hugging him close, still holding my hand. Theo stayed there the rest of the service, *making everyone laugh when Stefano kissed me, then him at the end. We were pronounced husband, wife, and son, much to Theo's delight. He'd already started calling Stefano "Dad." The first time it happened, Stefano was so thrilled, his smile didn't fade for about an hour. He started the adoption process the next day.*

Kelly was at our wedding and took all our photos. She was talented and creative and set up a photo booth in the corner of the house, making sure to take pictures of everyone there. She did family and group shots for everyone as our gift to them for coming. She helped me create a collage of our pictures, which I hung in the bedroom. It was a special memento I treasured. She had blushed when I reiterated to her that she was too talented to be an assistant. I only hoped she struck out on her own one day. She deserved that.

After our wedding, we settled into the house and life. Living with Stefano was a new experience. His excitement over the pregnancy was contagious. Being able to share all of it with him was such a joy. He held my hair when I was ill. Laughed at my cravings. Cradled me when I cried, rubbed my sore back and aching feet. And he did it all with love and tenderness. I was never too afraid to speak, to share. He listened and absorbed. He made sure Theo was involved. He made me feel safe, loved, and protected.

Every day.

Warm lips ghosted over my cheek, and I opened my eyes, meeting Stefano's dark gaze.

"My girls are having a little nap," he murmured.

I yawned. "It was so nice in the sun. Not too warm, just pleasant."

He sat down, looking at me hopefully. Laughing, I handed Luna to her daddy. He'd picked her name, saying she was the moon in his sky. I thought it was pretty and suited her. Luna Marie was welcomed by everyone around her, and she knew nothing but love.

He took her, resting her on his knees as he cooed down to her. "Hello, my little moon. Enjoying some quiet time with Mommy?" He chuckled as she yawned the way I did, her little arms lifting. "Good plan. Your brother will be home soon from playing baseball with Uncle Chase and Uncle Brett. With the three of them here, there won't be much quiet time. He'll want some time with you, and so will your uncles."

"Charly, Maxx, and the kids are coming too," I reminded him. "And apparently, Kelly arrived this morning."

Stefano frowned. "I didn't know she was coming for a visit."

"Neither did Charly. She says Kelly told her she was on *hiatus* for a while."

"Hmm," he replied. "Wonder what that means."

"I'm sure we'll find out." I watched him for a moment, loving how sweet he was with our girl. "I wonder how Brett will react?"

He lifted Luna to his shoulder, smiling as she snuggled in tight to his neck. He stroked her back as he mulled over my words.

"I don't know. I thought they were getting tight at our wedding, then she left. Brett was really upset. I don't think they've kept in touch, and she hasn't been back since." He sighed. "I tried to talk to him about her, but he was pretty tight-lipped. Refused to say a word."

"Charly tried with both of them. Got nowhere. I think Brett told her to mind her own business. She was rather pissed about that," I chuckled.

Stefano laughed, the sound rumbling through his chest and making Luna squirm. He rubbed her back again. "Sorry, little moon." Then he grinned. "Ms. It-is-my-business-because-I-say-so wouldn't like that, I agree. But he certainly isn't talking. I guess we'll see what happens."

"I guess so. I hope they are at least civil."

He didn't look worried. "I am sure they will be."

We were quiet for a moment, then he spoke again.

"So, Mama offered to let the kids stay over one night next week," Stefano said quietly. "I was thinking about getting us a hotel room. Taking you to dinner."

"A night without the kids?" I asked, surprised and instantly worried.

He leaned over, taking my hand. "We could start with dinner, see how you're feeling. Go for a drink after and check in again. If you want, we could stay overnight, or go pick up the kids and come home. Whatever you're comfortable with."

I hadn't left Luna since she was born. I knew it had to happen, but she seemed so small and still too young. I met Stefano's eyes, seeing nothing but love and understanding.

"How about dinner this week, dinner and drinks next time, and maybe an overnight a few weeks from now?" he suggested.

I pulled in a deep breath. "How about if that hotel room includes a big tub like last time, we try it?"

"Yeah?" he replied, his eyes glowing. "I can have you all to myself for the whole night?"

I smiled at my husband. The man who had changed my life. Who became the father my son needed, the husband every woman dreamed about, and the daddy to the sweetest little girl on the planet. The man who loved us deeply, protected us fiercely, and asked for so little in return.

Dinner. A night spent concentrating on us. Him.

I nodded. "Sounds good."

He leaned forward and kissed me. "I'll book it."

"You do that."

"I love you, *Tesoro*."

I smiled. "Back at you, *Amore. Ti amo. Sempre.*"

He kissed me again, his mouth lingering.

"*Sempre.*"

Are you ready for Brett and Kelly's story?

Can he get her to stay in Littleburn? Brett Conner is hoping to tame her restless need to wander in SHIFTING GEARS.

Enjoy meeting other readers? Lots of fun, with upcoming book talk and giveaways! Check out Melanie Moreland's Minions on Facebook.

Join my newsletter for up-to-date news, sales, book announce-

ments and excerpts (no spam). Click here to sign up Melanie
Moreland's newsletter
or visit https://bit.ly/MMorelandNewsletter

Visit my website www.melaniemoreland.com

Enjoy reading! Melanie

ACKNOWLEDGMENTS

As usual, a few thanks.

Lisa, thank you for your patience. Let's face it, if I knew how to do it, you'd be out of a job. Think of it that way ,,,,,,,,,,,,, or . Whichever you like better – or best. Should there be a ? there? Or here? Is it a question? I am so confused. Anyway—love your face!

Beth, thank you for your feedback and support. Your comments make the story better—always.

Melissa, Trina, Carol, and Deb—thank you for your eyes and input. Your support is such a gift.

Kim, I am sorry about Karen.

Karen, be nicer to Kim. We need her.

Seriously, thank you both. Much love and gratitude for all you do (most of which is thankless, I know—but I still love you!)

Nina (Valentine PR), already many thanks are needed. You seriously rock.

To all the bloggers, readers, and my promo team. Thank you for everything you do. Shouting your love of books—of my work, posting, sharing—your recommendations keep my TBR list full, and the support you have shown me is deeply appreciated.

My reader group, Melanie's Minions—love you all.

Matthew—always and forever. That will never change.

ALSO AVAILABLE FROM MORELAND BOOKS

Titles published under M. Moreland

Insta-Spark Collection

It Started with a Kiss

Christmas Sugar

An Instant Connection

An Unexpected Gift

Harvest of Love

An Unexpected Chance

Following Maggie (Coming Home series)

Titles published under Melanie Moreland

The Contract Series

The Contract (Contract #1)

The Baby Clause (Contract #2)

The Amendment (Contract #3)

The Addendum Coming to Radish 2022 - Wide Release 2023

Vested Interest Series

BAM - The Beginning (Prequel)

Bentley (Vested Interest #1)

Aiden (Vested Interest #2)

Maddox (Vested Interest #3)

Reid (Vested Interest #4)

Van (Vested Interest #5)

Halton (Vested Interest #6)

Sandy (Vested Interest #7)

Vested Interest Box Set (Books 1-3)

Vested Interest Box Set (Books 4-7)

Vested Interest/ABC Crossover

A Merry Vested Wedding

ABC Corp Series

My Saving Grace (Vested Interest: ABC Corp #1)

Finding Ronan's Heart (Vested Interest: ABC Corp #2)

Loved By Liam (Vested Interest: ABC Corp #3)

Age of Ava (Vested Interest: ABC Corp #4)

Men of Hidden Justice

The Boss

Second-In-Command

The Commander

Reynolds Restorations

Revved to the Maxx

Breaking The Speed Limit

Shifting Gears

Mission Cove

The Summer of Us

Standalones

Into the Storm

Beneath the Scars

Over the Fence

The Image of You (former title My Image of You)

Changing Roles

Happily Ever After Collection

Heart Strings

ABOUT THE AUTHOR

NYT/WSJ/USAT international bestselling author Melanie Moreland, lives a happy and content life in a quiet area of Ontario with her beloved husband of thirty-plus years and their rescue cat, Amber. Nothing means more to her than her friends and family, and she cherishes every moment spent with them.

While seriously addicted to coffee, and highly challenged with all things computer-related and technical, she relishes baking, cooking, and trying new recipes for people to sample. She loves to throw dinner parties, and enjoys traveling, here and abroad, but finds coming home is always the best part of any trip.

Melanie loves stories, especially paired with a good wine, and enjoys skydiving (free falling over a fleck of dust) extreme snowboarding (falling down stairs) and piloting her own helicopter (tripping over her own feet.) She's learned happily ever afters, even bumpy ones, are all in how you tell the story.

Melanie is represented by Flavia Viotti at Bookcase Literary Agency. For any questions regarding subsidiary or translation rights please contact her at flavia@bookcaseagency.com

facebook.com/authormoreland

twitter.com/morelandmelanie

instagram.com/morelandmelanie

bookbub.com/authors//melanie-moreland

Made in the USA
Monee, IL
21 May 2022

96804571R00193